The Story and Me

Pamela DuMond

The Story of You and Me

Copyright © 2013 Pamela DuMond

All rights reserved.

Photography and Cover Art Design: Regina Wamba of Mae I Design http://www.maeidesign.com

No part of this book may be used or reproduced by any means, graphic, electronic, or mechanical, including photocopying, recording, taping, or by any other means, without written permission of the author, except in the use of brief quotations used in articles or reviews. You can contact the author at Pamela.DuMond@gmail.com

All rights reserved.

ISBN: 1492789186
ISBN-13: 978-1492789185

DEDICATION

For Carol "Cookie" DuMond

Because you believe.

The Story of You and Me

a love story

ALSO BY THE AUTHOR

The Messenger (Mortal Beloved, Book One)

Cupcakes, Lies, and Dead Guys (A Romantic, Comedic Annie Graceland Mystery, #1)

Cupcakes, Sales, and Cocktails – A Novella (A Romantic, Comedic Annie Graceland Mystery, #2)

Cupcakes, Pies, and Hot Guys (A Romantic, Comedic Annie Graceland Mystery, #3)

Cupcakes, Paws, and Bad Santa Claus (A Romantic, Comedic Annie Graceland Mystery, #4)

The Girlfriend's Guidebook to Staying Young

CHAPTER ONE

"Screw you, Alejandro!"
The beer bottle whistled past my ear and smashed into the wooden bench behind my head, showering me with shards of glass. I dropped my e-book reader and ducked as a second bottle flew over my head and exploded onto the booth behind me.

"Thanks for asking, but you're not my type. Give me your keys," a guy said.

Multiple slivers of pain popped on my head and face. I mopped back my beer-drenched, long, chestnut-colored hair that was plastered onto my cheek and glanced down—my fingers were now covered with specks of blood.

"I SAID I ams fines for the drivings," the screw you boy slurred.

I wasn't all that thrilled about leaving my mom, Nana, friends, my safety net and moving to Los Angeles for a couple months. I certainly hadn't come here to be in the middle of a bar fight. I could do that back in my hometown in Wisconsin. Even an average Wisconsin chick could throw a punch.

A twenty-something, curvy, African-American waitress maneuvered her way through the crowd of flip-flop and T-shirt attired college students who'd suddenly shut up and stared at me. She hustled to my booth wearing a heavy dose of concern on her face. "You okay, baby girl? Oh, no. You're bleeding." She turned around. "Thomas Taylor, so help me God, you're not coming back in here until you clean your frat boy ass up. Get him out of here, Alejandro. Now!"

There was scuffling and more slurred swearing. "Dude, you're three sheets to the wind," the guy—Alejandro—said. "You're not driving. You'll thank me in the morning."

The pretty waitress squinted at me through black-rimmed glasses. "Honey, you don't look all that good."

"I'm fine, I'm sure I'm fine," I said. "Just one tiny cut."

She frowned and shook her head. "That is way more than just one cut." She turned toward the bar and snapped her fingers at a portly balding man. "Freddie. Call 911. This girl needs to go to the ER."

"No. No." I waved my hands. I hated hospitals. I tried to avoid them like the plague. "I'm not going to the hospital."

"You have to. It's close," she said. "Only a couple blocks away."

"I know. But—" I looked down at my e-reader. The screen had gone black. I tapped it. Dragged my finger across the screen. Nothing happened. I sighed. "It's been a long day. I'll clean up when I get home."

If I could find my way back there.

It took the whole day to travel from my home in Oconomowoc, Wisconsin to L.A. I cabbed it from the airport to the realtor's office where I picked up the keys to my summer session sublet that was about ten blocks from the USCLA campus. I asked the assistant for a recommendation to a local eatery where I could score a decent meal without breaking the bank.

I deposited my bags at my new crash pad and called my mom to tell her I arrived safely. I changed out of my sweaty traveling clothes into a modest sundress and grabbed my jean jacket. I bolted the lock, threw the keys in my purse and said hi to my new next-door neighbor—a handsome metrosexual named Cole who clutched his scrap of a dog. "This is Gidget," he said.

"Oh, hey, cute furball. My name's Sophie. I'm your new summer neighbor." I wiggled a couple of fingers at the dog.

Gidget narrowed her eyes and growled at me in a soprano tone.

I pulled my hand back. "Sorry," I said. "Animals usually like me."

"Oh, she does!" Cole said. "Gidget only growls at new people she thinks she might like." He scratched her ears. "Everyone else she simply ignores."

"Oh good!" I said.

Funny. That description sounded a bit like me.

By the time I walked to the Westwood Grill the sun was setting and I was exhausted. Based on the assistant realtor's description, I'd expected a semi-quiet night with a good book and a decent but not great meal. I didn't expect to be soaked in beer with glass shards embedded in my face and head. I pinched my forefinger and thumb together and attempted to pull one out of my cheek. Something squished and I felt a little woozy.

The waitress blinked. "Those wounds need to be flushed," she said. "You might be Wonder Woman for all I know, but you can't do that on your own." She grabbed my hand and pulled me to standing. "Will someone please call 911?"

"No! Don't. I'm all right." But she pulled me up too quickly and now I was definitely dizzy. I swayed for a few seconds when someone else with bigger and stronger arms grasped my shoulders from behind.

"You okay?" a guy asked.

"How many times do I have to say I'm fine?" I tasted blood trickling into my mouth, my knees buckled and just like that—I was falling.

But he caught me. His strong hands that had been holding my shoulders wrapped tightly around me—one circled my waist, the other crossed my chest as he pinned me back against what felt like his brick wall of a chest.

"Right. Because everyone's who's 'fine' collapses," he said.

I looked down. A complete stranger with built forearms and tan muscular hands was holding me up. *Way to go, Sophie.* This was such an auspicious start to my most excellent adventure in the City of Angels.

"I got you," he said.

"Thanks. You can let me go."

"You need to sit down. Cheyenne—pull out a chair, please. This booth is soaked."

The waitress pulled out a vinyl chair from an unoccupied table. "Where's Thomas? You didn't let him drive? I do not want that frat brat back in this bar, but I don't want him dead, either."

"Me either. Freddie locked him in the storage room."

"Freddie's got a hernia. No way Freddie could have carried Thomas "The Incredible Hulk" Taylor into our storage room."

"Freddie's hernia did not prevent him from locking the door after I pulled Thomas over the bar, dragged him into the storage room and propped him against the wall next to a large sack of potatoes."

"Hello?" I tapped my index finger on the guy's hand that was firmly planted between my boobs. "Do you people not realize that you are talking about stuff like I'm not here?"

"Oh, I definitely know you're here, Bonita. While I think the cute fingernail thing you're doing to my hand is kind of sexy, I'm not thrilled that you're bleeding all over my favorite Rolling Stones T-shirt."

"Sorry!" *The Stones? A grandpa-aged dude had his hand between my boobs and was practically feeling me up? My new life was totally not starting out the way I had hoped.* "Thanks for catching me, Mister. You can let me go. Now."

"Mister?" He lifted me up six inches off the ground like I was a stuffed animal, or a cat, walked me a couple of feet over to the table and deposited me gently onto a chair. "Mister is a word people use for someone's uncle, or a disheveled man on the street who hits you up for spare change. I'm not old enough to be called 'Mister.'" He released his grip on my waist and chest and shifted one large, firm hand onto my shoulder. "Hold still. You've got a piece of glass sneaking down the front of your dress. I'm going to save you from another cut. You can thank me later." His fingers inched down under the neckline of my sundress, brushing my skin, under my collarbone, headed toward my bra.

Seriously? Thank him for copping a feel? I held my breath.

"Breathe. I almost have it."

I glanced around. The young California flip-flop diners were staring at me like I was one of those embarrassing videos on YouTube. Oh crap, one guy actually had his iPhone pointed at me—I was going to be on YouTube. I probably looked like a bleeding, drowned rat and really hoped my mom wouldn't stumble across this online.

"Got it." His hand pulled out from the top of my dress and flicked a piece of glass away.

A round of applause and a few wolf whistles erupted from the crowd. "Chalk up another save for Alejandro!"

"Dude, she's bleeding all over your T-shirt and you haven't punched her. When I spilled my margarita on your Sticky Fingers T-shirt you punched me."

"I punched you, Paul, after you took three swings at me when you were hammered at the Memorial Day picnic."

"Whatev. I think this means you like her," Paul said.

"Hey, Alex!" A sun-kissed blonde girl wearing a plunging halter dress that displayed a scary amount of bulging cleavage placed the back of her hand to her forehead, batted her eyes and pretended to swoon. "If I happened to fall, would you catch me, too?" Three nearly identical Barbie friends seated at her table giggled.

I winced and turned my head away from the onlookers. *Could this get anymore embarrassing?*

Cheyenne caught my look, turned and snapped her fingers high in the air. "Show's over," she said. "Get back to it." They returned to their drinking, eating, hair tossing and flirting.

"Where's my purse? I need to pay for my burger," I said. My face was starting to burn more.

"Your burger's on Thomas's tab," Alejandro said. "Along with a new e-reader and your visit to the ER."

"I'm not going to the ER." *I tended to be stubborn about these types of things.*

"Hey, Cheyenne! Can I get another round over here, please? Some chicken wings, two veggie wraps and a Caesar salad with the croutons and dressing on the side?" Blondie shouted from the opposite side of this smallish, informal bistro.

Cheyenne regarded me with one eyebrow arched.

"Go. I got this," Alejandro said.

She nodded and walked away.

It was beyond time I called it a day. I had an appointment with a pair of tweezers, some rubbing alcohol, drugstore antibiotic creme, as well as shampoo and conditioner back at my new apartment. If I could even remember where that was. "Thanks for your help, Alejandro." *You big, strong, sweet and kind, Rolling Stones' loving, old grandpa.* I stood up. "You can take your hand off my shoulder."

He did. "Let the record stand that I do so reluctantly."

"Sorry for ruining your T-shirt." I plucked at my dress's neckline and shook off some glass splinters. "Why don't you give me your e-mail? I'd like to reimburse you."

"Even better, why don't you give me your name, number and email?"

I squeezed my eyes shut and frowned. *Maybe my mom was right. Maybe coming to L.A. wasn't the smartest move in the world.* I ground my teeth, but that hurt my face. "My name's Sophie. You're a nice guy and all but I keep the other stuff private."

I turned toward him. My gaze traveled up about six inches until I looked into the most stunning pair of hazel eyes I'd seen in my entire life. Alejandro wasn't a grandpa—he was close to my age. His black, shiny hair curled behind his ears, tapering down his neck. His cheekbones were high, his lips bite-able—I meant—full. His V-neck T-shirt revealed a hint of that wide, rock solid chest that had sheltered me for a minute or so. "Maybe I can Play pal you." I bit down on my lip. "I meant PayPal."

Alejandro smiled, leaned down and whispered into my ear. "I like your first suggestion better."

"Oh crap, just get me the hell out of here!" When I realized I'd said that out loud.

"Why don't you drive her someplace picturesque, Alex?" the booby blonde said. "After all, you're so good at driving."

Alejandro grabbed a set of keys from his pocket, held them up in the air and jangled them. "Yo, Freddie!"

The bartender looked up. "What?"

"Call a cab before you let Thomas out. I'm officially off duty. I am not driving his privileged drunk ass home."

Freddie saluted him. "Got it, Alex."

Alejandro, aka Alex, shoved the keys back in his pants pocket, grabbed my purse from the beer soaked booth and placed my dead e-reader inside it. "And now we're on our way to Emergency. I'm driving."

CHAPTER TWO

"I do not want you to hold my hand!" I lay semi-reclined on a gurney in the USCLA emergency room area for non-life threatening wounds. After the resident doctor examined me, a young intern had injected my face in seven locations with lidocaine or cocaine or whatever-caine combo they used at this teaching hospital. Now he was pulling out beer bottle splinters from my face with gleaming stainless steel tweezers as I tried not to flinch.

"Actually, you do," Alejandro said. "You're in the passenger seat tonight. Stop hitting your imaginary brakes."

"Don't move, Sophie," Dr. Dewitt said. "And unless you want these cuts to leave some scars, I'd be quiet if I were you."

"Good luck with that one." Alex squeezed my hand. "You could not have gotten all these out on your own. You would have screwed up your beautiful, pale, midwestern dairy queen face."

The waitress was right about the hospital being close by. The ride from the Grill to the ER took all of two minutes. Alejandro asked about my accent. "What accent?" I asked. "That accent," he said.

So I told him I had just flown in from Wisconsin. I'd

arrived two hours before my flight at the Milwaukee airport and was patted up by TSA. I flew to Denver and then had a lay over. My flight to L.A. was delayed due to tornadoes or thunderstorms, or whatever always delayed flights. By the time I boarded the plane I was seated next to a screaming toddler whose ears kept popping. Neither of us had a relaxing flight.

"And... voilà!" Dr. Dewitt smiled and held up a tiny piece of colored glass with his medical tweezers. "We have captured the last culprit." He plopped it into a small, pristine, stainless steel dish, then leaned in and fussed over my face. "No stitches. I'm prescribing a round of oral antibiotics, a topical antibiotic creme and Mederma to reduce chance of scarring."

"Oral antibiotics?" I asked. "Research has proven the overuse of oral antibiotics has paved the way for superbugs. Why do I need oral antibiotics?" I yanked my hand from Alejandro's and pushed myself to a seated position.

"Do you know how many people, places or things that beer bottle came in contact with before its fragments penetrated your pretty face?" He pulled out a pad of paper and wrote a script. "Hand this to the pharmacy on your way out. Don't leave here without your drugs. Here's a card for Dr. An'gel Ducote. She's the best plastic surgeon at the hospital should you change your mind and want a consultation. Call her assistant tomorrow to get a prompt appointment."

"Thank you," I said. *No way I'd be calling another doctor.*

"In regards to physical restrictions you need to forget about yoga or hitting the roller-coaster rides at Magic Mountain for a couple of days."

I rolled my eyes. "Got it."

"Nice of you to drive your girlfriend here," he said to Alejandro. "I'm sure you have only the best intentions. Do I need to spell out the rest?"

"I'm not his girl—"

Alex shook his head. "Apparently, you do?" "You need to curtail sexual activity for the next couple of weeks so her wounds heal properly."

My eyes widened. "He's not my boyfriend and we're not—"

Alex nodded, somber. "Thanks, Dr. Dewitt. Will do." His mouth squirmed, an impossibly sexy dimple formed in his cheek as he shoved back a smile. "Sophie didn't want to go to the ER. I had to convince her. Now she's going to be even madder at me." He cocked his head and winked at me.

I shot him a look that could kill. Or, at least, hopefully maim. "I'm not like that. I just met him tonight! I cannot believe that—"

"Yes, yes, young love will survive." The doctor scribbled notes on my chart.

"We are *not* having *any*—"

"You already argued with the good doctor about the antibiotics, Bonita. Pick your battles." Alex stifled laughter and shook his finger at me. "No sex. You're just going to have to live with that."

"I will not—"

"Everyone says that," Dr. Dewitt said. "Patients and their significant others consent. But then it's a special occasion, or an anniversary and everyone boards the passion train. Those wounds that were healing? Break open. Some even get infected. I see them back here or at the clinic, but it's usually too late. Then, good luck with the plastic surgery. I recommend either abstinence, or if you can't manage that? Just make do for a week or so with some basic foreplay." He pointed to Alex. "Yes, she's super pretty. Practice restraint."

Alex slapped his hands up in the air like he'd just been arrested. "I'll try my best to abide by your rules, Doc. But Sophie's her own woman, very opinionated. She does what she wants. That's one of the reasons I like her."

I blasted Alejandro with my most evil death glare, grabbed the prescription forms and business card, yanked the stupid, cubicle curtain out of the way and stomped toward the front desk. "Worst. Day. Ever."

* * *

I sat in the passenger seat as Alex drove his Jeep down yet another residential L.A. block filled with short apartment buildings that looked exactly alike. "Do you have your new address written down somewhere in your purse?" He asked. "Your wallet? Your phone?"

"All of the above. I even embroidered it onto a pillowcase while I was delayed in Denver. Because I, Sophie Marie Priebe, am so freaking organized that if I was only twenty-five years older, I could be the head CPA for The Container Store. I left the paperwork in the apartment with a copy of the lease. I've landed in Stepford, haven't I? Shoot me now. Oh wait! That one looks familiar. Pull over, please!"

He parked the Jeep at the curb. I got out walked onto the grass and squinted at the building. "This is it. There's something super familiar about it." I walked up, grabbed my keys from my purse and they slid wet across my fingers. Lovely—they too were soaked in beer. I stuck one in the front door lock of the first-floor walk-up and turned it.

Five minutes later, I was still finagling the key in the stupid lock.

"Are you sure this is your apartment?" Alex asked

"Damned if I know? *Boyfriend.*" I glared at him and stuck out my tongue. "I've been up for twenty-one hours, been in Lost Angeles for eight of them and I'm the next thing to brain-dead. Yes, this looks like my apartment. But guess what?" I threw my hands up in the air and then pointed to another apartment building across the street. "So does that one." I gestured at another complex a block away. "And, that one does too!"

Alex reached out and took a hold of the keys. "Hand 'em over. Let me try."

I yanked them from him like I'd touched a lit burner on the stove. "I appreciate all your help, Alejandro, Mr. Driver, don't-know your last name. But, hey?" I returned to wrangling the key in the door. "You allowed—no—let me re-phrase that." I swiveled and jabbed the key toward his chest. "You *encouraged* an ER doctor to think I'm a stupid-headed slut. Which, I'm not. How dare you! What if I run into him again?"

"I know you're not a stupid slut. You need to stop threatening me with a violent keychain and put that weapon back in that door. If we play our cards right, your cuts are going to heal just fine. You're never going to see that doctor again." Alex said. "Look. Sometimes I get carried away. Stupid things pop out of my mouth because I'm going for the joke that will hopefully make people forget whatever their problem is and find a little peace for a moment. A little calm in their storm. I'm sorry."

I grumbled. "You don't have to stay here. I'd lay odds California Barbie's still at the Westwood Grill tossing back Coronas and shots with her triplet friends. I'm sure she'd let you to take her for a ride."

"I already took that ride," Alex said.

I paused for a moment. *Of course he did. Forget Magic Mountain and Disneyland. This guy was so smokin' hot that he was probably the most favorite ride in town.*

"Shocker."

"It's not a ride I want to take again."

"Doesn't matter to me." When my legs that already felt weak started to tremble ever so slightly. *I had to get rid of him. Now. Before—* "Oh, look the door is opening! Yay! Thanks so much for your help. It was great meeting you, Alejandro, Alex, whatever your name is. See you around the neighborhood."

If I played my cards right, I'd never be seeing him again.
I jiggled the keys dramatically. "Home sweet, home!"
"If the lock's opening why isn't the door opening?" He peered at me, perplexed. "You're lying to me. That lock is still locked and that door is totally not opening. We're not even dating and you're lying to me? Is it just you, or are all Wisconsin chicks this devious?" He frowned. "I'm staying."

A small smile snuck onto my lips and almost betrayed me. I quickly erased it. "You've helped me just about enough for one day. Leave." My face ached. My bones were weary. My legs were so tired I prayed they wouldn't start twitching or worse—give out underneath me.

"I'm not going until I know you are safe and sound inside your new apartment."

I turned and stared at him. The streetlight shone high above and behind Alex illuminating his black hair, his earnest, handsome, chiseled face and his wide, muscular shoulders. In combination with the moonlight, he was almost too beautiful to be of this world. He looked like a dark, dangerous angel. I half expected wings to pop out of his back. I blinked and squinted at him. No wings. Just one hundred percent stubborn human male gorgeousness.

He was funny, smart and stunning. The Deadly Dangerous Guy Trifecta. Totally not fair.

But then I remembered my secret power, which could get rid of a guy like Off!, the mosquito repellant. I had it down to a science.

The nice boys, the sweethearts who I called the Beta Boys, would give up easily.

"Hey, Sophie? So, um, want to go to a party with me this weekend?" Beta Boy would ask.

Me: "Thanks, can't. Got family in town visiting."

Beta Boy: "Okay."

I felt bad about letting them down, but it only would have been more hurtful for them down the road.

The Alpha Boys were tougher. Their sub-categories

included: Brilliant. Boneheads. Bad boys. Broken. As well as all combinations, thereof. I'd turn the Alpha Boys down over and over. I'd make fun of the ones that wouldn't take no for an answer. I'd insult their manly egos. I'd be standoffish. After all, it was for their own good. With enough work and the right technique I could get an Alpha Boy—oh hell, I could get any guy to stop asking me out. Walk away. Leave me alone.

Yeah, I got called some names. "Frigid bitch" seemed to be pretty popular. Eventually I'd hear the obligatory gossip about how they told their friends that I was obviously gay. Actually, that might have made it easier. *Unfortunately I just wasn't wired that way.*

But now, looking up at Alejandro, I couldn't even think of cruel words let alone say them. And I wasn't sure if it was him, or if it was me. Maybe I was just overly tired. I'd been told a hundred times not to get too stressed: that it could do a number on me. I'd been warned this trip might not be a good idea. That it might trigger anxiety, additional symptoms or be too much for my system to handle.

But I didn't listen to the naysayers, because I had hope. And hope can make you do weird things. Hope made me take this journey two-thousand miles away from everyone I knew and loved.

So what if tonight started with a small misstep, a little trip to the ER? I was here. I would confront my fears. I would stagger through them one misstep, one shard of glass in the face at a time.

"Are you okay?" Alejandro asked.

"Yeah. Why?"

"Because you've been talking non-stop ever since I met you and suddenly you're quiet. Too quiet."

I shook my head and sat down on the front stoop. "I'm fine." I told my brain to get a grip and admonished my heart to stop pounding like a stupid teenager's. Oh wait—I was still nineteen, so maybe that last reminder didn't count.

Cut it out, Sophie. You didn't come to L.A. for romance. "Thank you so much for your help, Alejandro. Let's stay in touch. Right now all I want to do is bury my head in a pillow and go to sleep."

"Where do you plan on doing that if you can't find your apartment? I don't live that far away. You could come to my place. I have plenty of room—"

"No."

"Okay." He paced back and forth in front of me on the sidewalk. His legs were long, his jeans were fitted and showed off his body that was blessed by nature and enhanced by working out, being an athlete, or both.

Maybe God only wanted to hear big important prayers, but I couldn't help myself and uttered a silent "thank you" for the fact that Alejandro didn't wear his jeans half way down his ass like some gangsta wannabe.

"You want me to take you to a motel?"

"Um..."

He stopped pacing, stared at me and gestured with two fingers from my gaze that was locked on his posterior... up to his face. "Eyes up here, Bonita."

"Oh. Perhaps I was dozing for a moment." *Or perhaps a sinkhole would appear underneath me and swallow me whole.* "What were you saying?"

"Do you want to go to a motel?"

"That would be a definite no."

"Do you even remember your new address?" He asked.

"2132... 2138... 3821..." I dropped my keychain into my lap and my forehead into my hands.

"Stop!" Alejandro grabbed my wrist and pulled my hands away from my face.

I smacked his hand. "You stop! What are you doing?"

"I don't care how tired you are. You've got to be careful with your face. Have you taken your drugs, yet? Where are your drugs?" He grabbed my purse and rifled through it. "You need to swallow a damn pill and apply those cremes to your cuts."

"You're overreacting. I don't have any cuts on my forehead or my hands. Just a few on my face and my head." When exhaustion rolled over me like a big monster truck. "I totally appreciate everything you have done for me. I've officially passed tired and am headed toward a coma." I lay down on the concrete porch, pulled my knees up into my chest and rested my cheek that had the fewest wounds on my forearm.

His eyes widened. "What the hell are you—"

"The drugs are in the zippered side pocket inside my purse."

He unzipped the side pocket and pulled out the creme. "You will not spend your first night in L.A. like this," he said. "You cannot lie down on a stranger's front porch, in a strange city and go to sleep. They'll find your body in a dumpster tomorrow or next week. And then because I helped you—I'll be the main suspect. It'll be on all the news shows. 'Local young man's the main suspect in pretty midwestern girl's demise. News at ten.'"

"You're a dork," I said. "Perhaps the reporters will say, 'Alejandro whatever-his-last-name-is was *never* a quiet young man. He didn't keep to himself enough and too frequently intervened in the business of others. But the ladies seemed to like him something fierce. Although he banged too many stupid girls, he seemed to have a kind heart and he was a good driver.' Nighty night, Alejandro." I smiled into my forearm.

"You can't do this! The writers from *Law and Order: SVU* will copy this case and some bit actor who longs to be on the CW Network will play my role." I squinted one eye partially open and observed as he twisted open the cremes, squeezed a little of each onto his index and third fingers. "I hate those shows." He leaned in toward me.

Oh crap, he was delicious.

I tried to keep my breathing regular. Not stop breathing.

Not inhale with a loud gasp as he touched my face. For a big guy with large hands, I was shocked at how gently he dabbed the ointment onto my cuts.

I closed my eyes. Every place he patted on my face tingled. I flushed and felt warm all over: from head to toe. From heart to groin. But then I felt something almost miraculous. Something I feared was lost for good.

I felt safe. I felt protected.

When out of the corner of my eye I spotted a small scruffy dog poke its head around modern brightly colored curtains in the living room adjacent to my apartment and bark in a squeaky soprano.

I lifted my head. "Gidget?"

Alejandro frowned. "Sorry?"

I pushed myself to kneeling, flipped through my key ring. I found a different key—almost identical to the first one, shoved it into the lock and turned it. The door clicked open like magic. "Oh hallelujah! This is my place! Yay!"

CHAPTER THREE

I groped the wall next to the door and flipped on the lights, illuminating my tiny crash pad. "Gidget's my new next-door neighbor's dog. I'm home! I'm home!" I wanted to dance, but instead twirled around the small living room that featured a beat up love seat, an ancient recliner chair and some area rugs on the scuffed hardwood floors.

"Hang on." Alejandro stepped inside my door and looked around. "You're not supposed to be doing activities like yoga, or dancing or roller coasters or—"

"Twirling? The doctor didn't say anything about twirling." I was so incredibly jacked to be home. Even though technically my real home was two thousand miles away from this pricey step up from a closet that sported yellowed polyester lace draperies.

I honed in on his confused but happy face. This impossibly gorgeous young man was standing in my living room and looked like he didn't know what to do next. A couple of years ago I might have been super brave and offered him a suggestion like, "Shut up and kiss me." But a couple of years ago I was a completely different person. "Thank you heaps, Alejandro. For catching me. For driving me. For making me go to the ER. For helping me find my home."

He waved his hand dismissively. "Happy to help a tourist in need. In fact, I could show you around town—"

"I'm not a tourist. No time. I'm here for the USCLA summer session."

That statement was kind of true.

"What are you taking? A required core class? Then catching a tan and learning how to surf? I can teach you how to surf, you know."

"I'm taking Genetics 300 level with Professor Schillinger. I'm not the best swimmer in the world. In fact, I suck at it. So, thanks but I'll hold off on the surfing lessons for now."

"Genetics 300. Guess you're not just a pretty face." He grabbed my purse, pulled out the bottle of antibiotics, popped the childproof cap open and shook out one monster-sized pill. He walked into my kitchenette, opened the fridge door and peered inside. "Do you have any bottled water in this place?"

"I have nothing in this place but my luggage," I said.

He sighed and looked at the pill in his hand. "I'll be back in five."

"Tap water doesn't scare me," I said. "Another thing about midwestern chicks."

He cocked his head and eyed me like I was a little nuts.

I pointed to the kitchen sink. "Feel free to fill a glass with L.A.'s finest."

He did. He handed me the glass of tap water and the pill. I took it from him and swallowed it. I shuddered.

"Tap water sucks."

"Tap water's fine. It's the monster scary pill that sucks."

"It's healing," he said.

"According to you," I replied.

"Professor Schillinger is the smartest, coolest professor on campus. I can help you with your swimming. You just need to get in that ocean water and paddle around for a bit.

Get your confidence up. Once you do that, I can get you up on a board in no time, Bonita."

Drinking tap water and swimming and genetics and surfing. Two were the truth and two were a lie. I was so freaking tired I was practically hallucinating. And now I had to find a way to say goodbye to the most handsome guy I'd ever met. *Oh suck it up, Sophie. You are no stranger to tough times or stubborn Alpha Boys. Just get rid of him already.*

"Hey Alejandro?" I asked.

"What?"

"You know where I live. You know my name. You know where to find me."

"True," he said. "But, I'm not a stalker type. Got too much on my plate. Too many things I need to get done. Tonight, with you, has been kind of an exception for me."

Not the answer I expected. But I nodded like I completely understood. "I need to crash. So thanks and good night." I took his hand, stroked the base of his thumb and sighed. *This was one of my signature bye-bye moves. It worked with every single Alpha Boy I'd ever met.* "Maybe next time we meet, you could tell me a little bit more about you. I'd love that."

Especially considering I never planned to see him again.

"Agree. You've had a hell of a day, and you totally need to sleep."

Alejandro was a total pushover. He was cake. "Thanks for understanding."

"Oh, I definitely got it." He squeezed my hand, placed his other hand on my forearm and pulled me toward him.

"Um?" I frowned as my face came within an inch of where the narrow part of the V started in his T-shirt. I was breathing into his chest that was so wide and strong, I felt dwarfed next to it.

"I can't leave yet, Bonita."

"Yes, you can. You have to."

He placed his finger under my chin and tilted my face up toward his. I had no choice but to look up into his ridiculously gorgeous, hazel eyes rimmed by long, black eyelashes. Take in his high, sharp cheekbones, the way his thick, black hair was tucked behind his ears, and the fact that he would not take his eyes off me. And I wondered two things. One. Could you hate a guy for being too hot? And, two.

Why now? Why after the past eighteen months was the Universe, God, a Higher Power, the Fates handing me this tough card? I had enough tough cards to build a tough card deck. I had so many important things to accomplish in L.A. And unfortunately, getting involved with Alejandro wasn't one of them.

"I just have one more thing to do before I leave," Alejandro said.

He did not just say he had *"one more thing to do"*? I was so punchy I giggled.

"Hey! Stop laughing. You just popped open one of your cuts. It's bleeding again. God dammit, Sophie! I'm serious."

"Okay. Okay," I said. "You're serious. What's your one more thing? Lay it on me." *Oh craptastic with the sexual innuendoes.* I started giggling again, tried to shut it down but instead, snorted. Well if nothing else could get rid of this guy, I bet snorting while laughing would totally do the trick.

"Just one more simple thing. After that, I promise you— I am out of here."

"Your one more simple thing does not involve anything the good ER doctor said I couldn't do?"

"I promise. He never mentioned this."

* * *

My sublet was, just as Alex suggested, old. The apartment complex had probably been built sixty years ago. The walls painted over dozens of times with multitudes of colors ranging from eggshell white to eggshell blue to eggshell yellow. The oversized kitchen sink was accented with small spider vein cracks in what was probably the original porcelain. I leaned forward over the vintage Spanish tiled counter with the discolored grout. My head dropped forward into the sink while Alex stood next to me and massaged shampoo onto my beer soaked hair.

"Okay," I said. "I think you got it all out."

"I poured the shampoo on your head five seconds ago." He leaned in a little closer and pressed his leg, hip and then his torso firmly against me. "Keep your hands around your face. Like a mask. Or a shield. We don't want this sudsy stuff to get on your cuts."

I fidgeted. "Are we done yet?"

"No. You still smell like a brewery from a block away."

"Maybe you need to go a block away and try that smell test again," I said. "Why does everyone call you a driver?"

"Because I'm a Designated Driver. A couple of my friends and I do this to help fellow students." He turned the water back on and rinsed my hair. "I don't drink anymore. Don't do drugs. Everyone knows I'll drive students and their friends home if they've had too much. Or take their keys if I have to. As long as they don't abuse the privilege. Just like what happened tonight."

Interesting. Alejandro wasn't your typical, college, party boy.

He leaned his face into my hair.

"What are you doing?" I blushed and prayed he wouldn't notice.

He pulled away from me. "While I have nothing against Coronas—you still smell like one. Just one more wash." He poured more shampoo onto my head and massaged my scalp. "I will never understand how you women tolerate this stinky stuff."

"In defense of girls everywhere, I have five words for you," I said.

"What?" His nails scratched gently on my scalp and I suddenly understood why Gidget the dog liked her ears rubbed.

"Axe body wash for men."

He rinsed off the shampoo. Thoroughly. So thoroughly I calculated how many ones I had in my wallet to tip him. "Thank you. That's great. Now I don't have to go to bed with beer head."

"Or pop your cuts open. Again." He'd managed to find a towel somewhere, and dried my head with it while I was still bent over the counter, my head in the sink.

I was getting used to this head-rubbing thing. This felt pretty darn good. After all the stress of today, I figured I should at least make the supreme effort to stay awake and take this kind of attention for another hour or so. But he wrapped the towel around my head and tucked in the corner like a turban.

"Head out of the sink, please."

I heard the sound of a chair scraping across the linoleum floor.

"Sit here. Are you woozy? I'll guide you."

"Um…" I wasn't woozy. I was in love. Okay, I wasn't in love. I was simply infatuated. Truth be told, I just needed him to do this head-scratching thing for a bit longer. "You forgot the conditioner," I said. "Thank you so much for getting rid of my beer-head, but you totally forgot the conditioner. It's because you're a man. And I'm not sure if men even use conditioner. But girls do. And it's super important. And if I don't get conditioner, my hair will—"

Alejandro's phone belted "Gimme Shelter" by the Rolling Stones. He yanked it from his pocket and looked at the message. "Sorry, Bonita." He strode toward my front door. "It's an emergency. The conditioner will have to wait."

And just like that? Alejandro was gone. And my first day in L.A. had officially ended.

CHAPTER FOUR

I walked out my door the next morning and nearly tripped over a bouquet of white daisies jammed in a mason jar filled with water. Next to it was a small, white envelope. I opened it and pulled out a greeting card. It was a cartoon of a man who stood next to a dog that had a perplexed look on his face. The man pointed to a well. "Get well!" was inscribed in the dialogue bubble above the man's head.

> *Dear Sophie:*
>
> *Hope you're feeling better. Meet me at the Grill tonight? I want to see your beautiful, dairy queen face.*
>
> *Best,*
> *Alejandro*

Beneath his signature were his phone number and email.
I smiled, but that quickly faded when I realized I'd never go back to the Grill. I needed to cut Alejandro off quickly. Don't give him a reason to hope, or pursue, or expect anything from me that I wasn't able to give him. Besides, today was going to be jam-packed with all sorts of

adventures. Just not the kind I had last night.

***

I walked down what felt like miles of sterile white hallways, past white-coated interns, doctors and a few folks in medical scrubs. I headed toward a modern desk at the end of the hallway where a trim man and woman sat behind a counter next to computers and talked in hushed tones on their headsets.

I smiled at both the receptionists, waited my turn at the counter and glanced around. There was a small waiting area tucked into the corner with wood-like chairs and a few side tables covered in magazines. Cheap watercolor posters featuring soothing seascapes and knock off vintage prints of Santa Monica back in the day adorned the walls. A few folks read weathered magazines. One man surfed the Internet on his iPhone. Another lady slumped forward and rubbed her temples with the heels of her hands.

The male receptionist concluded his call first and turned his attention to me. "How can I help you?"

"I have an appointment for the study."

"Great." He reached across the desk, grabbed a stack of paperwork attached to a clipboard and handed it to me. "Sign in on the roster. Fill this out and we'll get you up and running. I'll take your insurance card. Remember to print the name of the person and their contact information in case of emergency. You can have a seat over there." He pointed to the waiting area.

I signed in, took a seat and started filling out the forms. "How long have you had symptoms?" *A year and a half.* "Please check the boxes next to the symptoms you have experienced." *Check. Check. Check. Check. Check.* "Has anyone else in your family been diagnosed with this condition? If your answers is yes, please fill in your relationship to this person as well as if they are still living?" *Yes. Grandmother.*

Very much alive. About a half hour later I finished filling out the mile-high pile of forms and stood at the counter watching Phil the receptionist enter my data into USCLA hospital's system.

"Strange," Phil said. "Looks like you already have an account and a chart with us." He leaned in and squinted at his computer screen. "ER visit just last night." He peered up at me, really looked at me for the first time, took in my face and winced. "Ouch. That must have hurt."

"You should have seen the other guy." I made a fist and flexed the bicep muscle in my arm.

Phil smiled. "We've got some really great plastic surgeons on staff here if you're worried?"

"Nah. Everything's healing. My face is going to be just fine. I just want to get on with the important stuff."

"Got it." Phil typed a little bit more and hit enter. "Done and... done. Go down that hall," he pointed, "to Room 342 on the left. Nurse Michaels will get you started. Good luck."

"Thank you," I said.

* * *

I sat in a small hospital room wearing an airy light blue hospital gown while Nurse Michaels attended to my every medical need. He took my blood pressure and my temperature. "Nothing to eat or drink since last night?" he asked.

"Nothing."

He pricked my finger, drew a little blood and dropped it onto a slide. "How many days since your last menstrual cycle?"

"Five," I said. "No, I'm not pregnant." *Unless I was the reincarnation of the Virgin Mary.*

He cinched a tube around my bare arm and tapped the underside of my elbow. "You have thin veins."

"So I've been told."

He found a good one and inserted a needle. I squeezed my eyes shut and tried not to make a face. "Did you get it?" I asked.

"Your veins have a tendency to roll," he said. "Sorry. I'll get it this time."

I hoped so because my arm felt like a sausage in a casing that was too tight.

"Darn," he said. "Third time's the charm."

I gritted my teeth and reminded myself to breathe.

* * *

I tried my best not to be nervous as gowned hospital techs wheeled me down the hall on a gurney. I already had an IV inserted into the back of my hand and an ID bracelet on my wrist as they rolled me into the operating room. It was a small, white space with multiple, box-shaped monitors craning down from the ceiling all focused at the operating table in the room's center.

There was a crash cart with electric paddles should my heart decide to tank during the procedure. Stainless steel carts were filled with instruments. Large round lights beamed down on me like I was about to be interviewed for a TV show.

But I wasn't. Instead I was about to have stem cells injected into my spinal cord in multiple locations.

A couple of techs helped transfer me from the cart to the operating table. "Hi, Sophie," a friendly female voice said from behind a medical mask and goggles. "I'm Dr. Kristin Warren and I'll be in charge of your anesthesiology today. You have to be absolutely still during the procedure so I'm going to knock you out for just a little bit. You won't feel a thing. I promise."

"Sounds good." I gave her a thumbs up.

"Hello, Ms. Priebe." A George Clooney type wearing a

mask leaned down and must have been smiling because I spotted deep crinkle wrinkles etched next to his eyes. "I'm Dr. Goddard and I'll be performing your procedure. Thank you for participating in this study. We're hoping to help a lot of folks, just like you, in the future."

"Thank you, Dr. Goddard."

"Sophie," Dr. Warren said, "I want you to start at ten and count backward."

It was officially too late to turn back.

"Ten. Nine." The lights on the ceiling wavered. "Eight." I felt a little funny. "Sevvvv—"

* * *

I woke with a shudder in the recovery room on a skinny cot. My senses came back pretty quickly. The room smelled antiseptic, was painted white and accented with stainless steel carts and stands. A nurse asked me how I felt. Frankly, I felt surprisingly well—just a little achey on my back where I'd been injected.

"Can you roll onto your side?" she asked.

"Sure." I gingerly turned over.

She pulled off the gauze and checked my injection sites. "They look good." She placed a few cushy bandages over them. An assistant brought me orange juice and some crackers. Told me to rest for a bit longer and get dressed when I was ready. Just take it easy. Don't over do anything for a couple of days.

"No problem," I agreed. "I just have one simple thing I need to get done this afternoon."

* * *

I sat on the hard, industrial plastic and metal seat next to a wide, unwashed window on a Blue Line Bus. I'd boarded at a main intersection on campus and headed toward Venice

Beach, which technically wasn't all that far away. I peered at a hard copy of the maps and schedules of L.A.'s bus routes that I'd grabbed from the Student Union.

There were about forty stops on the route. I knew from researching and Googling that traffic in L.A. was a fickle beast. The kind that when you lopped off one head, seven more materialized and took its place. Every blog I'd read about L.A. traffic said you couldn't beat it, so it was simply best to leave early and arrive on time instead of screwing up all your important appointments.

My summer journey here involved a lot of important appointments. I'd just spent most of the day at my first. Getting admitted to the USCLA Stem Cell trial study for early onset multiple sclerosis was huge. I'd signed a butt load of paperwork promising, swearing, declaring, that I would not participate in any other healing modalities while I allowed USCLA doctors and their staff to pump me full of stem cells, draw vials of my blood several times a week and MRI my brain and spinal cord in order to monitor my progress.

But I'd already decided before I flew out here to break their rules. Because, while I'd had MS for only a year and a half, my Nana was diagnosed thirty years earlier. She'd been highly-functioning until she landed in a wheelchair five years ago. Don't get me wrong. I was thrilled to be part of the stem cell research, but I really didn't know how much time my grandmother had left. And I couldn't just sit still, do nothing and lose her without a fight.

I was on a full-fledged journey to find help or healing for the both of us and nothing would stop me.

I planned on exploring the cornucopia of alternative medicines and treatments that could help stop the progression or even cure MS. Yeah, acupuncture and chiropractic were the basic standards and available everywhere—including Wisconsin. While it would have been fun to go to India or China to explore alternative

healing—it would have killed my budget. That left L.A. as the closest and probably biggest mecca for unconventional therapies.
You named it—Los Angeles had it. There was acupuncture with dry cupping. Acupuncture with wet cupping. Shamans. Peyote. Vision Quests. Brujerias and their concoctions. Gurus: Eastern Indian. South American. North American. Sweat Lodges. Re-birthing. Craniosacral. Thai massage. Chinese massage. Yoga—every freaking variety. Shakti-fests in the desert. Ecstatic dancing. Oxygen chambers. Hyperbaric chambers.

* * *

The sun was sinking toward the horizon as I stepped off the bus in Venice at Lincoln and Brooks. I stood on the sidewalk next to Patsy's Pet Store and Exotic Creatures Emporium, with an "Adopt a Kitten" banner in their window situated above a large cage filled with kittens. I pulled my handwritten directions from my purse but couldn't resist leaning in and ogling the fur babies.

Some napped. An orange fluff ball wrestled a tabby in the too-cute-for-words kitten version of a WWE fight. One longhaired, fat, fuzzy black kitten toddled to the edge of the cage, put his paws up on the rungs, gazed at me determinedly through the window and meowed, which sounded like, "Eep."

"I don't care how cute you are. Someone will adopt you soon. Just not me," I said. "I have too much to do in L.A." The bus squelched clean-gas fumes in my face as it pulled away from the curb and teetered into bumper-to-bumper Lincoln Avenue traffic. I examined my directions.

Exit bus at Lincoln and Brooks. Check. *Walk on Lincoln three blocks south to California Avenue.* I walked. Check. I looked up at the Triple XXX Hot Porn Store that featured "Going Out of Business" banners in its murky, tinted windows.

Once again the all-mighty Internet was beating the tar out of local businesses and forcing mom and pop places to close. Times were changing. I was changing too. *Turn right on California Avenue.* Check.

I strolled another couple of blocks, rounded a few corners and considering that I wasn't the best with directions, still somehow found my way to my destination.

The house was small with a tiny, fenced-in yard overgrown with flowers in a rainbow of colors. Fat sparrows, hummingbirds and a few bees visited a fountain and a birdbath. I buzzed #2 on the security keypad next to the gate. A hand inscribed sign hanging from the gate's entrance read, "Namasté. Please enter and leave QUIETLY so as not to disturb our neighbors." I was beeped in, pushed the gate and entered QUIETLY just as I was advised.

***

Native-American dreamcatchers dangled from the latches on two, small, older windows that were cracked half way open. Sturdy, metal bars painted a flaking white were bolted on the outside. No one was breaking in here without some effort.

I stood in a smallish living room furnished with bookshelves filled with books on healing, cultivating a positive attitude, as well as an impressive assortment of crystals. I wondered what I'd be dreaming about tonight while I waited for my appointment with Lizzie Sparks, medical intuitive extraordinaire.

A darker skinned woman with a bindi mark on her forehead wore yoga attire and a headset. She typed vigorously on her computer situated on top of an ergonomically designed Ikea desk, paused and smiled at me. "I'm Ms. Spark's assistant. My name's Indira. She'll be with you soon...." She squinted at her computer then looked back up. "Miss Priebe?"

I nodded.

"Have a seat. Can I bring you some tea?"

"Oh, thanks. No, I'm fine. I got here a little early." I sat down on a worn green vinyl couch and its tired springs squeaked in protest.

Indira nodded. "Good intuition on your part. Most first-timers arrive late. L.A. traffic."

I'd read and re-read Lizzie Spark's books since I stumbled upon them several years earlier. Her first: *You Can Heal—No Matter What.* Her second: *Heal Your Disease—Naturally.* And her third: *You are the Healer—Not a Disease.* And now here I was, in her waiting room, just moments away from talking in person with the woman, the legend, the diviner.

The light was fading outside in a muted display of colors over the Pacific Ocean, maybe only a mile or so away. Wow. Gorgeous. Even though I had been nervous as sin about doctors injecting my spinal cord with stem cells, everything about today had gone easy peasy. The polar opposite of yesterday.

Indira touched her headset. "Okay. Yes." She nodded at me. Goosebumps grew on the back of my forearms. "Lizzie can see you now. Come with me." She beckoned. I followed her as we walked through a doorway and down a narrow corridor lined with framed healing symbols on the walls. Indira opened a door for me. "Good luck!"

It seemed wherever I went in Los Angeles someone was wishing me good luck. I wasn't going to complain. I'd take all the luck I could get and then some.

* * *

I was in a small room with one barred window that was cracked open. I sat scrunched forward on an older, upholstered chair. A single lamp rested on a side table next to a big cushy armchair where Lizzie Sparks sat across from me and held my hand. Even in this dim light, considering Lizzie was close to seventy, she was gorgeous. She had silver hair, high cheekbones and looked fit. I knew she was the medical intuitive to the stars but she wore unpretentious khakis and a floral peasant top. I hoped I would be lucky enough to look like her when I hit her age.

If I hit her age.

"You've traveled a long distance to be here, Sophie. You want answers about a disease that you were diagnosed with not too long ago. Your disease is early onset, but I sense it has already given you several debilitating symptoms."

"Yes," I said. I really enjoyed the tremors that would come out of nowhere, the weakness, fatigue, dizziness and quite possibly my favorite symptom: a random seizure.

Lizzie's face was still. "You fear your symptoms will increase."

"Yes."

"You've been through radical change in the past year. You had seizures, experienced blind spots. Your boyfriend left you. This hurt. Caused you pain. But you knew he wasn't the one."

I nodded.

"You came to L.A. to find someone."

"No." I shook my head. "I came to L.A. to find healing."

"Healing doesn't necessarily arrive in the package or the pill that we think it will come in. We picture how our lives are supposed to play out. How healing is supposed to look or feel. But you know the old saying?"

"Which one?"

"Tell God your plans and then listen to her laugh." Lizzie squeezed my hand and smiled.

Laugh about this, God. I wasn't expecting MS. Yes my Nana had it, but my mom didn't and I thought I was free and clear. I was graduating high school and accepted at U of Wisconsin, Madison. I wasn't anticipating that I'd have to stay closer to home and go to U of W, Whitewater. I was planning on majoring in pre-law—not being a guinea pig in a medical study.

"Ms. Sparks. Do you have any intuition or feelings or a sense of who I should see or where I should go while I'm here in L.A.?" I asked.

"Close your eyes," Lizzie said.

I did. We were both silent and held hands for a few awkward moments.

"Your heart is closed," Lizzie said. "Your heart is closed down, shut tight, locked up. And you are scared to open it. Go to the healers who can open your heart." She released my hand but rubbed my arm maternally. "Does that make sense?"

"No. I don't know who can open my heart."

She was being too generic. She could be saying these things to anyone. I came here for answers. I didn't come to be coddled.

I pulled a list of names of healers and healing clinics from my purse that I'd printed out and thrust it in front of Lizzie. "These people, these types of healing? I've read about all of them. They all claim to have success for diseases like MS, Lupus, even Huntington's and/or certain types of cancer." My hand that held the paper shook a little.

I heard the nurse's voice in my head, "Take it easy for a few days, Sophie. Give your body a chance to rest. This isn't a suggestion. It's an order."

Lizzie beckoned to me with her index finger. I gave her the list. She picked up a pair of glasses from the side table, slipped them on her face, clicked her table lamp to a brighter level and perused it. Shook her head, grabbed a pen from the table and drew brisk lines through people's names, their occupations and contact information.

"Don't ask me why I'm doing this. I don't want to badmouth anyone. Feel free to ignore my recommendations. Let's just say I've been in this business for a long time and know the good ones, the opportunists, and jury's out on a lot of other folks." She handed the paper back to me. About a third of my potential saviors had inky black slashes through their names and contact information.

"Thank you," I said. "Out of all the people left, who should I go to? Who should I trust?"

"Considering you don't trust anyone right now—including me? I'd say that's going to unfold pretty quickly. You already set your intention to explore healing. You put it out into the universe and prayed about it. The wheels are turning and the right people—and believe me that does not mean they're all loving and kind—but they are exactly the folks you need because they facilitate your lessons. The right people are being cast, just like actors in a play. I bet they're already showing up in your life."

"Okay," I said. *Why wouldn't she be more specific? I wasn't here for something I could read in one of her books.*

"What happened to your face last night?" she asked.

My hand flew to my cheek. "Some drunken asshat pitched a beer bottle at another guy. His aim was a little off."

"That's not the easiest way to spend your first night in a new city. Even though you hate hospitals, looks like someone took good care of you."

There was a gentle knock on the door. "Come in," Lizzie said.

Indira cracked the door open and whispered, "Your next client is here."

I got up from the chair and walked toward the door. "Thank you, Ms. Sparks."

"Wait," Lizzie said.

I stopped in my tracks and faced her.

"I don't make a habit out of asking folks this but you're on a bit of an extraordinary journey. Keep me updated on how it's going? I'm primarily a medical intuitive but only possess a pinch of psychic ability. And by the way, no extra charge for future check-ins." She pointed to Indira. "Note that."

Indira nodded, pulled a card off the side table and handed it to me. "This is Lizzie's private e-mail."

"Use it," Lizzie said.

"I will." I palmed it. "Thanks so much."

"You're welcome. Be sure and tell me his name when you realize who he is."

"Huh?"

"Come with me." Indira reached for my hand and gently tugged me out of the room, down the hallway.

CHAPTER FIVE

I paid Lizzie Sparks's two hundred dollar consultation fee on my Nana's credit card. And just like that I was back out in Venice proper. The sun had set and there was a chill in the air as the beach fog had rolled in, obscuring light and buildings and further confusing my sense of direction. Or lack of it.

According to my research, Venice was this super cool place that was the surfer capitol of the world—Dogtown—like thirty years ago. I longed to see its funky boardwalk with tattoo parlors, grungy art and T-shirt shops, tarot readers and medical marijuana stores (I might or might not inhale), as well as Muscle Beach. But I wasn't in that section of Venice. Technically, I was in the 'hood section of Venice—after dark.

I squinted at my hand-written directions as I tried to walk back the way I came. But it just wasn't happening. The houses looked different. The streets appeared similar, but dissimilar, all at the same time. Maybe because it was nighttime? I pulled my phone out of my purse to check an app for directions. But my phone was dead. The idiot from the night before now owed me a phone as well as the bill for my ER visit.

I paced down small blocks, rounding corners. But no matter what street I turned on, I still couldn't find Lincoln Avenue. Lincoln was the thoroughfare with the buses that would take me back to my new, temporary home close to USCLA. I trudged past a big, unkempt park where some older kids and young men in sleeveless T-shirts and shorts sunk low on their butts played a pick up game of basketball. "Hey guys! Could you point me in the direction of Lincoln?"

Their game stopped for a second as they checked me out. "You a tourist?" A twenty-something, white guy with a shaved head whose arms and neck were tatted up asked, as he bounced the basketball. "You lost?" He cocked his head, eyed me up and down and licked his lips. He walked toward me, still bouncing the damn ball.

I was not only totally lost, but now also freaking out. Crap.

"No, not a tourist! Definitely not lost!" I said. "My ride's on their way. I think I just missed the cross street where I was supposed to meet them. Where's Lincoln? Could you just point me in the direction of Lincoln?"

"I do believe Lincoln's in a tomb some where and has been for a while." His shorter, uglier and even more inked up friend also ambled toward me.

"Hah!" I backpedaled. "You guys are hysterical." I pulled out my phone and punched a number. "Hey, yeah, it's me. You're right around the corner? Great!" I said into my dead phone.

"I'll show you where Lincoln is, sweetheart." The first guy smiled and kept moving toward me, a smug look growing on his face.

"No problem. I'm cool. Thanks!" I turned and resumed walking. Fast. I broke into a sweat and reached the chain-link fence that surrounded the park. Passed it. Phew. I was in the clear.

There was a loud, rapid shuffle of feet as two rough hands grabbed me, spun me around and slammed me face first into the metal fence. Their owner pressed himself against me from behind. I felt one of the bandages on my spine rip away from my skin. "Most of the tourists are a little closer to the beach. You coming here, all by yourself tonight, is kind of a treat." He ground his pelvis against my backside.

He was growing harder by the second. Not a turn on. Definitely not welcomed.

I was nineteen, and like most girls my age, I'd been groped a few times—at a packed dance club, in the stands of a football game and once at a high school graduation party. I'd managed to make it through these random assaults with a little dignity and maintained my choice for *when* I decided to have sex for the first time, as well as *whom* I'd share that crossroads with.

"A treat that my buddies and I might not be able to resist." The skinhead grabbed the waistband of my pants with one hand and yanked them. But my jean capris weren't giving.

And neither was I. A wave of anger surged through me. Last night's assault was unavoidable. Tonight's didn't have to be. "Go fuck yourself!" I slammed the back of my head into his face.

"Ow!" He released his hold on me. "Bitch!" he exclaimed. Which was my opportunity to run.

And I did. I raced down the block. I still didn't know where Lincoln was and at this point I didn't care. Just needed to make tracks.

"You cunt! You broke my nose!"

I stopped for a heartbeat, swiveled my head and eyed him, panting. He clutched his nose, which was trickling blood. Probably less blood than my face had oozed the night before. "Then maybe, you *Pintdick loser*, you need to stop attacking women half your size."

His friends stopped in their tracks bent over, clutched their stomachs and laughed out loud.

I continued running. Yes, I was an idiot for stopping, let alone delivering fighting words, but my adrenaline was sky-high.

"Yo, Oscar! A chick half your size takes you out?" one of his friends said. "Instagrammed it. And I'm sharing it with everyone!"

"Pintdick?" another friend snorted. "You ground it against her and she didn't feel anything? It's confirmed. Pintdick Oscar it is!"

* * *

I found my way back to Lincoln Avenue and staggered toward a bus stop a little over a block away. I was sweaty, messy and sensing a pattern here. The stop and go traffic had let up and cars rushed past each other. The occasional jerk cut someone off and horns blared. Tall streetlights overhead sliced through the beach fog casting weird illuminations onto the pavement and people below.

I trudged past a crowd of trendy attired twenty-somethings who posed like zombies had bitten them. They stood in a block long line that snaked into the entrance of a two-story brick building.

I was so tired, so out-of-it, again, that the midwesterner in me found it comforting to see a brick building in L.A. I stopped for a second to catch my breath and took in the sign on its frontage. It featured a foreign name in large block styled font. "Is this is a local nightclub?" I asked a girl in line.

She wore too much makeup and huge black sunglasses. She slid them down her nose and regarded me like I was a bug that had splattered onto her windshield. "It's a sausage restaurant."

My eyes widened as I gazed up and down the long line of hipster people. "You're waiting in line for... sausage?"

"Thirty minutes. The chef worked at Zertie's before he

opened SpreckenZie. This place has the best sausages in L.A."

I shook my head. "You all need to visit Wisconsin." I resumed walking.

"Your face is bleeding, you know." The girl pushed her glasses back up her face, shrugged her shoulders at her friends who giggled and then ignored me.

I'd almost made it to the bus stop. My face hurt: especially the part that had been shoved up against the fence. I was outside the pet store and bright security beams fixed to the top of the building illuminated their parking lot. A tiny light in the store's interior hovered over the cage of kittens in the window.

All that lovely adrenaline was draining from my body, leaving me weak and tired. Or maybe my exhaustion was from going under general anesthesia while they pumped my spine full of stem cells.

My second night in L.A. might have been shittier than my first night.

But the store with its decent lighting seemed like a safe enough place to stop, catch my breath and rest for a moment. I glanced behind me—no Pintdick or his pals. Thank God. I rested my hand against the store window. I heard a few tiny squeaks. Oh, please, no rats or mice. But the peeps were coming from inside the store.

I peered into the window. All the kittens were sleeping with the exception of the longhaired, black one I'd noticed earlier. He wrestled a pink, fuzzy toy about half his size; gripping it with his two front paws, biting and kicking it repeatedly. "You are too cute," I said.

He dropped the toy, toddled to the window, looked up at me and meowed, mouth wide open. Something stirred in my chest.

"Your heart is closed down, shut tight, locked up…" Lizzie had said. "Go to the healers who can open your heart."

Lizzie Sparks' comments did not apply to a cat.

"No," I said. "No freaking way I need a cat right now. I give you major points for being charming and I'll say a prayer that the right person adopts you soon." I tapped on the window right over his fat, funny face. He stopped meowing. I swear he squinted and frowned. I frowned back, forced myself to leave and walked the few steps toward the bus stop.

A disheveled man wearing pink robes with a long gray beard that matched his hair stumbled from a doorway onto the sidewalk in front of me and yelled, "Hare Krishna! Hare Rama!"

I quite possibly jumped two feet in the air. "Hare awesome!" I veered around him and made it to the curb where I huddled on a small metallic bench under the bus sign as the Big Blue Bus approached.

* * *

I sat on that hard industrial seat through the forty-odd bus stops from Venice to Westwood. My bones ached. My back spasmed. My face hurt. My thighs cramped—probably from all the sprinting to get away from some asshat or crazy person that showed up in my play. Because this was, according to Lizzie Sparks, my intention. Hah! Like I really wanted a skinhead rapist and a man wearing pink robes to be in my play.

My mom had *not* wanted me to come to L.A. for the stem cell program. She said something would open up in Madison or Milwaukee or Chicago. But I hadn't told Mom about my other reason for coming here. She most likely assumed I was simply being a typical, stubborn nineteen-year-old college girl who needed to leave home and act out my 90210 fantasies. But that wasn't the reason I'd picked L.A.

I loved my mom. She was the hardest working single

mom I'd ever met. (Yes, I was prejudiced.) But there came a time in a girl's life where one had to move a bit away from parental approval, even if that meant doing something pretty big that one's parent didn't approve of. That time was now.

An hour later the bus pulled up at my stop and I held onto the handrail as I descended its tall stairs. It seemed like today was the longest day ever. But that couldn't be possible, because *yesterday* was the longest day.

Cole was outside my apartment with Gidget. She sniffed the grass, squatted and piddled as I approached my door. "You okay?" he asked.

"Yeah." I searched through my purse for my keys. "Why?"

"You look even paler than yesterday and you've got some blood on your cheek."

The poser girl was right. Pintdick's assault had re-opened one of my wounds. "I'm fine."

"Good. I saw flowers on your doorstep this morning and this afternoon a gorgeous man with shoulders I'd kill for dropped off cookies."

I glanced down and saw a basket on my doorstep with tinfoil tightly wrapped around something inside. "How do you know that basket has cookies?"

"Because I opened it and took one," he said. "Okay, two. Don't hate me. I have a thing about sugar and hot men. You just moved here yesterday, but between the flowers, cards, cookies, Mr. Gorgeous and Gidget barking at you last night to welcome you home? And trust me, I know this dog—she's practically frothing at the mouth in anticipation of becoming your best friend—" Gidget bared her teeth at me and growled. "—your arrival here, Sophie, is turning into a bit of a mystery. And I'm a little obsessed, slightly Nancy Drew-esque, when it comes to mysteries."

"No worries. I'm simply here for summer session. The only mystery is why I've been so unlucky since I landed here."

"That kind of statement sets a bad intention. You might want to eat one of those cookies with a glass of milk before you decide the state of your luck. Night." He picked up Gidget, tucked her under his arm and headed back inside his place. "Snack time for Gidget before we watch TV?" The dog yipped and wagged her tail.

"You're right." I plunked down on my front step, unwrapped the tin foil, pulled out a cookie and sunk my teeth into a chocolate chip morsel with some kind of secret ingredient that tickled my taste buds. A postcard was stuck in the basket, a "DRIVEN" logo printed on the front. The same email and phone number were on the back. Along with a note:

Dear Sophie:

Summer session doesn't even start for two days. And you're recovering from a truly crappy first night in a new town. I'm sorry if I was a bit pushy. I volunteer to show you around L.A., which is kind of a weird place to be, even if you're raised here—like me. So call, or email me, or track me down at the Grill where I tend to hang out.

I nibbled on another cookie. This was the best part of my day so far. Except for the daisies. Filling out reams of paperwork, being pushed down a hospital corridor on a gurney, having my spine injected with stem cells, taking ass-numbingly long bus rides and being accosted by a skinhead were not in the running for the top ten best things about today. But this cookie was delicious. What was Alex's secret ingredient? I turned my eyes back to his letter.

And, by the way? I made these cookies from scratch. And that wasn't easy, because I suck at baking. I hope you like them.

Best,
Alejandro Maxwell Levine

Because you didn't know my last name and kind of accused me of being a stalker. Which I'm not.

P.S.
After I dropped off the basket, I was driving down your street and witnessed your next-door neighbor stealing one of my cookies. You might want to double bolt your doors. I'm not sure I trust him. Or his dog.

I started giggling and then thought about my day. I remembered how scared I was counting from ten backward in a cold, sterile room before I blacked out and woke up shivering on a cot with a thin blanket pulled over me in recovery. I flashed to what it felt like to have my newly healing face shoved into a chain-link fence while some asshole restrained and tried to assault me. I touched my back where it ached. Put a hand to my face and saw a touch of blood on my finger.

Floodgates from someplace deep inside me broke open, and suddenly I felt lonely and angry and sad. Cole slid his kitchen window open. Gidget hopped in it, gazed at me and barked. I got up, grabbed the cookies, walked a few steps and knocked on Cole's door. He opened it, a questioning look on his face. "Got milk?" I asked. 'Cause I've got killer cookies."

He smiled. "Come inside, mystery girl."

What the hell? Cookies and milk might be the perfect way to end today.

CHAPTER SIX

I called my mom from Cole's place and gave her the update on the stem cell procedure. I skipped the bit about getting assaulted and promised that I'd pick up a new phone tomorrow.

Cole might have been a cookie-thief, but he was a sweet host. The milk was low fat, tasted farm fresh and I washed down another antibiotic pill. Gidget even allowed me to play tug-a-war with her and her favorite stuffed toy. I left after a half hour and went back to my place. I was exhausted and one-hundred-and-ten percent ready for bed.

Which is why I was confused that I tossed and turned the entire night. I stared at the two framed photos on my dresser that I'd brought with me from home. The first was a posed shot of my mom, my grandmother and me. The second was a selfie of my best friend and me mugging it up at a football game. I wondered how everyone was. I probably fell asleep around five a.m. and didn't even blink my eyes open until around three p.m. that day. I woke up feeling like a truck had hit me.

I trudged to the bathroom and examined my face in the mirror. Most of my cuts were healing. But the few that Pintdick had broken open had fresh little bloody scabs and faint purple and green bruises blossomed underneath them. I sported under eye circles the size of small Wisconsin lakes. I was so incredibly pretty. *Not.*

I showered, pulled on some jeans, a T-shirt and sunglasses. I grabbed a cookie and walked to the commercial center of Westwood to get a new phone. An hour and a half later my sole mission for today was accomplished.

I grabbed a salad and a falafel at a Mediterranean fast food joint and took a seat by the window by myself. I watched everyone inside the place sharing a meal as they chatted with friends or family. I left my trap on the stand next to the door and left. My heart tugged and I felt homesick. Perfect time to call my best friend back home: Mary Martha Mapleson.

She picked up on the second ring. "You miss me already, don't you? Changed your mind about your most excellent adventure. What time should I pick you up at the airport tonight?"

I smiled. "Triple M, I do miss you! What's going on back home?"

"Except for pre-season Packers' football starting it's same old, same old. Dull and boring. Done anything interesting? Met anyone exciting?"

The hottest guy I've ever met rescued me and made me cookies. The creepiest asshat attacked me. I've been to the hospital twice in three days. "You have no idea." I spotted a small park and plopped down on a bench. We launched into our typical hour-long chat.

Back at my new place my e-reader was still broken, so I read a paper book for a change. Flipped through TV channels, surfed the Internet. Wondered if Cole was home. Thought about knocking on his door and seeing what he was doing, but I didn't want to become the pathetic, creepy, new neighbor who always showed up unannounced. The sun set. I changed into PJs and surfed the Internet looking for more YouTube videos on the different types of healing I wanted to explore. Some looked great, some weird and frankly some looked downright Dr. Frankenstein scary.

It was ten o'clock and I was still wide-awake. And I thought about Alejandro. He was obviously an Alpha Boy, but there was something different about him. Something intriguing. It didn't hurt that he could be the poster guy for the California Tourism Board. "Enjoy your visit to SoCal. We guarantee you'll want to stay and play for a while!"

I had more appointments with healers lined up in Playa del Vista and strange places called Compton and Gardena. I really didn't know how in the hell I'd get to them without getting attacked or killed in traffic or surprised by more religious zealots. At least back home the Jehovah's ladies dressed in pretty dresses and hats and knocked on your door instead of jumping in front of you. An idea percolated in my brain. I wondered if… nah. That was crazy!

My stomach rumbled. I'd forgotten to go grocery shopping. I went into the kitchen, pulled out a cookie from the tinfoil in the basket and gobbled it down. Munched on a second one and picked up Alejandro's invite from the night before.

So call or email me, or track me down at the Grill where I tend to hang out…

Alejandro

I brushed my teeth, dabbed on some lip gloss, brushed my hair, pulled on jeans, and a stretchy long-sleeved V-neck top that would hide the bruises on my arms from the blood draw as well as the ones on my back from the stem cell injections. I grabbed a jacket, my purse, and walked out my front door. Locked it and heard a small growl. Gidget was in the kitchen window next door.

"Cut a girl a break. I'm just going 'cause I'm hungry. And I'm polite. Midwestern girls are polite." I said. She wagged her tail at me.

***

I stood outside the entrance of the Westwood Grill. It was Saturday, but later than my unfortunate incident from the previous night, which meant the place was packed, standing-room-only. I stepped inside its heavy, wooden doors and spotted some of the same characters, as well as many more.

"Hey girlfriend! Glad you're back." Cheyenne smiled and brushed past me on her way to deliver a round of appetizers and margaritas to a corner table packed with beautiful people.

"Thanks!" I said. Freddie was behind the bar pouring beers, cutting limes and sticking wedges into several large glasses on top of his bar. The booby blonde perched at her signature four-top surrounded by her triplet wannabes while a hive of horny, cute, college-aged dudes buzzed around them dropping off drinks, appetizers, cards, phone numbers and options.

I swept the room with my eyes, but I didn't see Alejandro. I pulled his card from my purse and reached for my phone when I felt a gentle tug on my elbow.

"You're Sophie, right?"

I nodded and looked up into the handsome face of a beach blonde young man who smiled at me with crystal blue eyes that had the beginnings of twinkle wrinkles. He rocked a surfer's muscular tanned body that his T-shirt and board shorts could not hide.

"Welcome back!" He extended a Corona bottle with a lime wedge toward me. "You're old enough to drink, right?"

I nodded. I had my fake ID in my wallet. So yeah, I was

old enough to drink. I normally didn't drink beer, but after today? A beer would probably hit the spot. I accepted it. "Thanks." I took a slug. "Your name is?"

"Nathan. I never thought I'd see you back at the Grill after the other night."

"Ditto that."

He nodded. "We're in a big city, but USCLA is basically a college town. Shit happens, but someone like you—an innocent bystander getting injured—is extreme." He bent down and peered at my face. "Alex did a good job helping you."

"Thanks." Nathan was handsome, seemed sweet, but he was leaning into my space. And way too many people had invaded my space for a wide variety of reasons the past several days. I backed a bit away from him. "I was looking for Alejandro. I wanted to thank him. And maybe grab a bite to go."

He looked disappointed, but nodded. "Got it. Alex swooped in and shepherded you through a rough evening. Just so you know? He's a great Driver, but he isn't the only Driver at USCLA. There's a bunch of us. We're dedicated. We're honest. We've been through our share of shit. But now, for the most part, we're clean."

"What does that mean?" I took another sip of beer. *No Alejandro meant I should just get out of this place and just hit a fast food place. What was I thinking coming back here?*

"Maybe you should ask Alex," Nathan said.

"I'd love to. But he's not here."

"Yes, he is." Nathan pointed to the opposite corner of the Grill. I craned my neck and saw a stunning, dark-skinned, young woman with a killer body perched on Alex's lap. Her black, shiny hair was cropped short just like her floral sundress. She draped one bare, tanned arm across his shoulders and whispered into his ear. He tilted his head back and laughed out loud.

My heart dropped into my stomach. Mr. Gorgeous was

with Ms. Gorgeous. Just as nature intended; just as the world was supposed to be. I broke out into a sweat. I felt every scab on my face, every puncture on my back, everything that was wrong with me as I stood here in this local eatery packed with impossibly beautiful people, the exception being me—Ms. Plain. Ms. Bruised. Ms. Diseased.

There was no way Alejandro would ever be interested in me. He was just doing his job. He was just being sweet. I was simply his latest rescue case.

"He's busy," I said. "Thanks for the beer, Nathan. See you around campus?" I smiled up into his face, beguiling. Friendly. Completely fake. Held my beer bottle up and we toasted.

He smiled at me. "Absolutely. Looking forward to it."

I turned to leave.

"Sophie?"

"What?"

"You're new in town. You probably know you're beautiful—"

Nathan had a sense of humor.

"—but you might not realize that you're different from most of the girls around here. All of us Drivers are intrigued."

"Who are the other Drivers?" I frowned.

He pointed to a nearby table. Two handsome college-aged guys were watching our conversation and tipped their glasses in the air toward us in acknowledgment. "Right now there are only four of us. That said—we have a short code of ethics. One: Don't drink and drive. Two: Do your best to take the keys away in a non-violent fashion. And three: The Driver who meets a pretty girl first gets dibs on her until he screws it up. I'm really hoping that happens tonight. Go talk with Alex."

I frowned. I was already a pawn on too many boards. I had not come here to be a player in one more game. "Another night."

"Reconsider?" Nathan asked. "The quicker Alex screws it up, the sooner the rest of us have a legitimate shot at you. Don't get me wrong. He's like a brother. But, you know how sibling rivalry works. You'd make three guys very happy by simply having a conversation with him."

I looked over at Alex and the gorgeous girl. Now she was whispering into his ear, their faces touching, both of her arms wrapped around his neck. One of his circled her waist. They were a beautiful couple. Healthy, attractive and would most likely live long, happy lives. They were made for each other.

"I've got a better idea." I chugged the rest of my beer. "Why don't you just tell Alex thanks for me. Tell him I said he can forget the other night ever happened." I placed the bottle on a table. "Feel free to tell him that."

Nathan looked confused and I walked out the front door.

* * *

The two cookies, sadness, disappointment and probably a touch of anesthesia that was still wearing off had killed my appetite. So I skipped the fast food and made my way back toward my apartment. This time I knew the route. Turn left at the Gap store. Walk four blocks. Turn right on the street with the three lemon and orange trees on the corner.

Hold on—every corner seemed to have three lemon and orange trees. But I remembered to keep on walking until I hit the street where the apartment buildings had yellow, dark red and pink rosebushes out front. This corner only had red rose bushes. But the overwhelming scent of lemons distracted me.

Grocery store lemons never smelled this good. Only lemony fresh furniture polish smelled this good. I stopped and reached up to snap one from the lemon tree. But it eluded my grasp.

"Wuss," Alejandro said.
Crap.
"What?" I slammed back on my heels.
"Wuss," he said from the sidewalk and stepped onto the grass as he made his way toward me. "You came to see me at the Grill but then you left? Why'd you chicken out?"
"I did not chicken out. What do you want?" I backpedaled into a rosebush and jumped when a thorn poked my butt.
"You totally chickened out. You're acting weird. What do you mean, 'The other night never happened.' Of course the other night happened. You're not telling me something. Be honest with me. *What do you want?*"
"I want you to go back to the Grill and leave me. Just leave me alone." I refused to let those seductive, hazel eyes of his suck me in and returned my attention to the lemon tree. I balanced on my tiptoes and reached up for a juicy one high overhead, slightly out of my reach. I was grabbing a lemon and going home. I don't care if he stripped naked right now in front of me and whistled the "Star Spangled Banner." I would Not. Look. At. Him.
His hand brushed against mine, snapped the fruit off the tree and held it out to me. Unfortunately, he was not naked. I sighed and took the lemon as my heels dropped back onto the ground.
"Your answer doesn't cut it, Bonita."
I suddenly missed Oconomowoc, my Wisconsin hometown. Where lemons didn't smell lemony and I already knew and had turned down the majority of the Alpha Boys. "Look Alejandro, Alex, whatever I should call you…"
"Call me whenever you want."
"…I'm not a wuss. I'm simply the new girl in town for summer session at USCLA who had one bad night."
Make that two nights in a row.
"Thank you for helping me," I said. "That's why I went

to the Grill. To thank you. And now you can leave."

"You're welcome. But I'm not leaving without an explanation why you left the Grill with your weird 'the other night never happened' remark."

"Fine. You're obviously a guy who has a lot of stuff going on, a lot of chicks coming and going, no pun intended." I stared up into his beautiful, now frowning face.

"How do you know the number of chicks I have coming and going?"

I shook my head. "Doesn't matter. I'm too young and I'm also too old for these kinds of games. You need to go back to the Grill, find a hot girl, maybe that raven-haired one that was all over you. You need to drive her some place, bang her and carve another notch in your belt."

"Are you talking about Lucina?" he asked. "The girl with the dark, short hair who kind of looks like me?"

Maybe she did kind of look like him.

"What's her name who was swirled all over you like icing on a freshly baked cinnamon roll."

Alex laughed out loud. Then covered his mouth and laughed with a snort. The same way I did. "Lucina's my cousin. Yes, she's gorgeous. She's also a lesbian. She pulls the whole fake seduction thing with me every time she meets a new girl that she's interested in and wants to test her. Will that girl fight for her attention? Or see her with me and simply let it go? Her technique separates the serious suitors from the 'maybe-I'd-be into it for a night' bi-curiosity."

"Oh," I said. "Smart on her part. Good technique."

"Right now, Bonita, I'm not seriously involved with any girl."

So—how many girls he was not seriously involved with? I stared at his chin because I couldn't look him in the eyes. "I know about the Drivers. I know you all compare notes, compare chicks you rescued and have a—" I did the quotation mark in the air thing with my fingers. "—code of honor. I don't know what goes on at your headquarters or if you even have one. 'Cause I don't really know what you do or why you do it. I also don't know if you record the girl, list your conquests on an Internet page and chalk them up on a board or whatever. But FYI? I am Not. That. Girl."

I walked away from him toward my apartment, which I now knew was only one block away.

"Are you out of your mind?" Alejandro followed me. "I will cop to dropping daisies on your doorstep, as well as cookies. But if you think I put your name on a board, somewhere? Anywhere? Well, you're just plain wrong. Wait. I did put your name on the ledger at the USCLA Emergency Room. Excuse me."

I glanced at Gidget and Cole who spied on me from behind the curtains through his open kitchen window. And I gazed at Alejandro who stood on my front lawn, a frustrated look on his face.

"You're funny. You're smart. You're different. I want to spend time with you," he said. "Is that a sin?"

"No."

"Then, why are we standing out here, *again*, on your front lawn, in front of your cookie-thief neighbor and his creepy dog while we try to figure out our next step?"

"Uh!" Cole grabbed Gidget, slammed his kitchen window shut and then his curtains.

"Do you have a next step in mind, Sophie? Because if you do, I'd really like to know what it is."

"Yes," I took a deep breath. "I want to know, I want to ask…Would you drive me?"

He frowned. "Why?" He leaned in toward my face, totally catching me off guard. His lips were an inch from mine. I bit my lip. Was he going to try and kiss me? But he didn't. Instead he sniffed my breath. "Are you drunk?"

"Are you high?" I pushed him away from me. He stumbled for a second and stared at me like I was a wacko. "Of course I'm not drunk. I had one beer."

"Some people can't even drink one beer—"

"That's not it." I threw my hands up in the air and paced back and forth on the sidewalk.

How much truth should I tell him? How much should I keep secret?

"You showed up at the Grill tonight. I understand the Lucina thing might have looked confusing. I hope I cleared that up," he said. "Now's the time for you to tell me what you really want. Because if you don't want anything from me? Now's also the time I need to move on."

I took the deepest breath I'd taken since I'd landed in L.A. "Look, Alejandro. I'm sorry if there have been misunderstandings. I don't know how you all handle things here, on campus, in L.A. Whatever. But—"

"But what?"

"I want to hire you."

"For what?" He cocked his head to one side and raised an eyebrow.

"For driving. People tell me you're a great driver."

"That's because I am. Which doesn't answer my question. Why do you want to hire me?"

"Because I can't drive here. This place is too big, it's too much. I get lost so easily. I don't have a car. I took the bus yesterday to an important appointment. I mapped out the whole trip. I arrived on time. I thought I had it all figured out. But on the way back I got lost and it was kind of a mess and almost a disaster. I can't do this on my own. I just can't."

I felt my face shoved up against the chain-link fence while Oscar restrained and ground up against me.

"You said I wasn't completely honest with you."

"You're not," he said.

"You're right," I said. "I'm not just here for summer school. I'm here to…" My mind trailed off.

I'm here to participate in a hospital study where they knock me out, inject stem cells cells into my spinal cord and the very best outcome is?

Cells don't proliferate next to my spinal cord. Malignant tumors don't grow into my brain. Nothing shitty happens to me.

Alejandro snapped his fingers. "Finish your thought."

"I'm here to research and interview alternative healers for a book proposal. My grandmother encouraged me to turn it into a non-fiction book that we are creating together. I need pages done by the end of this summer. I need an outline, chapters and a great pitch that we can send to lit agents."

I'm here to voluntarily be a guinea pig for any kind of healing. No matter how strange it is—I'm up for it—if that kind of healing could actually save a life.

"I'm asking you to drive me to places in L.A. where these people are," I said. "Because, after today, I don't think I can do this on my own." I gazed into his hazel eyes flecked with gold. Got lost for a moment before realizing I was me and he was him and we were two persons, not one. That I needed to pull myself out of a delusional fantasy and attend to the real reasons I came here.

Alejandro reached out and cradled my face in his hands. Brushed his thumb over my cheek. "Half your face is healing. The other looks like some of your cuts broke open. What happened?"

"I can't..."

"You *can*. Why *won't* you tell me?"

Because I wanted him to be part of my healing—not part of my fear.

I shook my head and pushed back tears of frustration. "Can I count on you? Will you drive me?"

He took my hand and held it between both of his. His touch was warm. Strong. My pulsed raced, but I felt safe. Like I was coming home.

"Yes, Sophie Marie Priebe," he said. "Yes, I will drive you."

CHAPTER SEVEN

"U of W, Whitewater?" Alejandro asked. "Why not Madison?" He drove his black shiny Jeep down Pershing Drive lined with squatty apartment buildings, gas stations and tall palm trees with more dead fronds than live ones. We were on the way to my appointment in Playa del Vista.

"I'd planned on Madison, but Whitewater was closer to home."

"Lots of people go even farther away for college. Why did you want to be close to home?"

"Maybe I get homesick easily? Besides, you said you're from around here, right? And you're going to USCLA."

"Point taken. What's your major?"

"I keep waffling. I was thinking about pre-Law. But then didn't think I'd be up for law school after."

"That kind of kills the pre-Law thing." He pulled into a turning lane and flipped on his signal.

"So I'm shooting for a B.S. and see where that leads me."

Probably back to another surgical room and a cold, hard operating table.

"You're thinking about transferring here in the fall, right? USCLA isn't that easy to get into. But if you have a good GPA and applied right away—it could happen."

"Nah. I'd miss the fall weather, all the leaves turning gold, orange and red, frost on the windows and Green Bay Packers' football."

"We have an awesome football team."

"They're not the Packers. I'm only here for the summer."

* * *

Alex maneuvered his vehicle into a small parking space at a tiny strip mall. In the distance you could hear the planes rumble as they took off and landed at LAX, L.A.'s behemoth airport.

"Thanks." I stepped down and out of the passenger door and walked toward the curb. "I'll be about an hour. What are you going to do?"

He looked up at the signs topping the small shops assembled in the mini-mall. There was a Spot-Out Dry-Cleaner, a Fresh Water Station, Airport Chinese Foot Massage, Sergeant Washington's Kung Fu Zone, Pete's Chicago Pizzeria and a door with mysterious markings but no name.

"You're not going to the Kung Fu place?" he asked.

I shook my head. "You Kung Fu-get about it."

"Dork." He laughed. "I like that in a pretty girl. I'm going to check it out." He hopped out of the Jeep, jogged across the parking lot and up the concrete stairs to the martial arts studio located on the second level.

* * *

I laid back on a long, beat up, reclining massage chair in a dark room with soft lights and heavy closed curtains. There were busts of Buddhas and Chinese lucky bamboo plants located on little plastic tables adjacent to ten massage chairs. My treatment area was far from private. Across the room from me an older Caucasian woman with helmet hair wearing large earphones lay with her feet in a tall bucket of water. Her eyes were closed but she smiled as a young Asian woman deftly massaged her forehead.

An earnest, middle-aged, Chinese man massaged my feet. He hit sweet spots, scary spots, sexy spots and incredibly tender spots that I had no idea my feet possessed. I moaned. I groaned. He dug his fingernail directly next to the top of my big toenail. Waves of energy, fear and something like ecstasy pulsated from my feet up into the rest of my body.

While I'd never experienced an orgasm before that was not self-induced, I think I might have just had my first one—all due to a Chinese man who had been introduced to me by the manager as Lao.

Lao stopped massaging. "Is too strong?"

"No it's great. Thank you." I gave him a thumbs up.

He nodded. "My English not good."

"My Chinese is not good either."

He hit some exceptionally tender areas on my ankles and legs. I assumed the most painful ones were reflex points that might actually make a difference in my immune system. Or, perhaps boost my co-ordination. At least that's what I read about Chinese foot reflexology. And Lao at Airport Chinese Foot Massage was supposed to be one of the best healers in L.A.

Yes, I knew this was all a crapshoot. But at the very least the relaxation part of today's therapy would do wonders for me. Soothe out the stresses from the past couple of days. Calm my worried mind.

When thuds and screams, grunts and yells pierced the ceiling and interrupted my Zen. The sounds of someone kicking a wood wall or cement bricks and pounding up and down on the ceiling above my head interrupted my healing experience.

The female manager waddled up to me and waved a pair of headphones in the air. "I am sorry," she said. "We had no idea it would be so loud during the day. We are here for you to feel better. That man upstairs...." She frowned. "That loud man does not care that our clients need healing and relaxation. He leaves at five p.m. The nighttime is quiet. Next time, you come back for Chinese reflexology at night. I am so sorry. Headphones? Yes? All clients say headphones make Chinese Foot Massage during the day much better."

"It's okay." I heard a muffled familiar laugh and a thunderous bang resounded directly over my head. It sounded like Alejandro was bursting through the ceiling and going to land on top of me at any moment. I might have welcomed that in the past but now I flinched and my shoulders tensed. I didn't know if it was from the bedlam or Lao's thumb pressed like a nail into the arch of my foot.

Forty minutes later I put my hands together at my heart and bowed to Lao and the manager. I paid for my massage, tipped Lao and wondered if my feet would be able to walk across the parking lot, let alone ever feel the same. I hobbled outside the joint just in time to see Mr. Loud—a middle-aged, tall, muscular African-American martial arts instructor—trot down the cement stairs next to Alex who followed him with adoring puppy eyes.

"You're a natural, kid. I'm happy to train you. You got spare time this summer? Want to learn more moves?"

Alex looked at me and winked. "Thanks, Sergeant Washington. I'm pretty busy this summer. I've got a couple of part time jobs. Here's one of them." He smiled and gestured to me.

I smiled at the loud man and stuck out my hand. "Nice to meet you, Sergeant Washington. My name's Sophie Priebe."

He shook my hand. "Pleasure to meet you too, Sophie."

"Oh, please. Just call me Miss Part Time Job."

Alex and Sergeant Washington stopped smiling and shot each other a knowing look.

"Not to go all fourth grade school teacher on you," I said, "but the tenants in the space below you are real people, running a legitimate business. Maybe you all should have a conversation on how you can both run successful businesses when you share a common floor and a ceiling."

"That's a good idea, Sophie," Sergeant Washington said.

Alex's face blanched. "Thanks for the awesome lesson!" He shook the man's hand and then grabbed my arm. "I've got your card, Sergeant Washington." He practically dragged me to his Jeep "I'll be in touch!" He opened the passenger door and practically hoisted me inside.

"Calm down," I said. "Did he mainline you on sugar before you turned into the Karate Kid?"

"You don't know who that guy is," Alex said.

"You're right. I don't."

He strode to the driver's side, hopped in and buckled up. He backed the Jeep up, turned and sped off into traffic on Pershing Boulevard. "He's a black belt as well as a decorated Purple Heart veteran from the Persian Gulf War. Sergeant Earl Washington was a radio operator who watched his squad blow up just feet in front of him during an IED incident in Iraq. He had a breakdown, ended up at Walter Reed, became homeless, but found his way out of Post Traumatic Stress Disorder through martial arts. He was featured in the L.A. Times. On *Fox News, CNN, 20/20* and there was an article in *Vanity Fair*. The rights to his life story have been optioned for a movie. And you confront him in a parking lot over a Chinese foot massage place?"

"The Chinese foot massage people need to make a living, too."

"He's a decorated veteran who nearly lost his mind."

"And they're in this country legally trying to find the American dream that we all sell to the world in little sound bites and big action-packed movies. They have as much right to succeed at their business as anyone. They just need to talk to each other."

"How do you know they're here legally?"

I frowned and crossed my arms tight across my chest. "I don't."

"What have I gotten myself into?" Alex slapped his forehead with his hand.

I stared away from him, stony-faced out the passenger window. "It's not too late. Drop me off, now," I said. "I'll find a way to do this on my own. It's California, after all. Home to dreamers and wishers and lovers of all things that seem impossible. And you all have the Pacific Ocean with all its beautiful beaches. Maybe I don't belong here. Maybe I should go back to Wisconsin. After I've seen the Pacific Ocean."

He grabbed one of my hands and squeezed it.

"Hey!" I said.

"I'm sorry. I shouldn't have introduced you that way. I was an asshole. It was stupid of me."

"Glad we can agree on something."

Alex smiled, released my hand, and made a sharp right onto a side street.

"This isn't the way we came. This isn't the way back to campus?"

"Detours can be interesting."

* * *

Alejandro and I sat on a faded Mexican blanket on chewed up grass in a small park in Playa del Rey. It featured some swing sets, a jungle gym and a few picnic tables next to a sloped hill. But the best part was its location: squatted next to a four-lane thoroughfare that lined a wide beach that bordered the Pacific Ocean.

"Wow. All the photos and videos don't really do it

justice," I said. "This is the first time I've seen the Pacific Ocean."

"Technically it's the Santa Monica Bay."

"Which the Pacific Ocean feeds into."

"Just 'cause you saw it doesn't mean you get to leave. There are too many things you need to experience for that book you're writing with your grandmother." He pulled some cardboard containers from a paper bag and placed them on napkins on top of the blanket. "Wisconsin has a lot of lakes, right?"

"Yeah," I said. "But nothing quite like this."

Alex had stopped at a hole-in-the wall Mexican restaurant on the way here and ordered take-out. He dipped a chip in a plastic vat of guac and held it in front of my lips. "Here's another thing you never experienced. Homemade chips and the best guac in L.A."

I graciously accepted and sunk my teeth into his food offering. I crunched down and decided that this must be heaven for taste buds on earth. "More," I said.

"Salsa?" he asked.

I shook my head. "No. My brain can't handle that amount of deliciousness."

He fed me another guac-loaded chip.

"Holy guacamole, this is good. Why does it taste so different?"

"From what? Taco Swell? Frozen Mexican food?"

I nodded.

"Paco's only makes their food from fresh ingredients. They've been doing it for fifty years. They're the shit."

"You've ruined frozen burritos for me forever."

He grinned. "Another reason you need to stay here for fall semester."

The Bay was dotted with small sailboats and behemoth tankers. There were a few surfers in wetsuits trying to catch a wave. A couple of families with their kids hunkered down on the beach: the parents sitting on brightly colored beach blankets squished into the sand while their kids ran screaming with joy in and out of the low surf. The sun arced down above the water on its journey toward the horizon.

"I like it here." I glanced around the park. There weren't that many people hanging out. "Seems like everyone prefers the beach."

"I love this place." Alex plopped onto his back and folded his arms under his head like a pillow. He patted the ground next to him with one hand. "Your turn."

My eyes widened.

"Oh, come on. It's not like I'm planning on making out with you." He circled his arm toward the other eight people and two dogs in the park. "At least not in front of this crowd. I just want to show you something magical."

"The guacamole was magical." I dipped and ate another chip.

"It's not going to kill you to lie down on this blanket during broad daylight. Lighten up, my little Cheesehead."

"Cheesehead?" I frowned. "I like Bonita better. Besides, it's not broad daylight. The sun is setting." I lay down on the blanket next to him. No body parts were touching.

I was not going to go there.

"In defense of highly strung Cheeseheads everywhere," I said, "I will share with you that I might have had an orgasm during the Chinese foot massage."

Alex coughed violently, cleared his throat and harrumphed.

Which made me smile. *Hah-hah, Alpha Boy. Go ahead and mess with the midwestern girl. Sophie: One. Alejandro: Zero.*

He popped up on one elbow and glowered at me. "Did he... Did you..."

"Oh, please," I said. "You're the one who needs to lighten up. Eat some more chips. Besides, logistically, how could that have happened when all I heard during my relaxing treatment were the sounds of you and the Sergeant beating the crap out of each other?"

"We were not beating the crap out of each other—" Alex shut up and dropped to his back on the blanket. He pulled on my arm with one hand and pointed up to the sky with the other. "Look."

A low rumbling emanated from the skies and grew louder as it moved toward us. I jumped. "What the—"

"It's okay." He took my hand. "Watch."

The muffled sounds increased to a shriek as a jumbo jet ascended through the skies directly over us on its way out over the low, choppy, indigo seas. "Holy crap!" I applauded.

"I know," he said. "We're lying at the bottom of an abandoned runway at LAX. Where we can watch the planes fly over us as they take off. It's freaking awesome."

"It's so freaking awesome!" I kicked my heels and clapped my hands as the airplane disappeared into the mist forming over the Pacific Ocean.

"Tell me about your home. Tell me about you, what your life is like—back in Wisconsin?" Alejandro asked.

Right now was unexpectedly perfect. I didn't want to go there.

"Better idea. Tell me about you?" I asked. "Tell me who Alejandro slash Alex is. Why are you a Driver? How do you know about this park? And when does the next plane fly over?"

"I am boring, Bonita. I'm turning twenty-one in a couple of months. I come from your typical middle class L.A. family. Who, by the way, I love."

"That's not boring. That's refreshing. So many people only bitch about their families. It gets old. Why do you drive?"

"Because I'm good at it. Because I've learned and can pretty much predict who I can grab the keys from, who I can talk out of driving and who I'll probably have to throw a punch to capture the keys and keep them from driving drunk."

"But why did you—"

"Shh." He pointed to the sky. Another ginormous plane roared over our heads and caught some ocean mist.

"Whooh!" I thrust my fist into the air as the plane ascended over the ocean toward the setting sun. "That is so freaking cool! Another guac-chip, please?"

He smiled, pushed himself up on one elbow, dipped a chip in the guac and fed it to me.

"I bet you haven't been this excited since you were at a football game!"

"I haven't been this excited since the Chinese foot massage man stuck his thumbnail in my toe."

"Stop!" Alejandro made a face as I giggled.

We watched and I cheered the planes taking off well after the sun dipped below the horizon.

* * *

The Jeep's engine hummed in neutral parked curbside in front of my apartment. Alejandro stood next to me on the sidewalk. "Sure you don't want help taking that inside?"

"Nope." I held a slightly greasy paper bag filled with leftovers. "Thanks for today. Do you want me to pay you now? Will a check be okay?" I juggled the bag while I dug through my purse trying to find my checkbook. I grabbed it and thrust it out toward him. Like it was a symbol of my definite ability and desire to pay. Like I was a serious customer. Not a user-type.

Alejandro shrugged his shoulders. "We'll figure out our payment plan later."

"When later?" I asked. "I don't want to be that person who says I'm going to pay you and then for some reason I disappear or you disappear and there's this unfinished debt that hangs between us."

Like what my dad did to my mom. Courted her. Moved in with her. Knocked her up. Then left a couple of years after I was born because he couldn't deal with his boring life. I would not be the person who didn't keep my promises.

"That's not going to happen," he said. "I will camp on your doorstep and pelt you with cookies and guac chips until you pay me."

I thought about the real reason I was in L.A. And the real reason I asked him to drive me.

"But, what if I don't live here anymore?"

"Then I will hunt you down and find you," he said. "I have class tomorrow and so do you. What time are we driving?"

"Tomorrow late afternoon? Three p.m.?"

"I will pick you up here. We are on for three."

I liked that he said "we".

"That works," I said.

"Goodnight, Bonita."

"Goodnight, Ralph." I smiled and walked to my apartment's door and put the right key in the lock.

"Wait! Who's Ralph?"

I turned and regarded him. He looked confused. Gorgeous, delicious, but confused. *I was so good at messing with Alpha Boys.* "Oh, gosh. I'm just an innocent Cheesehead." I shrugged my shoulders, batted my eyes and pretended to swoon. "What do I know?"

"Apparently more than I gave you credit for," he said.

"About time." I opened the door to my place and stepped inside. "Thanks for—"

"What do I get when I figure it out?" He stared at me. "I mean—when I figure out the Ralph reference I should at least win a prize or something for my efforts."

"You're never going to figure it out."

"Don't underestimate me."

"What kind of prize do you want?" I asked.

"I want to kiss you," he said.

A shiver zipped up and down my spine. I thought about it for a moment. Realized he'd never find the right answer.

He'd also lose all interest in me the more he drove me. He thought I was exotic. I knew I was boring. So my reply was easy.

"Yes, Alejandro," I said. "Yes, you can kiss me if you figure it out." I shut my door, leaned back against it and smiled.

Sophie: Two.
Alejandro: Zero.
But who was counting?

CHAPTER EIGHT

The next day was officially the beginning of summer school. I sat in a small, somewhat claustrophobic room on the third floor of Walden Hall with twenty kids close to my age. We listened to Professor Schillinger talk about the syllabus for Genetics 300 that we'd be studying this summer.

Schillinger was in his thirties and handsome in that studious, slouchy, starting to lose his hair kind of way. This worked for me and most likely the rest of the girls in class as well as some of the guys. But the absolute turn on? Not sexually—just in general—was that Professor Schillinger was not only brilliant, but seemed earnest and kind as he discussed genetic markers, new medical tests and studies that were already in progress or on the horizon for difficult medical conditions. We were even going to have our own DNA evaluated by Spectrum Labs as part of our course curriculum. I might not only earn college credit hours but also gain understanding about my MS.

After class I walked the winding concrete pathways of this huge tree lined campus. Unlike the rest of the neighborhood, USCLA had plenty of brick buildings and leafy, non-fruit bearing trees. It almost felt like home. Preseason football was starting. Who knew if I could even find it on cable in L.A? I missed my mom, Triple M, and it hit me how much I missed my other best friend.

She hated texting, was always busy and yes—there was a two-hour difference between Pacific and Central Daylight time zones. I pulled my cell from my purse and hit a number. I expected it to go directly to voicemail. But miraculously she picked up.

"If you're a charity, I've already given, if you're a church, I've been saved, and if you're that guy who just breathes heavy, I suspect I've seen what you're doing before and frankly don't care," she said.

"Don't hang up! Nana, it's me!"

"Me, who?"

"Your favorite granddaughter!"

"I only have one granddaughter."

"So that should help you figure out who's calling."

"Sophie, my darling! How is it going in Lost Angeles?"

"It's going—interesting. It's...well, I can't wait to tell you all about it. I've just got a few minutes before a hospital thingie." I kept on walking. "Is this a good time?"

"Hearing from you is never a bad time. But first, please bear with your poor addled grandmother."

"You're not addled."

"You might think differently. I have a burning question that's poking at my brain the way a small child does in the grocery store when they're having a meltdown: screaming, crying and throwing things while their mother looks on aghast because she doesn't know how to handle what she perceives as her own public humiliation. Because she has not learned to separate from her child and realize that this is her child's doing and not hers."

Nana was perceptive. She was also a little intuitive. I hoped she wasn't going to ask about the stem cell study, or question the credit card bills for the healers I'd seen.

"Ask away." I bit my lip.

"I'm sitting in front of the TV watching more tornado coverage on CNN. I'm confused. Anderson Cooper seems like such a smart, young man. Why does he always go to areas that have fires, floods and tornadoes? Do you think he has an addiction to emergencies? I heard that some men have addictions to emergencies. His mother is an icon, you know. I worry this might upset her."

Phew. Thank God she hadn't figured it out yet. "Nana. He's Anderson Cooper. That's part of his job, who he is, a significant indicator of his entire persona."

"Oh, blech on the persona. How is your persona? Your mom told me you got in the middle of a bar fight your first night in L.A." She coughed. "Hang on. I swallowed my throat lozenge." She hacked and gurgled.

"You okay?"

"I refuse to die from a cherry flavored throat lozenge. Tell me your story."

"Well—it's been kind of strange and at the same time a little magical…"

***

We talked until I entered the building that housed the medical center. "I'll call you again soon. I love you!"

"Love you back, my favorite granddaughter," she said and hung up.

I made my way back to the same waiting room at USCLA Medical Center. Today was an obligatory blood draw day. Three tubes needed to be sucked from my skinny rolling veins. I signed in at the front desk. Smiled at Receptionist Phil and his female counterpart. And took a seat in one of the uncomfortable chairs as I waited for my name to be called.

A pretty girl about my age sat in a wheelchair and picked through the magazines on a side table. She grabbed one and stared at the cover. 'Jennifer Aniston's Hair

Secrets?' Gag me." She dropped it back on the table. Selected another rag and eyeballed the cover. "'Is Gwyneth Paltrow the most hated woman in Hollywood?' Do I really care?" She tossed that one too. Picked up a third. "'Twenty bathing suits to fit any body shape'." She pitched the magazine across the room. It smacked against the receptionist desk and slid to the floor. "Hey Phil!" she hollered.

"Yes, Blue. Your wish is my command. What is it this time?" he responded from behind his super duper state of the art command post.

"Got any magazines with swimsuit suggestions for girls in wheelchairs?" Blue ran her fingers through her blond hair streaked with blue.

"Anticipating that summer would soon be upon us, I've been researching that subject for several weeks now. I have not yet found that magazine article. In the mean time, I suggest you read about current celebrity couple breakups. I heard Miley Cyrus and what's his name broke up. Again."

"Dammit!" Blue threw another magazine against the waiting room wall. "I thought they would last. I thought they were young but meant to be together. That they were all about true love!"

"Stop throwing stuff," Phil said calmly. "Or I'll call hospital security and report that you're scaring patients and defacing hospital property. And you'll get in trouble. Again."

"No one cares. These magazines are five months old," she said.

"The waiting room was painted two months ago," Phil replied.

"My shrink says it good to vent my anger."

"Your shrink didn't pay for the paint job."

"Fine!" Blue wheeled up to Phil's desk and pointed at him. "I've got my eye on you, buddy. One little mistake? One nap on the job? One time I catch you using hospital time to surf the Internet? I can report you as easily as you can report me."

"Touché, cookie." Phil smothered a smile.

She smiled back at him, turned her chair and wheeled back into the waiting area.

"Hey," I said. "You're amazing how you handle these robots. My name's Sophie."

Her eyes narrowed and she took a few moments to check me out. "Doesn't look like cancer."

"Huh?"

"Well, you've got all your body parts—on the outside, at least. Two arms, two legs. No huge, obvious crevices in the rest of your body. You've got naturally pale skin with some facial scabs obviously caused by something like a bar fight or a jealous girl attack. But you're sporting splendiferous, shampoo commercial worthy hair. So if it is cancer? It's early stages and you haven't done chemo yet."

Blue wanted to know about me. This almost made me feel like I had someone who quite possibly wanted to be my friend here at the USCLA Stem Cell Study Lab. Which quite possibly might be a miracle. "You're right. I don't have cancer."

"Yes!" She held up her hand overhead to high five.

I leaned down and slapped her hand back.

"I called it," she said. "Forty-two out of fifty right." She pulled out a pen and a small notepad from a bag that was attached to her wheelchair. Flipped through the notepad. Until she found an empty page. "What's your name?"

"Sophie Marie Priebe."

She inscribed it in perfect cursive. "How old are you?"

"Nineteen," I replied. "What are you doing?"

"I get to ask the questions first. Email, please? I promise not to spam you or sell your email to any other list that will spam you."

I told her and she wrote it down. "Phone number and what state do you hail from? And I could care less about your emotional state. I mean like one of the fifty. Unless you're from Guam or D.C. or Puerto Rico."

"Wisconsin," I said.

She inscribed it in her book. "So." She stopped writing and squinted up at me. "Why are you here at USCLA Stem Cell Central? What lab study are you, their Cheesehead rat, enrolled in?"

"What's up with everybody calling me a Cheesehead?"

"Blue," Phil said, "you're up. Room 304."

"Got it." She nodded at him then looked back at me. "Even better? Don't tell me. Let me figure it out." She turned her chair around and wheeled out of the waiting area down the long white sterile hallway.

"Thanks for asking," I hollered after her.

But she didn't hesitate or turn around. She just kept on wheeling.

* * *

And then it was my turn. I was back in a small hospital room. This time I didn't have to strip naked, or wear a scratchy hospital gown, or bear my ass. The tech was female, middle-aged and a total pro at finding my skinny, deep, rolling veins. She only jabbed me once to collect three vials of blood.

"God bless you," I said. "You're good.

"I know." She wiped the inside of my elbow with a small gauze square drenched in alcohol. Grabbed a cotton ball. Peeled the plastic off a band-aid and secured it on top of my punctured arm. "See you in a couple of days."

* * *

I walked across campus, picked my phone out of my purse and saw Mom had called. I hit re-dial but she didn't pick up. I clicked on voicemail. But she hadn't left a message.

Not fair. I hit re-dial and left one for her. "Saw you called, Mom. Could you be a little less cryptic so I don't freak out when you *don't leave a message?*"

I paced outside the Student Union. "You know I worry. Just give me a heads up why you phoned. Like, 'We miss you, Sophie. Hope all is well. Love you, Mom.' Or—'There's been a tragic accident in our home town, Sophie. Alien centipedes invaded Oconomowoc. I barely escaped with my life, but was captured and am now a house keeper in servitude to the Head Pede.' And by the way? All is fine here in L.A. I think you would like it here. I think Nana would really love the Pacific Ocean. It's freaking gorgeous. Call me back and tell me everything's okay. I love you," I said and hung up.

* * *

Alex sat in the driver's seat of his Jeep and I was seat-belted in the front passenger seat as we drove through congested city traffic to my next appointment. This was becoming our norm.

Over the past ten days, he'd driven me to Hollywood where Dr. Susan Deffer, a middle-aged chiropractor, adjusted my spine with gadgets that sounded like power tools. He'd chauffeured me to Mrs. Sweet Tea, an aura healer in Compton and then to Stanislaus, a Phrenologist in Gardena who studied the bumps and grooves on my head.

The power tool chiropractor gave me a womping headache (yes, this could have been a healing "crisis"). Mrs. Sweet Tea said I had a gaping hole in the third chakra of my aura, which sadly, was a dark golden color. This hue signified that I'd been trying to make up for lost time. She waved her hands over me slowly and intensely for about forty minutes as I lay on a cotton-braided rug on her living room floor. At the end of our session she advised me to stay out of the sun for a day to allow my aura to knit. Then offered me peaches from her fruit tree in the back yard. I took her up on the peaches.

Stanislaus gave me a scalp massage for a half hour (very nice, but not as great as Alex's shampoo,) oohed and aahed over the bumps and dents in my head (I was a klutzy child) and declared I was over-thinking everything and was predisposed to anxiety. Should I continue on this course, I would most likely develop an autoimmune disease someday. Spot on, Stanny!

While my explorations were yielding a variety of results, I had to admit that ever since I'd hired Alejandro to drive, everything was going smoothly.

Until today.

Today we were stuck in gridlock traffic on the 10 Freeway as we snaked onto the 110 Freeway East into downtown Los Angeles. Apparently, getting anywhere in L.A. could take either a half hour or two hours. It all depended on the time of day, local disasters including earthquakes, helicopter chases of bad guys (yes, they really did this in L.A.,) or streets that were shut down for TV and or film shooting.

"Do you think we'll get there in time?" I asked as we crept along the too-tall, sweeping, concrete curve of the 110.

He looked at the clock on the dashboard. "When's your appointment scheduled?"

"Six p.m."

"Well, we're a quarter past five with a couple miles to go. We could get there ahead of time, on the dot, or completely miss your meeting. I'm sorry. It's L.A."

"But this is one of the reasons I hired you!" I fumed. "I don't know this city. You know it like the back of your hand. These appointments are important."

"You already admitted I gave you a better scalp massage than Stanislaus."

I shook my head. "Not every healer's for every person."

He glanced at me, skeptical. "I thought this was for research. For your book."

"It is," I said.

Even if technically there was no book.

"Maybe there's someone out there who might read our book and find a healer or an experience that resonates with them. Maybe these interviews might help people. People who are sick or going through something painful or debilitating," I said.

"You're sweet," Alex said.

I'm also a liar.

"I'm trying my best," Alex said. "But you need to realize you're not in Wisconsin anymore."

"Trust me, we have crappy traffic in Wisconsin," I said, knowing full well it was nothing compared to this. I stared at the bumper-to-bumper traffic on a nosebleed high ramp next to a huge building with a sign on it that read "The Staples Center." "Isn't that the place where you all have basketball games and hockey and concerts?"

Alejandro nodded. "I saw the Rolling Stones there a couple years ago. They blew my mind."

A flatbed truck merging from a ramp swiftly angled in front of a Prius with a "Give Peace a Chance" bumper sticker and cut him off. The Prius man slammed his horn.

"Perhaps they blew his, too," I said.

"Hah! Okay. I'll get you there in time." Alex veered onto the exit ramp.

I clutched one hand to my chest and raised the other to white-knuckle the handle above the side window. "Trusting you here."

"Good. You need to put your trust in the right person. Got to be careful with that kind of shit." He maneuvered down a few side streets. We passed skinny lots covered in litter. He gunned it—and we flew past a few, disheveled, homeless people pushing shopping carts. He hit the brakes when man in a BMW turned in front of us with no warning. Alex flipped on his turn signal and changed lanes as he accelerated around the asshat.

I flipped something different to Mr. Bad-Driver Beamer—my middle finger.

"Relax," Alex said. "He's just a bad driver. One out of a bazillion in L.A. Save your third finger salute for the real assholes."

I felt a little nauseous, squeezed my eyes shut and put one hand on my stomach as we rounded a corner. "Did you know that Lambeau Field where the Green Bay Packers play is the only professional, football stadium in this country that is still owned by a consortium of little people like you and me? Not some mega-corporation that's touting office supplies or cell phones."

"I admire that about Wisconsin." He braked abruptly.

I whiplashed forward, then back in my seat.

"You should be proud to call yourself a Cheesehead. Open your eyes and drink in the majesty that is…"

I opened my eyes and gazed up at an overhead sign. "Chinatown," I said. A large metal overpass that featured two golden snakes with dragonheads hissing at each other swooped over the road. "No way!" I said. "You got us here…" I glanced at the clock on the dashboard. "…ahead of time!"

"I promised." He pulled up next to a car and parallel parked. "And score. Metered parking space." We were officially in L.A.'s Chinatown surrounded by Chinese signs, restaurants and emporiums. He hopped out of the car, jogged to the curb, opened my door and stuck change in the meter. "What's the address?"

"Hang on." I fumbled through my purse for my notepad.

"Why don't you just enter everything into your phone?"

I pulled my book from my purse, flipped open to the page that was marked with a ribbon. "Because I like paper and pens, Ralph. I'm a little old-fashioned that way."

"The infamous Ralph." He followed on my heels. "I'm hoping this doesn't mean that I make you nauseous. Like—" He opened his mouth and pretended to vomit.

"Oh, stop it."

***

I'd filled out all the paperwork forms at Dr. Tung's Acupuncture and Cupping Healing Center. (Could some university somewhere just award me an undergrad degree for filling out paperwork forms?) There were diplomas and a few framed pictures on the walls: A photo of Dr. Tung needling a famous athlete. A newspaper clipping of Dr. Tung smiling and shaking hands with the former Govinator.

Alex sat in a chair next to me and read a Chinese newspaper.

"Like seriously? You know Chinese?" I asked.

"No," he whispered. "But thanks to my mom, I can spot coupons in any language. Maybe there's a two for one coupon in here for acupuncture or whatever you're here for at Dr. Tung's Healing Center."

"Have you ever been to an acupuncturist?" I asked.

"No. Needles scare me." He flipped through the thin Chinese newspaper, scanning it from top to bottom. Then bottom to top.

"Me too, sometimes," I whispered. "So why do you want a coupon?"

"Because I need to know more about your research. Understand more about what you're doing. You know—for this book proposal that you and your grandmother are putting together. Maybe I could help you with that, too." He flipped a page. "Found it." He tapped the middle of the paper. "This ad features the name and contact info for an acupuncturist and it's a two for one promotion."

"Jeez, you're good," I said.

"You have no idea." He winked at me.

"How do you know it's a two-fer?"

"Because it says right here, 'Two new patients treated for price of one'."

"How can you know that unless you know a little Chinese?"

"Because it's printed in English," he said.

I elbowed him in the ribs.

"Ow! What was that for?"

"Smart-assery. Use your detective skills to find a Chinatown Dim Sum restaurant with two for the price of one," I said.

I didn't want Alejandro figuring out what I was really doing. I also didn't want to lose him. He'd helped me so much—without pushing himself on me. He was hot, he was Alpha, but so far—he was safe. I wanted our relationship to stay that way. Casual. Helpful. Safe.

"Do you want me to ask Dr. Tung's receptionist if they'd do a complimentary first time customer two-for-one needle thing?" I asked him.

He shook his head. "No."

"Okay."

"Wait a minute," Alejandro said. "*Ralph.* Why didn't I get this before?" he smacked his palm to his forehead. "Ralph's that actor from *The Karate Kid*? Ralph Macchio? It's him, isn't it? It totally is. If it's not him—and you have to be honest with me? Then you can ask the receptionist if they would do a two for one." He smiled. Smugly.

I stood up, grabbed the newspaper from him and walked three feet to the receptionist's desk "Excuse me. I found a two for one coupon for a first time acupuncture appointment. Do you think Dr. Tung would honor… "

CHAPTER NINE

I lay on a flat table on my stomach in a thin gown in a tiny room that had two, narrow, treatment tables. Posters of acupuncture dummies with meridian lines drawn down their bodies and little notations for needle spots like LI6, or BL5, were noted on the mockups.

Dr. Tung was an older gentleman with a thin, earnest face and a crew cut of thick, white hair. He poked acupuncture needles into my head, back, forearms, wrists, knees, ankles and feet. He twisted the needles until I felt burning, sizzling and tingling on most of the insertion points.

"Ow!"

"You are here for healing," Dr. Tung said. "Healing sometimes hurts."

"Yeah there, got it." I breathed through my discomfort. I glanced at Alejandro who lay on his back on a table next to me also clad in a threadbare patient gown. Strangely, it suited him. His eyes widened as he watched what I was going through, most likely realizing—he was next. "Dr. Tung," I said, "please be super gentle with the needles on my friend, Alejandro. He's not here to heal. Or research. He's just here to experience… life. I think."

"Yes." Dr. Tung gently stuck in a needle in Alex's forehead. "Yin Tang. Third eye point."

"Hey!" He jumped halfway off the table. "What are you doing? This feels weird."

Dr. Tung put a hand on his shoulder and gently pushed him back down. "You have energy shut off from accident that happened about four years ago."

"You were in an accident?" I asked.

"You're not an official Angeleno until you've had your first fender-bender," Alex said. "It's practically a rite of passage."

Dr. Tung stuck a needle in Alex's chest and then—*bam, bam, bam*, three needles in his right ankle and foot. "You need to release that energy so chi flows. So life flows."

"I'm not a human pin-cushion, you know?" He squirmed.

"Stop moving," I said. "You're going to screw up the needles. You don't want to do that."

Alex frowned but stopped fidgeting. "Fine. But, I'm doing this for you, Sophie."

Dr. Tung stuck a few needles in his ear. And one in his nose.

He sneezed, which didn't help matters. "Dammit!" He was filled with needles, half naked and wearing a stupid gown. He looked at me like a miserable puppy that was getting shots at the vet.

I started giggling. I knew it was wrong. Very wrong. But I couldn't help it.

"Stop laughing," Alex hissed. "You're going to screw up the needles. God knows you don't want to screw up the needles. Because we could actually be having a normal date."

"But we're not on a date," I said.

"Whatever. We could be catching a movie. Going to a party. But no, we're in Chinatown. And not for Dim Sum. We are quite possibly screwing up the needles."

I couldn't stop laughing. "Dr. Tung. Dr. Tung?"

"Yes?" he asked.

"I think Alejandro needs his Yin Tang opened a teensy bit more."

Dr. Tung moved toward Alex and eyeballed his forehead. He twisted the needle deeper.

"Ow!" He hollered.

"I come back in fifteen minutes. You two be quiet. Do not scare other patients." Dr. Tung quickly left the room.

"This is like hitting me with the kickball in middle school, isn't it?" Alex asked as a grin grew on his face. "I think this means you like me."

"Get over yourself," I said.

***

Summer school continued. I learned about genotypes and genetic predispositions. I even heard about the time, several semesters back, that a student taking this class discovered the man who was raising him wasn't, technically, his dad.

I talked to my mom. There had been no alien centipede invasion of my hometown but she did have news. Nana had decided to move out of our house into an assisted living retirement community.

"Why didn't you talk her out of it?" I asked. "What are we going to do without her? She'll miss us. This isn't good for anybody! If I was home I could have talked her into staying."

"When's the last time you talked your grandmother out of doing something she'd already decided?" Mom asked.

"Oh," I said. "Right."

"I tried, Sophie. But she does what she wants when she wants. Besides, I think she's tired of me mothering her. Or as she calls it, 'smothering.'"

"What about coming out here to mother…I mean…visit me?" I cringed because I sounded like a needy child asking for attention. I didn't want to be that person. Unfortunately, I was spot-on, exactly that person.

"I'd love to visit, kiddo. But right now I'm not going anywhere without your Nana. Talk her into it and I'll book the flights."

I called Nana and left numerous messages, which apparently she didn't pick up or return. I yakked into her voicemail about the Pacific Ocean, the park where you could watch airplanes take off right over your head and even tempted her with the magical guacamole. When I finally got her on the phone I begged her to visit me in L.A.

"Sophie, my favorite granddaughter, I would give my left foot to see you."

"Don't do that, Nana. Promise me."

"Okay. I'll keep the foot. I'm finally unpacking the last of the boxes and settling into my new home."

Duh. What was I thinking? Moving was a huge life transition, a shock to anyone's system. Especially someone older, in their seventies. "You're right. I'm sorry. I should have been there to help you."

"You've got your own important things going on. Have you met new friends?"

"I think."

"Be nice to them. Don't be cactus-Sophie."

"I am not cactus-Sophie!"

"Sweetie, you are beautiful. Strong. Resilient. A little prickly—like a cactus. You get that from my side of the family," she said. "Don't apologize for it. Just be aware of it."

"Okay." I knew she was totally right. "Have *you* met any new friends?"

"Yes!" She coughed deeply. "Hold on." She coughed some more. Blew her nose. "Damn allergies." She sighed.

"Are you okay?"

"Never been better! I have met new friends here, but they speak a foreign language. Because life is regrettably short, I've decided to immerse myself in Berlitz to learn their foreign tongue. I hope to be able to converse with them in a more authentic fashion."

"Nana, that's awesome," I said. "What language are you learning? Spanish? Italian? Chinese? Where are they from?"

"Skokie, Illinois, my bubbelah."

"You're learning Yiddish?"

"It's a mitzvah, I tell you. Learning new things keeps one young. We'll see each other soon. Oh, I received a couple of charges for—"

"Are you still okay with that?" I asked. "Me going to the healers?"

"Stop asking," she insisted. "You are young and following your dream. I want you to have that."

She was astute, but she hadn't figured it out yet. Which was a good thing.

"But—"

"No buts, Sophie. We've already had this conversation. You need to be exactly where you are, doing precisely what you're doing. I must go. Esther Rosenstein is hosting a game of cards. I asked what I could bring and she suggested I give her a holler."

I shook my head and smiled. "Challah, Nana. It's a kind of yummy bread. I'm guessing she wants you to contribute some snackies. Have fun. I love you."

"I love you too, my favorite granddaughter."

I hung up the phone. I felt sad and happy and nostalgic all at the same time. And then I felt grateful I was here in L.A. On my journey.

***

Alex drove me to some more appointments: a yoga class where we breathed and examined our every movement, body posture, joint alignment and then chanted funny words. It felt wonderful and I felt incredible the day after class: no twitches. No leg weakness. No lethargy. I wanted to go back as soon as possible.

But the next day I was scheduled to be at the generic waiting room at the vanilla medical center waiting to get my dreaded, ear-killing MRI done. They wanted to ensure that the stem cells hadn't turned from good to bad. Because, apparently, stem cells could be deceptive.

These cells that were meant to be potential healers could, once in a while, morph into monsters and form tumors that would further disable or even kill patients. Yeah, life was a laugh a minute in L.A. as I lay on the imaging tube, was shuttled into the MRI tunnel and tried not to grimace through the machine gun and explosion noises as the medical device took pictures of my spinal cord. My mind desperately needed to escape from this freaking hellhole and that's when I thought about him. To be honest, started to obsess a little about him.

He was not only impossibly cute, but we seemed to have some strange connection. I knew this wasn't right. I knew I shouldn't be doing this. I hesitated. But finally gave in to my desires. I was out of the tube, yanking my clothes back on in a dressing room cubicle while I picked up my phone and hunted down the number.

I called as soon as I exited the USCLA medical building, walking on concrete paths that wound around the brick buildings and green, grassy landscapes.

"Patsy's Pet Store and Exotic Creatures Emporium. My name's Patsy. How can I help you?"

"Hey, Patsy," I said. "I saw your Kitten Adoption sign in the window about two weeks ago. There was a longhaired, black kitten that was up for adoption. I'm sure he's already found a great home. But I had to call and check on him. Just in case."

"Oh. You're talking about Napoleon," she said.

"Huh?"

"The bossy, black, long-haired, male fuzzball who thinks he's the ruler of an empire?"

"That totally sounds like him." I smiled. "He's obviously been taken."

"No," Patsy said. "You do know that black and tuxedo cats have a tougher time being adopted than other kitties?"

"No." I shook my head. "Why?"

"Old-fashioned superstitions... Juan!" Patsy hollered. "Do not let Mr. Tweets out of his cage! He acts all nice and sweet, but he'll fly off on a moment's notice and try to attack the lovebirds. Keep his cage door shut."

"Yikes," I said. "Sounds like you've got a lot going on. Does that mean Napoleon's still at your store?"

"Sorry for the bird drama," Patsy said. "In regards to the kitten you're calling about? No one wanted Napoleon. Store policy. We sent him to West L.A. Animal Shelter a couple of days ago."

"But, but...." my palms broke into a sweat. "Is that a kill shelter?"

"Sorry, yes." She screamed, "Juan! Mr. Tweets just attacked my hair! You let him out—"

I hung up the phone and hit one number.

"Bonita! What's up? Need a ride? I've got plans with the guys this afternoon. I promised. I can't break it. I can do sometime tomorrow afternoon. Or the day after? Where do you want to go? What do you want to do? More research?"

My heart sunk. For some reason I thought Alejandro and I were cool, on the same page. Like—he'd always be there for me. Because, so far he had. But no one can *always* be there for someone else. That's a fairytale. And my life definitely wasn't a fairytale. "Can't wait. It's urgent," I said.

"How urgent?" he asked.

"Walking out my door and headed to the bus, urgent," I grabbed my purse, keys, strode out my door and slammed it shut.

"Shit. I—" Alex said.

"Don't worry about it," I said. "I'll handle it."
"I'll call you—"
"Thanks." I hung up. Things needed to get done. Things that couldn't wait for one guy, or one hospital. One research study. One alternative healer.

Sometimes you couldn't wait, because the only way things would get done? Would be if you did them yourself.

* * *

I was back on the Big Blue Bus that headed toward Venice. I'd researched where the West L.A. Shelter was—Pico Avenue, approximately where Ocean Park Boulevard dead-ended a few blocks from it. I checked my phone. Four thirty p.m. This time I had to get there before closing time—5 p.m. Because this time the price for punctuality wasn't a charge on a credit card. This time the stakes were life or death.

My phone buzzed and I glanced down. It was Alex and I picked up. "What?"

"I'm in my Jeep. I'm driving. I'll pick you up. Where are we going?"

"Where am *I* going?"

"Okay. Where are you going?"

"West L.A. Animal Shelter."

"Why?" he asked.

"I can't really talk right now." I hesitated, my index finger poised over the disconnect button.

"Don't hang up! I know where it is. I'm like a mile from there."

"I've got to get there before five p.m. Or they'll kill my cat."

"I didn't know you had a cat?"

"I didn't, either."

"What's it look like?" Alex asked.

"He's black, fuzzy, round, about ten weeks old. His

name is Napoleon. He thinks he's the king of the universe."

"I like him already, Bonita. Must drive fast. Hanging up now."

CHAPTER TEN

The bus stuttered to a stop a couple blocks away from the shelter. I'd relinquished my seat ahead of time, made my way to the front and clung to one of the poles near the exit door. But six people didn't care as they pushed and squirmed past me. I checked my phone. 4:53 p.m.

The bus driver opened the doors. But the pushy people suddenly became the slow-to-exit people and I didn't have the benefit of time.

"Excuse me! I have an emergency!" I shoved my way past several, large men and elbowed a few, surly teens as I tripped down the bus's stairs. "Sorry!"

I ran down the few blocks to the shelter. My heart was pounding as I reached the front door. Yanked on it. But it was already locked.

I looked down at the hours printed on the door.

"Open Monday through Friday 11 a.m. to 5 p.m. Sat. 11 a.m. to 4 p.m."

I grabbed my phone. The time read 4:57 p.m. I pressed my face against the glass door. Saw a reception desk. But no one was behind it. I heard barking and howling coming from inside. I pounded on the door. "It's not five p.m. You cannot close your doors before you state that you will close your doors! That's just plain wrong!" I hollered. "Help!" I slammed my fist on the door over and over again.

A petite woman around thirty years of age, with multi-colored hair, wearing beat-up scrubs and earbuds exited the side of the building and whistled along to a song.

"Hey!" I yelled to her and waved my hands in the air.

She pulled the buds out of her ears. "Can I help you?"

"Yes! I'm here to rescue a kitten before he's euthanized. I got here on time, but the front doors are already locked and frankly this is freaking me out, because you shouldn't lose your life if help arrives in time. And you shouldn't have to die if help arrives at the last minute or is perhaps just a little bit late."

"I agree," she said. "The early door-locking thing? That's Mr. Littleton's doing. He volunteers here. Has for years. Which is great. But whenever he's in charge he closes the front door five minutes early. I think he has a small penis and this is his way of showing that he is important, like the ruler of his universe or something. I'm not supposed to do this, but what the hell." She motioned to me with a small wave of her hand. "Come with me."

***

"My name's Sadie." I heard a cacophony of barking as she unlocked and opened the door to the shelter's side entrance next to the dog wing.

"I'm Sophie. Nice to meet you and thanks." My heart was pounding as I tried to catch my breath.

"Back at ya."

We walked past dogs of all descriptions: mongrels, old dogs, puppies, small ones, huge ones. "They're all up for adoption?" I asked.

"Some," she said. "Others are scheduled for euthanasia." She bit her lip.

"How do you deal with this? Because I couldn't."

"I deal because I can help rescue a lot of lives. The other part? I don't deal with it all that well."

We walked past a pen that held a skinny, but at the same time bloated, Rottweiler mama who lay on her side, looking exhausted while five squirming puppies sucked on her engorged nipples. "What's going to happen to them?" I asked.

Sadie sighed. "We're pretty confident we can adopt out all the puppies. If we're lucky, perhaps the adoption gods will smile on us and someone will still want the mama after she's spayed."

Moments later we were in the pound's cat wing standing in front of a small, wire cage located two tiers up from the ground. A paper sign stuck in a little slot in the cage read, "Napoleon. Feline. Mix-Breed. Longhaired. Color: Black. FIV Neg. FeLV Neg. Age: Ten weeks. <u>Status</u>: Relinquished. <u>Reason</u>: Did not sell at pet store."

There were two little bowls. One had some dry food at the bottom. The second some water. There was a tiny box with a sprinkling of cat sand. But there was no black, fuzzy kitten with a badass attitude. "Where is he?" I asked.

Sadie shrugged and looked at her feet.

"No," I said. "There's no way this kitten is being killed."

"I don't know," Sadie said. "Maybe he was adopted out?"

"Oh, screw that." I stomped my foot. "Take me to the room where they do the euthanasia."

"I can't," Sadie said.

"You have to. Now."

"I can't, Sophie. I'm sorry. I'd lose my job. I'd never be able to help another animal here, ever again. I know this totally sucks. But you cared. You cared enough about another being that you totally went out of your way to help. If there's such a thing as karma, I think you scored major points."

I started crying. Just a little. I couldn't help it. I plopped down cross-legged on the floor in front of Napoleon's empty cage and wiped tears away as they slipped from the corners of my eyes. I wondered why I was so freaking selfish about my journey here in Los Angeles that I couldn't, actually I *wouldn't*, let someone else's journey make a dent in my plans. Especially that of an innocent. I was a selfish, coldhearted person and now Napoleon was dead because of me.

"It's okay," Sadie said. "Seriously, I cry about two times a week here, too." She tugged on my arm. "But I need to get you out of here before I lose my job."

I got up and followed her down the corridors that smelled of harsh cleaners, animal pee and poop, all the while more disgusted with myself than any of the odors.

I made it back to the bus. Found a seat in the back and hunched over nauseous. Then we hit rush hour traffic. Two hours later I exited my stop and walked home, sniffling the whole way.

I rounded the lemon trees and saw the rose bushes. Alex sat on my front stoop, his arms stretched in front of him while he actively warded off Gidget who kept lunging toward him.

Cole stood a couple feet away. "Gidget, my darling," he said. "Come to papa."

Gidget turned, bared her teeth and growled at him.

"You need to put your dog on a leash." Alejandro extended his arms, keeping the dog at bay.

Cole glared at him like he'd said, "I pronounce that you're a witch and I will now burn you at the stake. And your little dog too."

"I think..." Cole leaned down and grabbed Gidget. He tucked her under his arm, pulled his shoulders back as he stood up tall and sucked in his stomach. "...that because you are gorgeous, Alejandro, and most likely popular, you believe people will listen to your every word like you are a savvy politician, a charismatic self-help author, or a

Kardashian."

Alex frowned. "You did not just compare me to a Kardashian."

Cole sniffed. "Because you are charming with your cookies and flowers, you most likely believe your every suggestion will be obeyed. But I am here to tell you that you don't really understand what it's like to love an animal. A pet. You probably don't even know what it's like to love *anyone*. Probably not even another human being."

"Cole!" I exclaimed. "Stop being a douche! Alejandro's my friend. You're my neighbor and my friend. And frankly, even though Gidget only growls at me, I believe we're pals. I'm here until the end of summer. Could you all just play nice until I leave? Someone needs to apologize to someone else. And that suggestion is meant for all of you."

"Not me, not Gidget, not tonight." Cole disappeared back inside his apartment and slammed the door.

That left Alex seated on my front doorstep, awkwardly shifting from side to side. "Look," he said.

"Thanks for trying," I said. "Today was a tough day. I need to be alone."

"I disagree."

And that's when I heard it. A single tiny, "Eep."

"Oh my good God," I said. "No freaking way."

"Mew. Eep. Mehhh..." The sounds emanated from behind Alejandro.

"You rescued Napoleon, didn't you?"

He smiled. "Yes."

I couldn't help myself as I jumped up into the air, crouched back down and high-fived Alejandro.

He edged to the side of the concrete step revealing a cardboard cat carrier that featured round air holes carved in its sides. A tiny, pink nose stuck out of one opening. It was Napoleon, his nostrils widening and narrowing as he sniffed the air.

"The head guy was closing the place early, Bonita, and I

had to make a decision. So I got him. I signed the forms and adopted Napoleon. And now I'm giving the little bastard to you."

"Oh my God!" I threw myself on Alex and hugged him hard. He fell back against my front door and I landed awkwardly in his lap. He grabbed me around my waist and stopped me from dropping off the porch onto the concrete.

"Oops," I said my lips inches from his. I looked up into his eyes. "When I was a kid I was a bit of a klutz."

"There is nothing remotely klutzy about this moment," he said. "I wouldn't mind catching you every time you fall." He leaned toward me and his lips brushed mine. I felt the stubble on his chin on my face: It was rough but intoxicating.

I suddenly couldn't breathe, and falling I was.

There were small, insistent scratching sounds, claws on cardboard, followed by one pathetic mew.

I pulled my lips from Alejandro's, backed away and ripped myself off his lap. "Thank you, thank you..." I knelt down next to the cardboard carrier and peered though a hole at Napoleon who was eyeing me suspiciously with one round yellow-green eye. "You are mine!" I exclaimed.

"You're welcome." Alex looked a little befuddled. "If I had known you would have plastered yourself all over me like Saran Wrap, I would have gotten you a cat a couple of weeks ago."

"Any cat a couple of weeks ago wouldn't have mattered. Napoleon matters. You matter. What you did for me today matters." I broke into a sweat and fanned myself. "When did it get so hot out? I need to take him inside. I'm so excited! We need to get cat food and treats and a litter box and catnip."

Alex stood up and pointed at two giant grocery bags behind him. A large scratch pad poked out the top of one bag.

"Oh, my God!" I hugged him again.

"Damn, should I get you *another* cat? I can only fantasize what might happen if I got you *a second* cat."

I shoved the key in the door, opened it and picked up the cat carrier. "I don't want another cat. I want this cat. You didn't do just good, Alex. You did great. Want to come inside?"

He shook his head. "I thought you'd never ask."

* * *

"You owe me," Alejandro said. "I saved your cat." He drove the Jeep, top down, as the summer sun blasted down upon us.

Per usual, I rode shotgun in the passenger seat. He wouldn't tell me ahead of time where we were going but he suggested I dress casual. I wore shorts and a halter top with a flared hem that landed at my waist.

"I tolerated your bitchy neighbor," he said. "I attended yoga classes with you and did downward dog in front of complete strangers. I spotted three people checking out my ass. Jeez, that was embarrassing."

I pretended to stare saucer-eyed at his butt. "Oh my God, has anyone ever told you what a fine behind you have?"

"Stop!" He covered a laugh. "I even took needles for you. This afternoon is *my call*."

Strands of my hair whipped across my face and blew behind me under my new straw hat that I held onto with one hand on top. I discovered it wrapped up in tissue paper in the bottom of one of the bags with the cat supplies and bottled water. I pulled it out thinking it was an awfully big cat toy.

"You're in L.A.," Alex had said. "You're going to be a beach girl and you need a hat. I wanted something a little different for you. Hence the cross between country-western and a typical, floppy beach hat."

"I love it!" I plopped it on my head and rolled up the woven rim. "But I'm from Wisconsin—a state squarely in the northern part of the Midwest. What about me screams 'country-western'?"

"Your take no prisoners attitude," he said.

Now we drove through funky narrow streets where ramshackle apartment buildings were plopped between modern four level houses with pristine rooftop gardens. I smelled the ocean air and leaned back against the seat. I kicked my bare legs up and draped my feet out the passenger window. "I agree, Ralph," I said. "I totally owe you for the Napoleon rescue. Where are you taking me?"

"Venice, Bonita. Because you haven't lived in SoCal until you've experienced the splendiferous, crazy Venice Beach scene."

I thought about Pintdick Oscar and his friends, and despite the heat from the sun glaring down on us I suddenly felt cold. I closed my eyes and remembered how scared I was a couple weeks ago when I was lost and assaulted. "I heard Venice has a bunch of gangs. Are you sure it's safe?"

"Venice Beach is technically part of L.A. Every big city has gangs. Hell, even small cities have them. And bullies know no boundaries—they're everywhere." He reached out and squeezed my arm. "You're with me today. I'm your Driver. I'm your protector. I saved your cat. Stop questioning your safety. At least for today."

"Okay." I smiled and shook my head. "Today I am in your hands, Alejandro." I placed my hand on top of his that was on the wheel.

He smiled at me from behind his Ray-ban aviator sunglasses: the faintest twinkle wrinkles etching next to his eyes, the dimples in his cheeks deepening.

I'd pushed every guy out of my life for the past year and a half because I was scared to death to fall for anyone with a beating heart. Now I'd fallen for a fuzzball with a beating heart—a kitten. But worse, I feared I was surrendering my heart to a real man.

The last boy I dated—let's just say the relationship didn't turn out so well. When I told Joey, my old boyfriend, that I had MS? He sprinted so fast from my house that I don't think he even put on his running shoes until he was easily a half a mile away. And to top it off, he had a new girlfriend on his arm within a week, hanging out at all our old haunts. Showing her off to our mutual friends.

I sincerely hoped Joey had developed a nasty case of blisters from all that running. Everywhere.

I wasn't sure I could stay open to a new guy in my life, especially someone who was warm and sweet and strong. Like Alejandro. A man who *did not know* my life's reality. And I was still uncertain how much I should share if any of my deets with him.

Deet #1: The Girl (Me) who you're driving is keeping secrets from you.

Deet #2: Same Girl (Me) has one secret you might not be all that happy about upon discovering. In fact, you might even bolt and leave Same Girl high and dry. Just like my dad left my mom.

"I trust you, Alex," I said. "But I'm not as tough as you think." I pulled my legs back inside the car, placed them firmly on the floor and sat up straight in my seat. "Not to be a bitch, but don't screw it up."

"What is the mysterious 'it' that I might screw up? If you give me a warning, I might be able to avoid screwing up whatever, 'it' is?"

"You'll figure it out as soon as you figure out the Ralph thing," I said.

It is whatever we are right now. It is the beginning of something between us... or maybe it is nothing.

He shot me a look that made my heart pound. Stop. And restart again. "I will figure that out you know. Soon."

"Good. I've been anxiously waiting."

"Look," he said. "I've had my share of girls and screw-ups, but overall I'm not a bad person. I'm actually kind of a good person. Or at least a person, who, maybe if I'm lucky, will find meaning in the mundane of everyday life."

"I'm not trying to—"

"I got 'it.'" He shook his head. "I'm human, Sophie Marie Priebe. I'll *definitely* mess it up. But when I do?" He slid his sunglasses down his nose with his index finger and stared down at me with his impossibly sexy hazel eyes. "Remind yourself, Bonita, that you're hanging out with a guy who has not only the heart, but also the balls to make it right." He smiled at me and laughed out loud. Which made me laugh too.

Mick Jagger crooned "Symphony for the Devil" on the Jeep's sound system. Alejandro dialed up the volume. "Hang on!" He thrust one arm across me holding me back in my seat. "Short cut." He whip-turned the Jeep onto a side street and we careened down a hill on a narrow one-way street lined with parked cars.

CHAPTER ELEVEN

The sun was bright, the beach air warm but oddly enough, at the same time cool. It wasn't like summertime in Wisconsin with ninety-nine percent humidity. Alejandro and I dangled our shoes from our fingers as we walked barefoot through the sand. We trudged past the famous Venice Beach boardwalk on our way to the ocean in the near distance.

The choppy water had long rolling waves topped with white caps.

"God." A dreamy look grew on his face. "It's a surfer's paradise today."

A pod of wet-suit attired folks held onto their surfboards and bobbed in the ocean water a decent distance from the pier while they waited on their next wave. "I need a picture," he said. "I need a picture of you in that hat with the ocean in the background."

"I'm not very photogenic," I said.

"Come on! It's a freaking, perfect day. I want something to remind me."

I grumbled. "Okay."

He backed away a couple of yards and aimed his iPhone at me.

I smiled. Awkwardly.

"You look like you're at the dentist's office. Could you do something kind of cheesecakey for me, my little Cheesehead?"

I stuck my tongue out at him.

"Tempting," he said. "But not quite what I had in mind. Humor me."

I bent my knees slightly off to the side, put one hand on them, leaned forward, displayed my modest cleavage, puckered up and blew him a kiss.

"Way better!" He snapped the shot, checked it and smiled.

When Alex's friend Nathan waved to us from the wet, hard sand a hundred yards away.

Alex waved back. "Ready?" He held out his hand to me.

"I thought today was about us."

"It is," he said. "Come on!" He grabbed my hand and we jogged across the sand toward his buddies. "I want you to officially meet my fellow Drivers. They're my best friends."

"They tried to steal me away from you two nights after we met."

"Of course they did. I'd expect nothing less of them. We're a little competitive."

* * *

Alex and I stood next to his friends, Nick, Nathan, Tyler and Jackson just yards from where the choppy, cold, Pacific waters hit the sand. Nathan and Jackson already had their wetsuits on and were checking out Jackson's new top-of-the-line board. Nick and Tyler were partially suited up which meant they were also half-naked from the waist up.

They were built. Nick had exotic tats up and down his left arm. Tyler had one ear pierced—and not that hideous hole-in-the-ear the size of Wyoming fad. I tried not to stare, as that would be incredibly wrong considering I was officially under Alex's care today. What did they put in the water here that grew such yummy-looking guys? Was it a miracle potion of sunshine and sand and salt water mixed with magical guacamole?

When Tyler called me out. "Stop trying not to gawk, Sophie. Yeah, we're privileged sons-of-bitches from SoCal. And not necessarily in the monied sense. We range from poor to stinking rich. Well, at least our parents do."

"You must be mistaken, Tyler," I said. "I was checking out Jackson's new surfboard—*not you.*"

"Speak for yourself, Tyler," Nathan said. "I have my own money. Gawk all you want, Sophie. We've got a bit of a reputation for copping attitude, being smart as well as smart-asses."

"But we're the best Drivers in L.A. And sometimes that combo's a turn-on," Nick said. "An aphrodisiac of sorts." He yanked on the top part of his wetsuit. "We're kind of like firemen." He winked at me.

"Not to brag," Jackson said, "but the Drivers, and well, their best friend—lucky me—usually score the hottest chicks in a hundred mile radius."

I backed away from them as well as Alex. "Have I just meandered into the beginning of a low-budget porn movie?" I asked.

Alejandro and the guys looked at each other and started laughing.

"Nah," Nathan said.

"We're in Venice," Nick said. "The cheap porn's shot in Chatsworth. That's in the Valley."

"Whatev. You all need to tone down the self-promotion right now," I said. "Bragging about your this and that as well as how many people you sleep with makes you sound like dicks."

"You're getting the wrong impression," Tyler said.

"Maybe I'm getting the wrong impression," I said,

"because you all are giving that. So—what's it really like to be a Driver? Better question—why did you all become Drivers?"

Tyler shook his head and kicked one foot in the sand. He gazed at Nathan, who stared at Nick, who shrugged and tossed the gaze back to Alex like it was a puck in a hockey game during playoffs.

"Being a Driver is the best of the best, Sophie," Tyler said. "When it's not tough. Or humiliating. Or carving out a piece of your heart that you believed you already lost a while back."

Nick rubbed his tatted arm. "None of us here became Drivers out of good will. We became drivers out of need."

"Enough," Alex said. "I don't want to talk about the whys today. Just want to have some fun."

"Hey," Jackson said. "I'm not a Driver. I'm just friends with them. Got any cute, midwestern friends who might be interested in a road trip?" He winked at me.

"Shut up, Jackson," Nathan said. "Take your new baby out on the water."

"Yes!" I said. "Gorgeous board. Take it out immediately." I gave Jackson a thumbs up. "I'm dying to see what it does, how you do, you know, the whole shebang."

He smiled. "Thanks, Sophie!" He strode toward the ocean, clutching his board. Waded into the surf, one hand on his new toy as he guided it through the choppy waters.

"Your Cheesehead doesn't surf, does she, Alex?" Tyler asked.

I frowned. "Cheesehead has a name. It's Sophie," I said.

Alex pulled me even tighter into his side, if that was possible.

"They have lakes in the Midwest," he said. "Besides, she's taking Genetics with Schillinger this summer. And, researching a book on alternative healing."

"Sophie?" Tyler tucked a stray curl of his light brown

hair behind one ear. "Just one more question."

"Sure."

"You were checking out Jackson's new board, right?"

"Yeah."

"What color is it?"

Crap.

"Considering you all were huddled in front of it like the Wise Men at the baby Jesus's manger, I could only see the very top of it." I jutted my chin out. "Which appeared white."

I prayed for a long, hard second that the top of Jackson's new board was white.

The sea of gorgeous men standing around me parted as Tyler, Nick, Nathan, and Alejandro turned and squinted at Jackson in the water. He was deep out in the surf, sitting on his board, which appeared multi-colored, patiently waiting on his wave.

"Lucky bastard got the top of the line again," Nathan said.

"He ain't a bastard. His dad can totally afford it," Tyler said. "It looks red and blue to me."

"Yeah," Alejandro said. "But the top of it's solid white."

I said a silent prayer to the Saint of Confused Women Everywhere. "And that," I jabbed my index finger in Jackson's direction, "should be a God-given sign to stop testing this midwestern chick. I'm out of here, Alejandro," I said. "I'm dying to see the boardwalk."

"I'm coming with you." He stared somewhat wistfully at Jackson bobbing out in the Pacific.

"No." I pulled the list of healers from my purse. I knew there were a few in Venice. I'd find one to be a distraction and buy time for Alejandro to have some fun with his friends.

"My friend Javier has a tattoo parlor on the boardwalk called InkBaby," Nick said. "He did all my work." Nick's tats were extensive and amazing. "He even did Alex's tattoo."

"You have a tat?" I asked.

"Just one," Alex said.

"I've never seen it."

Alex raised one eyebrow. "There's a lot of me you haven't seen."

Tyler laughed but covered it with a cough.

Nick rolled his eyes and did the universal symbol for "zip it" across his lips. "You and Sophie should check out Javier's shop."

"I will, thanks," I said.

Nick smiled at me. Was I really winning over Alejandro's friends? Did I even want to be doing this? It just meant more connections that needed to be eliminated in the near future.

I scanned my list of healers, but the only one had three big black squiggly lines that Lizzie Sparks had drawn through the man's information. The address on Venice boardwalk was still visible through her scratchings.

"Let's go," Alex said.

"You stay. I'm going to knock down another thing on my to-do list." I said. "Meet you in an hour?"

"You sure?" he said, but didn't release his hand from my side.

I leaned into him and planted a kiss on his body part that was closest to my lips—his tan, muscular shoulder.

He jumped and for a second loosened his hold on my waist. Exactly the response I was looking for.

"I'm positive." I extricated myself from his arm and walked away from him and his friends.

"Kissing a man's shoulder has consequences, you know," Alex called after me.

My back was to him when I smiled, attempted to wipe that smile from my face and in a moment of gloriousness, realized it was okay to smile. *It really was.*

***

I walked down the Venice boardwalk. It was the most amazing group of shops, eateries and kiosks run by folks selling tarot readings, sunglasses, funky art and jewelry. The people seemed to be of all ages, cultures, and socio-economic groups. There were sunburnt tourists and dogs dressed up in clothes. People should not dress their dogs up in clothes.

It was stranger than the Mall of America and had more tourist shops than the Wisconsin Dells. It was kind of what I imagined the funky section of Amsterdam was like but without the legal hookers. Which most likely meant that Venice had illegal hookers. But I really couldn't be sure. They just might have been tourists wearing super high heels who didn't realize their shorts were too short. Frankly, I didn't care because I wasn't on a hooker quest.

I was, however, looking for Dr. Carlton Kelsey, vision quest master, guru for more than four decades to the masses, author of at least seven, best-selling books. Dr. Kelsey, the mid-sixty something, former USCLA professor who experimented with a wide variety of psychedelics back in the day and purportedly cured himself of cancer. He was donating a free lecture tonight in a meeting hall somewhere above a store on the boardwalk.

I squinted at the address through Lizzie Sparks' thick, black scratchings when I spotted a spit-polished, brown Mercedes SUV with two, behemoth bodyguards standing next to it. They wore plain khakis. Their steroidy-muscular arms crossed against the front of their short-sleeved, T-shirts while their purple veiny head-necks popped out of the necklines. The bodyguards looked like attack dogs: thick around the chest. Serious. Complete with a reputation to rip you open if you messed with them.

"Hey," I said. "I'm trying to find Dr. Carlton Kelsey's lecture. You all appear... informed. Do you know where this event might be taking place?"

They regarded each other and nodded. Meathead #1 opened his mouth. "There." He pointed to a turquoise building in front of us. It had a Vegan Delight fast food joint and medical marijuana clinic on the lower level. A tall concrete staircase was built into the side of the building. "You're late," he said. "Dr. Kelsey doesn't like late."

"Story of my life. Thanks." I waved at the both of them as I climbed the stairs.

"Dr. Kelsey really hates late," Meathead #2 said.

"Then he'll love trying to convert me."

* * *

I stood at the back of a smaller, weathered lecture hall and took in the surroundings. It was a plain, faded space with a few windows and creaky, old ceiling fans that wobbled like they might spin off at any given moment and decapitate someone. There were no posters, prints, or art of any kind on the walls. Ancient, convention-styled folding chairs lined up in rows in front of a small, unassuming stage.

If you were a wannabe speaker, upcoming author and/or aging guru—this was the perfect space to attempt to re-create yourself on a blank palette.

The lecture room was full—not packed—but definitely not hurting for people of all ages and many races. Some appeared healthy. Some appeared sick. Some appeared dying. Everyone clutched their Complimentary Welcome Package handed out by one of the two greeters. They stood at the back of the hall with spiffy stick-on nametags on their "KELSEY VISION QUEST: Give Life a Chance!" T-shirts.

I glanced up at the wobbling fans, located the one that appeared the least deadly and took a seat in the back of the hall a few feet away from it.

Dr. Carlton Kelsey paced back and forth on a small

stage in front of his audience. He was a big man, tall and thick, probably in his late sixties. His full head of hair was silver and pulled back in a ponytail that landed just above his shoulder blades. I sensed Dr. Kelsey was used to larger stages as he almost fell off the edges of the platform and more than once wobbled for a millisecond when he reached its borders.

"Kelsey Vision Quest," Carlton Kelsey said, "is the most powerful mind-bending healing experience you can go through in your entire life. We here at Give Life a Chance have been helping folks do this for almost forty years now. We open doors. We open lives. We open your... mind."

A few folks in the audience applauded.

"Life is hard," he said. "because we make it that way. We worry about things that we have almost no control over. We stress about people who basically give a shit about us. We live safe, tiny existences watching the years roll by as we develop conditions that are ticking time bombs like heart disease, depression, rheumatoid arthritis and cancers that stem from bad chemicals, bad water, bad genes, as well as all the restrictions and rules that we've placed upon ourselves."

Dr. Kelsey paused in the middle of the stage and gazed at the audience. Dear God, I could swear he was looking straight at me. I glanced down toward my knees, cleared my throat and ducked my head into my hand.

"When is it time, people, to heal your disease, or nurse your loved ones back to health? When is it time to reclaim your life? What are you waiting for? A new drug? An experimental, surgical procedure? A miracle?"

I wanted all of the above.

CHAPTER TWELVE

A few people in the audience applauded. Some stood up. One man shouted, "Amen!" I wasn't sure how I felt, so I just stayed silent, butt in chair and watched.

A middle-aged, African-American woman a few rows in front of me slowly stood up. She had no eyebrows, no eyelashes and wore a bright yellow bandanna tied around her head.

Her nearly look-alike companion, dressed in the same gear but with a turquoise colored bandanna, poked her in the shoulder repeatedly with her index finger and whispered, "You can do this, Betty. Ask him. Go ahead. Just like we practiced."

"I'm not waiting, Dr. Kelsey," Betty said. "I was diagnosed with stage two ovarian cancer about eighteen months ago."

Folks in the audience turned toward Betty and eyed her. One woman sighed and dropped her forehead into her hands.

"I'm not going to say, 'I'm sorry'," Dr. Kelsey said. "Because that means I perceive you as a victim. And I don't. You're still alive. You must be doing something right. What are you doing right?"

"I'm exploring all my options. I had the surgery, chemotherapy. I enrolled in a clinical trail. I admit, however, I am still hoping for a miracle." Betty's friend squeezed her hand. "How can Kelsey Vision Quest help me, my friend, and others like us? Why is what you offer different than all the other alternative treatments?"

"I can't guarantee the Quest will cure your cancer. But I can guarantee, your mind will be opened to healing in a way that no other healer, including western medicine's traditional therapies or alternative therapists have offered you."

"Thank you, Doctor," Betty said as her friend put a hand on her arm and steadied her as she sat down. A smattering of applause rose from the audience.

Dr. Kelsey cracked a small smile and then turned back to a small table, grabbed a bottle of water, twisted the top off and guzzled some.

My legs seemed to have a mind of their own and I popped out of my seat. "Dr. Kelsey," I said.

He turned around and faced me. Something shifted in his eyes. "Yes? Your name is?"

"Sophie Marie Priebe," I said. "I've read a couple of your books. I've looked at your videos on YouTube. You have so many followers. Fans. Testimonies from folks who swear the Quest helped them break through problems, ranging the gamut from mind to body. From carb craving and binge-eating to types of arthritis, autoimmune diseases and even certain cancers. Would you elaborate on that for a moment, please? Thank you."

Now all the eyes in the audience flickered between Dr. Kelsey and me. In a perfect world I would have kept quiet and not asked anything. But my world was far from perfect.

"What an absolutely, splendid question, Sophie. Years ago when I was diagnosed with thyroid cancer, I went on a quest to find healing. Those journeys lead me to many places, techniques and teachers. When I finally tripped through a rudimentary vision quest, I realized my answers were already there. Always had been. I was just too stubborn to accept how simple it all was. After the quest, I desired to understand life and the world at such a profound level that I was able to release many of my pre-programmed and pre-conceived notions. Let them go. And that's when I found my healing."

"Thank you, Doctor. Your methods appear dramatic, but your YouTube videos seem to be from a long time ago. They're old. Have you made changes to your program? Do you have more recent, advanced techniques? Testimonials?" I sat down.

"Another great question. I personally am too busy working with clients to spend time marketing my program. However, as anyone knows, more people that need healing will be reached if we update our marketing. So yes, our healing techniques have advanced. The Quests are stronger. And we are actively looking to reach more folks who desperately need us." Dr. Kelsey nodded at me, a curious look in his eyes.

* * *

His lecture continued for another twenty minutes. I peeked at the time on my phone. I didn't want to be late for Alex. I snuck out the door while the audience applauded Dr. Kelsey. I traipsed down the stairs, hit the boardwalk and realized I felt different: buoyant, hopeful, almost high. I had to call my Nana and Mom and tell them about my latest discovery. Because this method might actually help my—

A meaty, male hand grabbed my arm and stopped me in my tracks. "Dr. Kelsey requests that you stay and have a word with him." I looked up at Meathead #1's red, sweaty face. He had an earpiece lodged into his ear and pushed on it.

"Thanks for your help," I said. "Dr. Kelsey's lecture was

supreme. But I can't stay. I need to meet some friends." I tapped on his arm until he released me. And I strode away.

"Stop!" he said.

"Why?" I asked.

"Dr. Kelsey says he wants to talk to you personally about your situation. No charge. He's a busy man. He doesn't do this very often."

An unexpected opportunity to heal. I had to stay. I'd find Alejandro eventually or he'd find me. "Okay," I said. "But only for five minutes. I can't be late."

He grunted and took my arm. I expected he'd lead me right back to the lecture hall. Instead he guided me toward the brown SUV.

A strange car. People I didn't know. I balked, ground my heels into the cement and imagined my legs were made of lead. "I have Dr. Kelsey's card. I will totally call or email him tomorrow, and we can talk then."

"But Dr. Kelsey wants to speak with you now." Meathead #1 gripped my arm a little tighter, and despite my metallic legs, practically dragged me closer to the vehicle.

I gazed at him. His eyeballs were wobbling in their sockets and his arms were twitching. Hell, I could appreciate the whole twitching thing, but truth be told, Meathead #1 wasn't all there. Something had happened to him. He'd disappeared into a steroidy, tough body, a determined mind, but also a brain that was a little Jello-y. Meathead #2 jogged toward us.

E-freaking-nough. "I plan on attending Dr. Kelsey's next event." I squirmed. "But right now I have to go." I yanked my arm free from his grasp and paced away, hoping to disappear into the crazy, Venice scene.

"Dr. Kelsey doesn't like people who walk away!" Meathead #2 caught up with #1 and yelled after me.

I plucked my phone from my purse and hit Alex's number. It went straight to voicemail. I hung up. He was probably still hanging with his friends. I peered up at the side street and realized I wasn't on Brooks and the boardwalk anymore. I was blocks south. How many, I had no idea.

I passed T-shirt shops, and a high-end surfboard gear store. Tourists and regulars swarmed passed me. I felt sunburnt, light-headed. I popped in a lemonade stand called Squeeze Me, bought a small fresh-squeezed lemonade and asked where I might find InkBaby. "Three blocks that way," the clerk pointed, "on the left close to the basketball courts."

The sun was nearly kissing the horizon when I found InkBaby, a small, tidy, tattoo parlor located on the eastern edge of the boardwalk in a dilapidated storefront. A twenty-something, buff Latino man with multiple tats and piercings was pulling in his displays from the sidewalk. He seemed to be shutting down his shop.

I decided to catch my breath inside the store. I peeked around the place and checked out the designs displayed on plastic covered poster boards. "These are good," I mumbled.

"Thanks," the man said. "Most are stock, generic and boring. But I designed a few that aren't half bad. What's your name?"

"Sophie. Are you Javier?"

"Javier Sebastian. Do I know you?"

"Nick told me about you. He's a Driver."

"Nick's my man. He's been through shit, but he's a good guy."

"He said you did all his tats," I said. "I read that Venice is home to a lot of artists. You're the first one I've met."

Javier smiled. "Not too many people call me an artist. I'll take that as inspiration for the future."

I pointed to one tat on a board: an elegant heart comprised of words. "What was the inspiration behind this?" I asked.

Javier laid his hand on the design. He took a deep breath but seemed to forget to exhale. "Inspired by the first girl I fell in love with. I thought we'd be together forever. Now, I visit her grave a couple times a year. On her birthday. On the anniversary of the day we met as well as the day she died. I leave flowers and remind Tatiana that no matter who or what happens in my life, she will always live in my heart." He wiped one eye.

I pretended not to notice and willed the tears welling in my eyes to just cut it out already. "She knows," I said.

"You've lost someone?" Javier asked.

I remembered peeking through Mom's barely opened bedroom door as I watched her crying alone in bed. I pictured my Nana who had struggled with MS for so long, had been through so many therapies, but still ended up in a wheelchair in a retirement home. I thought about my own mission to find healing. "Not like you. But in other ways, yeah." My hand shook a little. I covered it with my other hand to spare us both the embarrassment.

"Death seems to hover around certain people, ready to exact its toll on them or someone they love at a moment's notice." Javier crossed himself. "God, I'm morbid today. Sorry."

"No worries. You're closing up. I'll get out of your way." I nodded at him and headed toward the door. "Great to meet you, soon-to-be famous, Venice Beach artist." We shared a smile before I left his shop.

Back on the still crowded boardwalk I passed a performance artist covered in silver makeup, wearing silver clothes and moving in jerky motions like a robot. I circled around a kid spinning on his back in a break-dance routine while his father passed the hat to a small audience. When my phone rang. It was Alejandro. Yay! I picked up.

"Bonita, I'm on Brooks and the boardwalk but I don't see you."

"I just left InkBaby."

"Javier's place," he said. "Do you see the basketball courts?"

"Hang on." I wandered a few yards down and spotted them. "I'm right next to them."

"Take a seat close by. Maybe on the bleachers. I'll find you in five. I rode Jackson's new board. Oh, crap, Sophie, it's amazing. You need to experience this. It could even go in your book. Certain types of exercise have transcendent, healing qualities associated with them."

"Like yoga," I said.

"Like surfing," he said. "I need to get you out in the ocean on a surfboard. Let's talk about this."

I couldn't help smiling as I made my way toward the courts. I felt like I was talking to a four-year-old who just dug up his first earthworm. "You went in the water without a wetsuit?" I reached the metal bleachers bordering the courts and climbed each rung until I hit the very top. I stood on the skinny bench that had a view of the Ocean, the boardwalk and the Ferris wheel on the pier in Santa Monica a couple miles away.

"That board was so hot, I didn't need a wetsuit," he said. "Actually, the water was cold, but, hell. It was still awesome! I'll meet you in three minutes. You've got to try surfing, Sophie!"

I couldn't help but smile. "Maybe someday."

Someone mumbled in the distance. "Yeah sure," Alejandro said and our call was disconnected.

I knew that for me, getting in the water, getting up on a surf board and riding a wave—someday would never happen.

I hung up and ruminated about today's events. Dr. Carlton Kelsey seemed like the real deal. He was powerful. Didn't seem like a bullshitter. I didn't like his bodyguards, though. But really, whose bodyguards were supposed to be likeable, hip and smart?

And I realized—mine was! Alejandro was kind of my bodyguard and he possessed all those qualities. He had to be the exception. My mind returned to spinning. Why did Lizzie Sparks cross Dr. Kelsey off my list? When I heard a familiar voice that squashed all my mental gymnastics like bugs hitting a windshield.

"Hurry up, you pussies. Not every day we score a game on these courts."

I peered down from my perch and spotted a pack of bald young men with trousers hanging halfway down their butts, huddled around a park bench ten yards in front of me.

Oscar, aka Pintdick, jogged onto the court and passed a ball to one of his buddies. The rest of his pals poured onto the painted concrete and dove furiously into their game.

I froze. The asshole that attacked me and his skinhead friends were playing ball just yards away. I pulled my hat low on my head and tucked my body tight into a nondescript orb of a person. My heart raced, I started to panic but forced myself to think. Alex was close by, but not here—yet. If Pintdick or his friends spotted me? I was not only fair game—*I was revenge-worthy*. Maybe I shouldn't have called him out. Maybe I should have just run away.

I eyeballed the edge of the bleachers. But I was too high up and would definitely break bones if I jumped from this height. That left only a few escape options. The best one seemed to climb down five rungs, edge to the side, jump off and walk away. Slowly. Calmly. Quickly.

I gathered all my courage, stood up and pulled my hat as far down on my face as it would go. I slunk down the steps.

Pintdick and pals were hitting baskets, working up a sweat and shouting at each other. "You hit a basket the same way you hit your toilet," one skinhead said.

"That's because I was too busy hitting your sister."

"Dude, if you ever hit my sister I'll take you out."

"I meant nailing your sister, creepers. Do I have to explain everything to you?"

I made it all the way down to the fourth rung on the bleachers. My pulse raced. I looked over the edge at the ground. Technically I was only about four feet from the earth. Hell, even I could survive a four-foot jump. I just had to time it when the jerks were in the middle of a scoring drive on the court, so they wouldn't spot me.

"And score! Take that, Pintdick!"

"I told you never to call me that." Oscar's voice grew cold.

I scooted to the edge of the bleachers and gathered all my courage when I heard a small cry. I glanced down and spotted a little boy crouched in the dirt directly under my escape route. Snot bubbles escaped from his nose as he patted the remnants of a popped balloon lying on the ground next to him.

My heart went out to him and at the same time I felt frustrated and confused. If I jumped now, I'd probably land on the kid and flatten him. I had no problem deflating the egos of guys my age, but flattening an actual child was not in my repertoire. "Psst!" I whispered. "Go back to your mom. She's probably looking for you."

He gazed up at me and sobbed even louder. One of Oscar's buddies turned and eyed the boy. I glanced down, tried to hide my face under my hat and my arm. I prayed he didn't make me. It was past time to jump. I aimed away from the boy, catapulted off the bleachers and landed on my feet on the ground. I managed to walk about a yard away when someone grabbed my shirt and spun me around.

CHAPTER THIRTEEN

"Well, well. Still looking for the dead president?" Pintdick clutched my wrist and stared at me. A cruel smile spread across his ugly face. "All those little cuts healed up real nice." He ran his finger across my cheek.

"No thanks to you," I said. "You attacked me right after I got them. You made them bleed again. What kind of man does that to a woman?" I looked him square in the eyes as I broke out into a sweat.

He pinched the hat off my head and flung it onto the sand. "The kind of man whose nose you broke." He seized my shirt's neckline and jerked me toward him. "We have unfinished business." He clamped a hand around my neck and pulled me after him, away from the courts toward an alleyway in the near distance.

I screamed but he pressed his hand over my mouth, and my cries were muted.

"Oscar," a friend of his said. "Think about this, man. Do you really want to do this?"

"Oscar. Dude!" another friend said. "If the bitch talks? Parole violation board will be all on you like superglue. You'll end up back in jail."

"That's why the bitch ain't going to have an opportunity to talk." Oscar pulled a dull knife from his pants pocket and flashed it for a heartbeat.

No. A thousand times no.

I raked my fingernails across his hand and drew blood.

"You cunt!" He dropped his hand and I screamed. That caught the attention of a bunch of folks who stared at us, fear growing on their faces. The majority quickly gathered their belongings, their kids and raced away. But one guy pushed his way through the crowd twirling a baseball bat like it was a baton.

"Oscar Fuentes, you son-of-a bitch." Javier held the baseball bat high in the air and slammed it down on a metal, picnic table then continued to race toward us.

"Back off, Javier!" Oscar exclaimed.

"Fuck you, Oscar." Javier bolted toward us. "You are not hurting that girl."

I elbowed Oscar repeatedly. Most of my efforts connected with air. But a few jabs nailed his ribs. He grunted and slowed down for one long second.

I spotted Alejandro about fifty yards away with Nick right behind him. They raced like hell toward me. "Take care of my girl, Javier," Alex hollered then jabbed his finger in the air toward Oscar. "I can see you, skinhead prick, and I'll fucking kill you if you hurt one hair on her head."

Basically after that all I heard were roars and grunts and thuds, the sounds of fists hitting flesh, a baseball bat hitting bodies, and concrete and bones cracking. Someone slugged Oscar and he released his grip on me.

I hit the ground and rolled on the grass and sand onto my side. Police sirens blared in the near distance. People shouted. I felt weak. I felt like a victim. Once again, I felt like a stupid girl.

A young, pretty, Latina woman snagged my hand and hissed, "You're next to a picnic table. Get under it—now. Hurry! We'll hide you."

I crawled under the table. She and her friends threw their backpacks, purses, a dog carrier, a sand-filled blanket, and rolled up paper trash bags from their day at the beach on top of me.

I laid on the sand and dirt under the table until, in spite of Oscar's protests, the cops cuffed him and took him away. I huddled there while I heard a Venice police officer tell the rest of Oscar's gang to leave and instruct the crowd to disperse. Another officer told Alex and Nick and Javier that they had not yet found me, but the bathrooms had been searched and were cleared.

The girl who helped me hide didn't abandon me. She and her friends pretended it was just another day at the beach as they chatted about celebrity gossip, their own gossip, what movies they'd seen and who was hooking up with whom. At one point I pinched her ankle.

She bent down like she was tying her shoe.

"Can I leave?" I asked.

She shook her head. "Oscar's gang, the Lowriders, always keep a lookout on the scene. Wait a bit longer."

"Thank you. Would you tell my friends who are looking for me that I'm okay?"

She shook her head. "Boyfriends and friends always give it away. You gotta think like the bad guys right now."

Alejandro, Nick and Javier paced back and forth looking for me. I felt like a shithead for not telling Alex where I was. But when I asked the girl again, she whispered a story to me. A story about a girl that Oscar's gang had fucked up about five years ago. That girl's name was Tatiana. And that girl was dead.

It had to be after eight p.m. It was getting dark outside. Alejandro, his friends and Javier were still searching for me. Pacing the boardwalk, checking storefronts, asking folks if they had seen the confrontation. I squeezed my savior's leg. She bent down under the table and looked at me. "I think it's okay for you to go."

"I can't even find the words to thank you for hiding me," I said. "What's your name?"

"You're welcome," she said. "My name's Gabriella. I

was Tatiana's friend."

Two more female faces popped under the picnic table. "Hey," I said. "I'm Sophie. You are?"

One girl extended her hand toward me. "Rosie—Tatiana's friend." She shook my hand.

"I'm Naomi—Tatiana's friend," another girl said and handed me a bottle of water. I cracked it open, took a long slug and crawled out from under the table. We all hugged and I started crying. Then the rest of the girls followed suit. I was covered in mud, sand and was completely disgusting.

"Sophie?" Alejandro said.

I turned and saw him. He stood next to Nick and Nathan and Javier. Their jaws dropped.

"Sophie!" Alejandro raced toward me, grabbed me around the waist and pulled me tight into his chest. He kissed the top of my head. Placed his hands on either side of my face and tilted my head up as he bent his down. "Are you okay? Are you all right?"

"I'm okay," I said. "These girls hid me. They protected me."

Javier, Nathan, Nick, Tyler and Jackson joined us.

"Gabriella?" Javier asked.

She nodded. "We don't forget Tatiana. Never again."

Javier took her hand and squeezed. "*Gracias*, Gabriella."

It was practically a love fest. Everyone exchanged phone numbers and emails. We all agreed to meet up at the Grill in an hour.

***

Alejandro drove me home, the top of his Jeep back on. "If anything had happened to you, I was going to take that banger out," he said.

"Don't say those kinds of things. I never want something bad happening to you because of me," I said.

"Something bad just happened to you *because of me*,"

Alex said. "I let you down. I shouldn't have left you. I didn't show up in time."

It would have been easier to let him think that was the truth. But it would have been so wrong. A shiver traveled down my spine and part of my heart cracked open.

"No, Alejandro. That had nothing to do with you. That happened because of me."

"How can you even say that?" He slammed his hand on the steering wheel. "That Oscar asshole's the scum of the earth. A complete opportunist. Five years ago, Javier's girlfriend got into drugs. Tatiana was experimenting. Someone in Oscar's Lowriders gang sold her bad shit. She overdosed. He's been a mess ever since. This whole thing tonight was completely my fault."

"No, it wasn't," I said. "Remember the first night I asked you to drive me? You asked me why my cuts had broken open, but I wouldn't tell you."

"Yeah?"

"I had an appointment with a healer in Venice that day. I got lost. I ran into Oscar. He tried to, you know, take advantage of the situation and me—"

"Did he touch you? Did he hurt you?"

"He threw me against a fence, but no…I didn't want him to touch me that way. I've never… Not that that matters. So I fought. And I got lucky and broke his nose. And then I went a little overboard and called him Pintdick in front of his friends. He didn't forget. He's still pissed off at me."

"He's the one that broke your cuts open?"

"Yes," I said.

"I'm going to hurt him."

"You're not going to hurt him," I said. "Because if you hurt him, you'll go to jail. And if you go to jail, I'd have to find another Driver. And I'd really miss you. So promise me that you're not going to hurt him. Promise me that you and I are okay?"

Alejandro didn't say a word but ground his teeth while his jaw muscles popped. He was silent for the rest of the ten-minute drive until he pulled up to the curb in front of my place and threw on the parking brake so hard I whiplashed in my seat.

"I promise I won't hurt him, Bonita, but only if you swear to me you won't head back to that neighborhood on your own. I freaking love Venice. I've always wished we lived there instead of Bel-Air. But Oscar and his friends are in a gang. That's their turf, their stomping grounds and you're big-time on their radar. So if you need to go back there—take me or one my friends. Just promise you don't go there alone. Not forever. Just for right now. Yes?"

"Yes," I said.

"Good," he said. "By the way? No matter what happens—you and I will always be okay. Burn that into your memory," he said. "Like a mental tattoo."

I smiled at him.

He smiled back. "Hurry up. Everyone's expecting us at the Grill in a half hour."

"Let's just go there, now," I said. "Not to repeat, but I'm kind of tired after today."

"I hate to tell you…"

"What?" I asked.

"You smell a little like dog poop, McDonalds and Coppertone rolled together."

"Oh, my God!" I leaped out the passenger door and ran toward my apartment. "Back in fifteen minutes."

He cut the engine and walked toward me. "I want to see Napoleon."

"Okay. Come on in." I opened the door. "Just don't let him out. Can you even stand how bad I smell?"

"I can stand that you are alive and have a couple of fresh bruises." Alejandro scooped Napoleon up in his arms and held him in his arms like a baby. "He's growing on me, Bonita."

I scratched Napoleon's chin. He grabbed my finger with his front paws, leaned in and smelled it. "He's probably smelling the Mickey D's. Feed him while I shower?"

"Sure." Alex crooned baby sounds as he walked with Napoleon into my kitchen. I stared at Alejandro's beautiful face. Glanced at his hands and spotted some blood on his knuckles. He'd thrown a few punches for me. His T-shirt was ripped in a few places. He was my Driver. He was my bodyguard.

He was growing on me too.

* * *

The Grill was busy with old faces and new faces. Alejandro and the Drivers had commandeered a bunch of tables and pushed them together along the back wall. Cheyenne dropped off trays of drinks and appetizers. People passed the food around the table. I sat across from Alejandro and chatted with Gabriella and her friends.

Tyler stood up and held up his Corona overhead. "A toast," he said.

"A toast," everyone echoed back.

"I, for one, am sick of the bad guys always winning. Today, the bad guys didn't win thanks to Javier, Gabriella, Rosie, Naomi and all the people who helped shut down the asshole Lowriders today."

"Cheers." Nick clinked his Pellegrino bottle to Tyler's beer. "And to Sophie, who can scream and hide with the best of them." I nodded at Nick as another round of toasts and cheers circled our long table.

"And to my favorite Driver," I said and held up my beer bottle. "Here's to Alejandro, the best Ralph, ever."

"Why's she calling you Ralph?" Nick asked.

He shrugged. "I haven't figured it out yet."

Nathan squinted at us. "A mystery. I like mysteries."

"Me too," Alex said. "This is a mystery with a benefit.

When I figure out the Ralph thing, I win something."

"Ooh," Gabriella said. "Like a GWP."

"What's a GWP?" Javier asked.

"Gift with Purchase," Gabriella said. "They have them all the time at makeup counters."

"I don't get to a lot of makeup counters," Javier said.

"Well, you should. You could be doing a whole side business with permanent makeup tattoos."

"But, I'm an artist."

"I'm an artist too, Javier," Gabriella said. "Artists don't come in one shape, size or variety. I'm a makeup artist."

"What do you win?" Tyler asked.

"When I figure out the Ralph reference, I win our first kiss." Alejandro winked at me.

"But if I figure out the Ralph thing before you do?" Tyler asked. "Wouldn't that first kiss prize automatically transfer to me?"

"No." I shook my head.

"No," Alejandro said.

"It's a one time offer intended solely for one guy—Alejandro. It's not a Groupon. I'm not kissing the first thousand folks who purchase this deal."

"Hmm. Do you want to kiss him, Sophie?" Rosie asked.

I blushed and suddenly was tongue-tied. "I… I… Um…"

"I'll answer that," Alejandro said. "Yes, she definitely wants to kiss me."

"Let the girl speak for herself. How long has Alejandro been driving you around L.A.?" Naomi asked.

"Since the first night I landed in town. He took me to the E.R.," I said. "But that was unofficial."

"Why'd you ask him to drive you?" Naomi asked. "Couldn't you just rent a car?"

No way I could answer that question honestly.

"I totally suck at navigating. I got lost about five times the first few days I was here. I took a bus from Westwood to

Venice and got completely turned around."

"You took a bus in L.A.?" Jackson asked. "For real? I've never taken a bus in L.A."

"That's because your father practically owns L.A.," Nathan said.

"A bus. A driver." Gabriella looked off into space and thought. A look grew on her face and she giggled.

I eyed her. She totally knew.

Alex gazed at her. "One clue, Gabriella. I beg you."

She shrugged.

I smiled and nodded at her.

It was okay. Might as well get this over with.

"To the moon, Alice. Or should I say, Alex," Gabriella said as Cheyenne walked up shouldering a huge tray of drinks and appetizers.

Everyone at our extended table shut up, stared at the ceiling or squinted at each other.

"Nachos. Veggie Nachos. Gluten-free Nachos. One Caesar wrap dressing on the side." She deposited the dishes on the rare, open spots on our tables. "To the moon?" She held the empty tray above her head and pointed to Alejandro and me with her other hand. "They're the freaking *Honeymooners*, man."

Alejandro peered at me as a smile tore across his face. "Ralph Kramden! Bus driver played by Jackie Gleason. I finally got it, didn't I, Bonita?"

He did finally get it. I nodded. And steeled myself for the impending shit storm.

"Well played," Tyler said.

"Is it my imagination?" Nathan asked. "Or didn't you just win a kiss?"

"I did win a kiss," Alejandro said.

"A little congratulations for me and my girls over here," Gabriella said as they divvied up a plate of veggie nachos. "I do believe we helped you figure this out."

"Dude, are you going to kiss her, or do I need to pinch

hit for you?" Nick asked.

"You've always got my back, Alex," Jackson said. "I'm your loyal friend and I'd be happy to sub for you tonight."

My heart started pounding. All eyes in the Westwood Grill turned toward our table, turned onto us. Alejandro got up off his chair and walked toward me. Gazed at me with a look that could melt ice cream in the middle of a blizzard in January. My face flushed. The hotness spread down into my chest, my stomach into my groin. My knees felt a little weak. I knew I was blushing and had to remind my hand not to fan my face.

"For the love of God, Alex. Do it," Freddie said from behind the bar. "Kiss her!"

"Freddie, you are a pervert," Alejandro said. "I know this because you confessed you regularly watch little people porn."

"You told me that was cool," Freddie said.

"Nathan. Nick. Tyler. Shut this down, please?" I wrung my hands.

The guys nodded at each other.

"I don't know." Nathan covered a smile.

"Tough call," Tyler added.

"Sophie!" Alejandro said. "Ignore these assholes, my fellow Drivers, as well as the jealous people and voyeurs. Have I promised you anything that I didn't deliver?"

"No. But—"

"Look me square in my eyes," he countered.

"Okay." My voice quavered. He was my dark haired angel with the mesmerizing eyes.

"Have I hurt you in any way?"

"No."

"Then why do you think that I would ever injure or humiliate you over a silly bet?" He leaned into my face.

"I want to go home, Alejandro," I whispered. "Take me home." I shut my eyes.

"We're going there, Bonita," he murmured into my ear.

Trust me." He took my hand with his. "Open your eyes."

I opened my eyes. I knew he was holding my hand. But what I didn't know was that he wasn't standing next to me, towering over my head.

He was kneeling on the floor in front of me. *On one knee.* The kind of thing an old-fashioned guy did when he was about to propose marriage.

No. Way. What was he thinking?

CHAPTER FOURTEEN

But kneel he did on the floor of Westwood Grill in front of all these perfect people who were stared at us, practically drooling. In front of his fellow Drivers, the girls who'd rescued me today and the Grill's patrons including Nicole, the beautiful girl he'd slept with.

"Will you, Sophie?" Alejandro asked loudly.

"What are you doing?" I hissed.

He leaned into my ear and whispered. "You're supposed to play along with this. Remember?"

"Okay," I whispered back. "But you're a dork."

"I know." He whispered, then leaned away from me and smiled at our audience. "Will you, Sophie Marie Priebe, take me, Alejandro Maxwell Levine to be your lawfully, whole-heartedly, completely smitten-with-you…" He winked at me.

The entire crowd hushed. You could hear a freaking pin drop.

Oh, no. He was not doing this.

"…Driver?" Alejandro asked.

"Um…." I said.

"Will you take me, as your Driver, to transport and guard you through good times and bad? Through tough neighborhoods that have bangers, as well as good, kind-hearted people that give you peaches?"

A smile tugged on my lips, but I shoved it back. "Yes," I said.

"Will you take me, Sophie, in good traffic and shitty traffic? Good surf and no surf? To protect you from people that are trying to kill you as well as those that flirt with you too much?" He turned, pointed at Tyler and scowled at him.

Who burst out laughing and shrugged. "Can't blame a guy for trying."

"Will you take me, Sophie to be your lawfully vetted Driver?"

"Yes, Alejandro." I could no longer hide my smile.

"Here here!" Nathan held up his margarita glass toward us in a toast. "I declare Alex and Sophie are now united in driver-passenger bliss. Alex may kiss the bride."

"I'm not a bride!"

Nathan smacked his forehead with his palm. "Oops, sorry."

"Bonita," Alejandro said. "Eyes down here."

I looked back down at him on one knee on the floor. He stared up at me with something in his eyes I hadn't seen before. His look was intense. It almost scared me. "I'm claiming my kiss," he said.

My eyes widened.

He brought my hand to his lips and kissed the back of it. Sweetly. He kissed the exact place where the med techs had inserted the IV that shuttled the anesthesia and other drugs into my body.

He pulled me closer to him. His fingers traced a line from my hand up my forearm and stopped at the inside of my elbow that was bruised from all the blood draws. He kissed my black bruises. The green ones. Lingered on the yellow one.

Something was happening to my chest. I started breathing a little heavy. Another piece of my heart was cracking open. I prayed no one in the crowd would notice my reaction, no one would see I was losing my cool. "Alejandro—I don't know…"

"Alejandro Maxwell Levine," Cheyenne stomped toward us. "So help me God if you're messing with my girl I will kill you. After I kill you, I will drag your corpse from this Grill and shove it next to the dumpster. Where LADWP trash collectors will pick you up and you will disappear forever. Do you understand me?"

Alejandro's lips left my arm as he swiveled his head and gazed up at her. "This is what I like about you, Cheyenne. You are loyal and fierce and kind. By all means. If I mess with your girl? Throw me out of here, for good. Lock the door, lose the key and never let me back inside." He turned his gaze back to me and smiled. "But I promise you, I am not messing with your girl. Because, I am crazy about your girl."

Cheers erupted from the semi-tipsy college crowd.

Cheyenne's frown morphed into a small smile. She gestured with two fingers next to her eyes, and then aimed those fingers at Alex. "I'm watching you." She walked away.

Alejandro stood up, all six-feet-two inches of him and leaned down toward me. "I won our bet. I claim my prize. Which is a kiss," he said.

And that's when he finally kissed me. Sweetly. Slowly. Surely.

On the top of my head.

A few folks applauded, but more then a few groaned.

"Pathetic," Tyler said. "You change your mind, Sophie, and decide you want another Driver, or a better kisser, do consider me." He winked.

"Shut up, Tyler," Nathan said.

Alejandro leaned down and whispered into my ear, "And now, Bonita, I'm driving you home."

* * *

This time Alejandro's Jeep's engine didn't rumble at the curb. This time the Jeep was parked and he walked me to my door.

"Thanks for everything. Again." I stuck my keys in the door. My hand trembled just a little. Hopefully he wouldn't see that. I heard Napoleon's meows coming from inside my place. "The new kitten calls. Need to give Napoleon food and attention. You were right about calming the crowd down. You seem to be right about almost everything."

He put his hand on top of my hand that was on the doorknob. "I should probably come inside and help you with stuff."

"You helped me a lot already. With the exception of my family and my best friend, you've helped me more than almost anyone else I know."

"Go out with me, for real," he said. "Not a yoga class or a walk on fire event, or a palm reading."

I really wanted to say, yes. But, this would take us to a different place.

"We are so perfect right now," I said. "I don't want to screw up our relationship. I don't want—"

He pulled me toward him and kissed me. One hand cradled the back of my head. He ran his fingers through my hair with his other hand. His lips were full and insistent. His tongue slipped inside my mouth like it was meant to be there. Tempting me. Claiming me. He tasted sweet.

And suddenly I felt like I was falling all over again. I leaned back against my front door as his lips moved from my mouth, trailing kisses down my face, down my neck.

"Sophie," he breathed in my name. Then kissed me hard on the lips, his tongue exploring my mouth. One strong arm wrapped around my waist as he lifted me up a few inches off the ground, pulled me toward him, my T-shirt scrunching up toward my breasts, my bared abdominal skin pressed tight against his thin T-shirt.

"Life is short, Sophie Marie Priebe. We are not perfect people. We don't know how much time we will have together."

He had no idea how scary prophetic he was being.

"But I will guarantee you this. We have something far more special than the majority of people. Consider this to be your official invitation—" His warm breath and the pressure of his full lips brought a flush to my skin. His hand traced down my neck toward the top of my T-shirt. He pulled the neckline back as he kissed my shoulder.

Shivers raced up and down my arms. "This is me. Officially asking you, Sophie, to, please, go out with me." He tucked strands of my hair behind my ear. Kissed my ear. Kissed my hair. Kissed my shoulder.

"Yes, Alejandro. Yes, I will go out with you." I tried to find my footing. Which was a little hard to do when he was still holding me six inches above the ground.

Gidget barked and I heard a kitchen window slam shut, muffling her yips.

"Voyeurs," I said to Alejandro as his lips brushed mine.

He frowned. And slowly let me slide down his body. His gorgeous face. His dimpled chin. I closed my eyes because I just wanted to feel him: His muscular, solid chest. His tight abs. His hardness. When my feet hit the ground, he backed away from me.

I swayed for a moment and wanted to say, *"Fuck you, caution. Screw you, MS! You can't own me. This is my time!"*

"Gimme Shelter" blared from Alex's phone. I opened my eyes and reached for him, but he was standing a couple feet away from me the sidewalk. "What are you doing?" I asked.

"Someone needs a Driver. I can't believe it. Not tonight." He stared at his phone.

"You're leaving?"

"Sorry, Bonita. It's important. I made a promise. I've gotta go." He jogged toward his Jeep.

"Okay," I said as my knees felt weak and I leaned against my door.

"I'll call you tomorrow." He got into his Jeep and drove away.

* * *

"I'll call you tomorrow." The most commonly used words that meant, "Have a nice life. Because, there's a good chance I'll never see you again."

I fed Napoleon and watched him devour his fancy, wet cat food on a plate on the floor of my kitchen. I wiped tears away as I played with him. Dangled the string. Rubbed his fuzzy belly. Tore the cellophane off the cat scratcher pad and sprinkled a little nip on it. Watched him as he inhaled and scratched the cardboard pad with his front paws like he was the first fireman on the scene of a five-alarm fire. "You have nothing to worry about anymore you adorable opportunist."

I sat down cross-legged on the living room floor, pulled him onto my lap, held him up to my face and cuddled him. He meowed. "You have landed in cush-land, buddy. Where everything will be good. And you will be loved and fed and comforted. And no one will kiss you then leave you." And I thought about Alejandro. Our one, magical kiss. I had let my guard down. Maybe this wasn't such a good thing. I felt pretty awful right now.

Napoleon squirmed and meowed loudly, mouth wide open.

"What? More food? More attention? More nip? You are too..." the room suddenly went gray for a heartbeat. Then black. Then nothing.

* * *

I woke up to squeaky meows. My eyes fluttered open. I was

lying on my side with a black kitten standing on top of my chest, staring into my face. I was collapsed on the living room floor. I felt like I'd just been through my own personal earthquake. What I'd actually just been through was another MS related seizure.

Dammit.

It was a gran mal, not a petit mal. The petit were the "pretty" types of seizures, where one would just stare off into space and forget where they were for a few seconds. Yes, they were still dangerous. But I'd just had the kind where you'd blank as your muscles spasmed uncontrollably, twitching, flailing. The kind where you could hit your head and die or cause an accident, which is why I didn't drive.

Which is also why I didn't date.

But why now? Nothing like this had happened in at least six months. Well before I landed in L.A. Were the stem cells turning dangerous? Was it my MS? Was it bad pixie dust raining down on me for whatever rotten karma from a past life I needed to burn?

I was already scheduled for an MRI at the hospital later tomorrow. I was not going to the ER. I didn't want to call anyone to stay with me, including Alejandro. I decided to spend the rest of the night on my living room floor. It was low and safe. No place to fall. I grabbed some pillows and a blanket from the couch and settled in. I wondered if I'd have another seizure. Replayed how Alejandro's lips felt on mine. How he tasted. Remembered how my heart felt like it was opening.

And felt it slowly tighten back up.

***

I told the doctors at the study about my seizure. So today's MRI was a close up of my brain. I ignored the machine-gunfire-in-the-middle-of-a-thunderstorm noises as I lay in the imaging tube for forty-five minutes. I ignored the cage over my head that made feel like I was Hannibal Lecter behind his mask. I ignored the ache in my heart.

I exited the tiny room where I'd been examined, walked into the hallway and practically tripped over a wheelchair and the girl in it.

"Hey, Cheesehead," Blue said. "Keep your eyes on the road." She wheeled down the corridor.

"Sorry!" I said. "How are you doing?" I followed her.

She shrugged. "Do you know anyone in a wheelchair?"

Nana had been in a chair for about five years now. I had watched as she deteriorated from walking with a cane, to using a walker and then the chair.

And now she was in Assisted Living. I nodded. "My grandmother. It's not easy."

"No. It's not." Blue's eyes narrowed as she swiveled and eyed me. "You don't look all that perky today."

Seizure last night. Brain MRI today. Throbbing headache from deafening MRI. No phone call or text or email from Alex so far. "Far from perky, Detective Blue."

"Hah! Are you headed out of here?"

"That would be a thank God, yes."

"Got plans?"

"Other than tattooing an L on my forehead? Nope," I said.

"Lithuanian?" She wheeled down the hallway. "Lutheran? Lesbian? Longshoreman?"

"Loser." I trailed behind her.

"Someone's feeling sorry for herself." She stopped in front of the elevator and punched the button. The doors opened in seconds. She rolled into the elevator but stopped midway and looked over her shoulder at me. "I've got a solution for you. It's temporary, but so is everything in life."

The doors started to close on her chair. I panicked and waved my arm between them scared they would bounce off the sides of her chair. They slid back open.

"What's a little jolt? It's nothing." She snapped her

fingers. "Try to keep up with me, okay?"

CHAPTER FIFTEEN

About fifteen minutes and ten blocks later, I sat next to Blue at Star Hair and Nail Salon. The outside of the storefront looked about five thousand years old. The inside only dated back to the 1980's.

Photos of fancy women with big Early Madonna hair hung on the walls. There were advertisements for eyelash extensions, waxing services, as well as acrylic nails that would last one whole month if you never touched anything with your hands. Like—anything.

Blue spread her fingers on a white, folded towel on top of a manicure stand while a female nail-tech applied a clear basecoat to her nails. Blue's pants were rolled up her thin legs. Her feet were bare and resting in a basin of warm water.

I sat at the mani-pedi station next to her in exactly the same layout, except I sat in a regular spindly chair. I wasn't in a wheelchair—yet.

"So basically he's driven you all over L.A. for weeks, flirting the entire time," Blue said. "He finally made this big to-do at the Grill last night and G-rated kissed you."

"Yes."

"And then he kissed you again but for real. Like a PG-13 kiss? Or an R kiss?"

"PG-13."

"Decent smoocher?" Blue asked.

I nodded. "Beyond."

"But then he left?"

"Yes." I squirmed as a man scrubbed my feet with a pumice stone. "Why is this supposed to make me feel better?"

"Beautification, darling. Beautification generally helps a girl feel better."

"You are a wise woman."

Blue watched her nail tech carefully apply bright blue polish to her fingernails. "Does he know you're in the stem cell program?"

"No," I said.

"Did you tell him you had something stem cell worthy?"

I shook my head. "I wasn't planning on letting him get too close—"

"I know his type. These guys set their sights on you and lock in like you're the prize in a video game. I'm surprised he didn't make some kind of a bet with you to win you over."

"Um…"

"I knew it! You come to L.A. for stem cell research, you hire a guy to drive you because you can't drive, or you don't want to. And you're in the stem cell study because…" She peered at me. "You have an autoimmune disease. Something that makes driving difficult."

I swallowed hard and nodded.

"Being that you're not in a wheelchair, walking fine and just a little peaked, I'd say it's in its early stages. You're scared to drive, which is the original reason why you hired the hot guy."

I inhaled deeply, reflexively, and my chest stretched.

Quite possibly another heart cracking open moment.

I exhaled. "I've got early onset Multiple Sclerosis."

"MS. That sucks."

"Yeah."

Blue peered down at her feet as the nail tech expertly drew an elaborate flower on her big toe with nail polish. "So the guy you like."

"I didn't say I liked him."

"Of course you like him or you wouldn't be moping around imagining a capitalized L branded on your forehead. He hasn't called, or texted, or emailed you yet today?"

I just dropped my biggest bomb on her. I had a freaking awful, degenerative disease that left me with embarrassing symptoms that appeared out of nowhere. Yet, she was asking me about my love life.

I totally wanted this girl to be my friend.

"No," I said. "I haven't heard from him today."

"You know what that means?" Blue asked.

I shuddered as my mind skipped over the dreaded possibilities. "Not really. Kind-of. Maybe. What do you think?"

"Means you need to get flowers on your big toes."

"Um, why?" I gazed at my toenails: they were very pink.

"Because a flower on your freshly pedicured feet signifies you are alive, playful and super girly. Painting flowers on your big toes mean you embrace life and love and you are totally cool with whatever happens because of that."

I stared at the flowers that the nail tech was perfecting on Blue's feet. Her toes couldn't even move on their own and yet they sported splendiferous flowers.

"You want flower?" my opportunistic nail tech asked. "Only five dollar. Five dollar extra for flowers on big toes. Very pretty."

"Yes," I said. "I want flowers, please. Daisies on my big toes." I smiled and looked at Blue. Who watched the nail tech gently place her feet back on the foot pads attached to her wheelchair. My smile evaporated. "What stem cell study are you in?"

"Spinal cord injury. Paraplegic, obviously."

"What happened? You don't have to tell me if you don't want."

"Riding accident," Blue said. "I was jumping a thoroughbred that I'd never ridden before. He was big and beautiful and I'd seen him with other riders. Watching people ride him was like watching a painting come to life. I wanted to be part of that. Feel it. Be in it. At first everything seemed fine. We were walking. Then trotting. I encouraged him to step up the pace. He moved from a smooth canter to stopping on a dime. I wasn't expecting it. My foot twisted and I lost my grip on the reins."

She re-lived the moment on her face. It morphed from excitement dancing in her eyes to apprehension, followed by terror.

"I flew through the air and the next thing I knew I landed hard and twisted on the ground. Blacked out. Came to in ICU. Couldn't move my legs." She blinked and her face registered shock.

"Oh, Jesus. When?" I asked.

"Nine months ago. My parents and my doctor lobbied their insurance program and got me into the USCLA program. Apparently the stem cells work better for cord damage if you haven't been injured for all that long. Although I know other people who've been paralyzed for years and they're still trying it."

"How do you even deal with it? Are you pissed?"

"Of course I'm pissed. I'm also sad and freaked and worried and scared that people won't want to be with me because of this stupid chair. That people won't love me because they'll think I won't fit in. My parents make me see a therapist to vent my feelings."

I nodded. My mom made me go to a therapist after my MS diagnosis.

"On the flip side? I get to do a lot of fun things they wouldn't let me do before the accident," Blue said. "Parental guilt totally works in the favor of teenage accident victims. One of the few majorly awesome perks. You should make note of that. It would probably work for teens with shitty degenerative diseases too."

I nodded and thought of Mom who didn't want me to be out here. *But yet, here I was. Perk noted.*

"I can't be pissed at the horse," Blue said. "He's just a horse. It's still somewhat confusing that one day I was moving at the speed of light and the day after? I was dreaming of baby steps."

I nodded. "We need to toast to baby steps."

Blue held up an imaginary glass toward me. "Here, here."

I clinked her imaginary glass with mine. And I wondered, *Maybe I should confide in her? Maybe it would be okay to tell her the real reason I was here. All the healers. All of my baby steps.*

My phone buzzed and my eyes widened.

Blue said, "I don't care if it's him. Don't ruin your manicure."

I plucked it gingerly out of my purse. By the time I finagled the phone the message had already gone to voicemail. I jumped when I saw Alex's number.

Blue cast a knowing look at me. "It's your guy, right?"

I nodded.

She pointed to her feet. "Witness the flower power."

I clicked the button on my phone and listened.

"Sophie. I'm so sorry I took off like that. I apologize. Like one hundred percent, get down on my knees—again—and apologize. I have a good reason. You must forgive me! My folks are having a last-minute BBQ tonight. I really want you to come. Hang out, it's casual, have some great food. But I promised my mom I'd stay home and help her get ready. So it's going to be tough to pick you up. But it's close to your apartment. Maybe you could talk Cole into driving you here. He's welcome as well. But not Gidget. My mom has her own version of Gidget. We're at 212 Copa de Oro in Bel Air, about a quarter mile

from the gates. Let me know that you can make it? Thinking of you. Dreaming of you. Alejandro."

I clicked off. "Want to go to a BBQ tonight at his family's house?"

"Thanks, but I've got plans. Interesting. He just moved from stalled to fast forward," she said. "Aren't you glad you got the flower? Now you need to pick the perfect outfit."

"I'm not a fashion slave. I don't really worry about that stuff," I said.

"Big mistake," Blue said. "How much?" she asked the guy who ran the shop.

He calculated in his head. "Two mani-pedi with flowers? Forty dollar."

I reached back in my purse for my wallet.

"I've got this," Blue said. "Leave the tip."

She paid the manager on a credit card while I passed out cash to the techs. "Why a big mistake?" I asked her.

"Because you're meeting the parents, girlfriend."

* * *

I knocked on Cole's door and asked him if he wanted to attend a BBQ at Alejandro's house in Bel Air. He asked me the address. When I told him, he jumped like he was on springs about a foot in the air. I took that as a yes. We both retired to our respective residences to beautify.

What to wear? Oh crap, the last thing I needed was fashion stress. I thought I left that behind after I was diagnosed with MS. Because, who really cares what you're wearing when holes open up around your spinal cord? But tonight was different, and for a change, I really wanted to look pretty.

I yanked open my closet door and examined each item of clothing hanging on the rod. I sorted through them, pushing the hangers from right to left, occasionally grabbing one and tossing it onto my bed. One hanger, two, ten, forty. I picked an assortment of about twenty cute dresses, tops, skirts and pants.

I grabbed a matchy skirt and top from my bed, yanked them on and checked out my reflection in a skinny wall mirror.

Choice #1: Both the skirt and top were short. Really short. I struck a come-hither pose. "What's up, Alejandro's parents? My name's Sophina. I know you're expecting your brilliant, gorgeous son to graduate at the top of his class and get a bitchin' job with benefits. However, I'm making him my beck and call boy as well as my personal shampooist. The job has benefits. Get over it." *Too sexy.*

I ripped off that outfit. Tossed it and shrugged on different clothes. Choice #2: A pair of black, loose lawyer-esque pants and a fitted, white, buttoned up shirt. I looked in the mirror. "Awfully nice to meet you, Alejandro's parents. My name is Miss Priebe. I am here to do your taxes, walk the dog, stare slack-jawed, aka Forest Gumpish, at your son and then disappear into a hole-in-the-wall somewhere never to be heard from again." *Too bland.*

I stripped those off and tossed them on the bed. Looked for something in-between. Choice #3. I pulled on a family friendly but super cute sundress. It was a poly-cotton blend, soft colored floral print without being fussy. A T-shaped back showed a hint of skin on my shoulders. I accessorized it with low-heeled sandals and simple small hoop earrings. I turned to the mirror. The reflection of a somewhat sane and kind-of pretty girl stared back at me. "Hi, Mr. and Mrs. Levine. I'm Sophie Priebe. You have a wonderful son and I'm so pleased to meet you. Thanks for inviting me. Anything I can do to help with your BBQ?" *Perfect.*

I applied minimal makeup, peered into the bathroom mirror and pulled my hair back into a goddess-styled modest bun with wisps and tendrils hanging down my back. I grabbed an elegant, black, cropped, cotton sweater in case things got cool the way they always seemed to during an L.A. summer night.

I fed and cuddled Napoleon. Looked at the clock—yikes, the way things were going I might be late again. I really didn't want that, tonight of all nights. Meeting family was huge. And big. And scary. Or maybe it wasn't.

Maybe Alejandro had invited all his friends, the Drivers and even Nicole. Perhaps there would be so many people I would just disappear like a fly on a wall into a vast party, the plain girl in the middle of all the sparkly, exciting people.

I walked the few feet to Cole's place and knocked on the door. Gidget jumped up and down on the windowsill and barked excitedly from behind the screen. "Three more minutes!" He hollered from somewhere inside his place.

"Hurry up! I don't want to be late."

"And I don't want to show up wearing the wrong shirt. Priorities!"

I trudged back to my place and clicked on my laptop's email. Saw a correspondence with the Kelsey Vision Quest address. Opened it. There was a personal email from Dr. Carlton Kelsey to me. Hmm. How did he get my—oh right. Sign in for the free seminar on the ledger. Print your name. Include your email contact info. Check the box that says you will accept emails from us in the future.

> *Dear Ms. Priebe:*
>
> *I regret we did not have a chance to further discuss your medical situation and how I, as well as The Quest, could best help you. You mentioned endorsements of The Quest featured on YouTube. I've enclosed a link to our channel. Feel free to check them out. We will be updating our site after the next Quest. I'm inviting you to a less public, more private gathering the day after tomorrow at The Century City Plaza Towers Hotel at noon. I do hope you will be able to join us. Please*

THE STORY OF YOU AND ME

R.S.V.P.

Sincerely,
Dr. Carlton Kelsey

P.S. On a more private note, a little bird informed me that my bodyguards might have been overly zealous and conducted themselves unprofessionally with you. I apologize. Being a bodyguard isn't the easiest profession in the world and the job description doesn't always attract the sharpest tools in the shed.

Huh.

A knock on my door broke my thoughts. "Hurry up!" Cole hollered. "We do not want to keep this beautiful, Bel-Air family waiting. I bet their BBQ is catered."

I grabbed my sweater and purse. Kissed Napoleon goodbye on his gorgeous, fuzzy face and exited my front door. "Who the hell has their BBQ catered?" I asked.

"Practically everyone who lives on Copa de Oro in Bel-Air." Cole rubbed his hands together as we walked toward his immaculate Prius parked at the curb. "The appetizers will be to die for. Unless Alejandro's family is vegan, the hamburgers will be made with Kobe beef. I can't wait to get the grand tour. I sincerely hope they give a grand tour. What if no one offers the grand tour?" He aimed his keychain at the car and pressed a button. A beep sounded followed by clicking sounds as the doors unlocked.

"Calm down. He probably lives in a tract house like the majority of us grew up in." I got in his car and belted up. "Okay. Make that a tri-level tract house. With…" I thought about it. "…lemon trees."

Cole laughed and closed the passenger door. "Have you ever seen photos of Bel-Air?"

"Nope."

He laughed again. "You're in for a surprise."

CHAPTER SIXTEEN

Alejandro Maxwell Levine's last minute, family BBQ was not catered. I determined that after we were buzzed in at the security entrance. I ascertained that during our excursion through the automatic Spanish styled security gates, down the driveway that was approximately half the length of a football field and parked on the left side of the house next to Alex's black Jeep. I figured it out when a short man wearing a sombrero waved at us and said, "As much as Mr. Levine would love to greet you at the front door, he is currently grilling. Follow me, please."

We did. The man wearing the festive hat led us though a small, side gate, past a dozen, wooden, planter boxes filled with a cornucopia of green and red vegetables and fruits. We entered a massive back yard that stretched behind a large, Spanish-styled, two-story house.

My eyes swept over the property. I suddenly wondered if there'd been a mistake with the sombrero man. Perhaps we'd ended up at a small museum.

Cole hacked and clutched his chest with one hand. "Are you okay?" I hissed.

"I think I might have swallowed my tongue."

The grassy lawn sloped down toward a pool at the bottom of the estate. A couple of kids goofed around in the water, splashing each other, diving and dunking. There was a pool house adjacent to the tall, black, wrought iron fence that surrounded the property's perimeter. Families, couples and single folks of all ages chitchatted around casual picnic tables and lawn chairs. An ancient, fat, Shih Tzu mix dog with a fancy, sequined collar waddled from person to person, sniffing the ground next to their feet, nibbling crumbs.

A middle-aged man who resembled a shorter, weathered version of Alejandro wore a chef's apron and flipped burgers on a fancy grill. "Alida!" he yelled. "Where are the vegetables?"

"They're in the ground," a woman said.

"What are they doing there?"

"They're still growing. We planted too late." A stunning, middle-aged, curvy woman with black hair that swirled to her waist walked up to the man. She carried a turquoise platter covered in Saran Wrap.

"Why'd we do that, Alida?" He smiled, leaned down and smooched her on the lips.

"Because, Jacob. You couldn't make up your mind what kind of tomatoes you wanted. Or if you wanted to grow zucchini, or corn, or both."

"I'm a piece of work and you still put up with me."

"Yes you are and yes I do. For you, Señor Levine. Fresh vegetables from the farmer's market."

Cole clutched my arm. "Oh my God!" he whispered as he swiveled and gazed at the Spanish styled house. "I've seen pictures of this house before."

"Oh my God!" I said. "I love that Alex's parents seem so cool."

"Whatev. I could swear this used to be Gary Cooper's house."

"The movie star Gary Cooper?" I whispered.

"No, the guy who invented Mini-Coopers," Cole said. "Of course the movie star Gary Cooper."

"Bonita!" Alejandro popped out of the pool house and

strode toward us. He took my hands in his and squeezed them. He eyed me up and down and smiled. "You look so pretty." He leaned in and kissed me on the cheek, his lips lingering just a little too long. "Am I forgiven?" he whispered into my ear. "I have a great explanation I plan on sharing with you very soon."

"That depends on the awesomeness of your explanation," I said, "as well as how great this BBQ is."

"Ahem," Cole said.

"Oh, hey Cole." Alex shook Cole's hand. "Thanks for hanging out with us and chaperoning my girl here." He wrapped his arm around my waist and pulled me tight into his side. I spotted Alida watching us. Like a hawk.

"I can't believe you live in Gary Cooper's house. I need the tour," Cole hissed.

"Rumors," Alex said. "For the tour you need to ask the lady of the house."

Alida took a few steps toward us. "Where are your manners, Alejandro? Introductions, *por favor*."

"This is my mom, Alida Hernandez Levine."

Alida nodded at Cole and me. "I'm pleased to meet any of Alejandro's friends."

"Mom, I'd like you to meet Cole..."

Cole stuck his hand out, "Cole Frederick. Thank you so much for sharing a meal as well as your beautiful home with us, Mrs. Levine."

She shook his hand. "You're welcome, Cole." Alida smiled at him and turned to me.

"Mom, this is Sophie Marie Priebe. I told you about her."

"So nice to meet you, Mrs. Levine." I stuck out my hand.

She took my hand but then pulled me to her and gave me a quick, warm hug. Then pushed me away for a second, looked me square in my eyes and smiled. "Call me Alida. You're exactly how Alex described you. Come with me for a few of minutes, yes, Sophie? I'll give you the tour."

"But..." Cole entreated.

"Later." Alex slapped him on the back. "Let me get you something to drink and introduce you to some folks. Dad's making burgers, brats and veggies."

"Organic?"

"Hell if I know."

"I really wanted the tour. Gary Cooper... Oh. My God." He pointed. "Is that who I think it is? Is that Johnny De—"

Alejandro put his hand on Cole's shoulder and spun him around. "It's like being at the zoo, Cole. Don't disturb the celebs. And definitely don't feed them. I hear they have special diets." He steered him toward the kitchen away from Johnny, who munched on his burger.

* * *

I followed Alida from the dining room through an archway that led into a cavernous but casually decorated living room. It smelled of rich leather that covered the comfy couches, as well as jasmine and sage. The wood floors were dark, distressed planks. A massive fireplace was built into the front wall. Hand-painted Spanish tiles in brilliant, jewel colors comprised its hearth. The back of the living room was filled with windows and wide doors that opened onto the deep informal back yard.

"Alejandro doesn't bring a lot of girls home," Alida said. "The last one was several years ago when he was just out of high school. She was older than him. It lasted for a couple of months until she left him and hooked up with a producer who got her onto a show on the CW."

I nodded. *No wonder he was worried about the CW.*

She nodded. "Alejandro's been sharing bits and pieces of your adventures with me. You went to Chinatown together?"

"Yes."

"He wasn't all that thrilled about the acupuncturist."

"I know. But he was the one who found the two for one advertisement in the Chinese newspaper."

She laughed. "I taught him well! Follow me." She walked toward a hallway at the opposite end of the room.

I gazed out the windows into the back yard and spotted Alejandro staring at me as helped his dad at their BBQ. He raised his eyebrows and shot me a questioning look.

I shrugged my shoulders. I thought things between his mom and I were going okay. I really couldn't be sure because I hadn't met that many moms since I was diagnosed. Honestly? I hadn't met any.

The wind picked up, swerved and carried the BBQ's smoke right into Alex and his dad's faces. They turned away and coughed. His dad dropped the lid down on the grill. "Another ungodly hot, dry summer. Don't want to be starting a fire."

"Highly unlikely that would happen in lower Bel Air, Mr. Levine." Cole was upwind and untouched by the smoke. He held a colorful plate filled with food and munched like his life depended on it. "It's much worse in canyon country and the mountains."

"Do you want to see the rest of the house, Sophie?" Alida asked.

"Yes!" I ripped my eyes off Alejandro and turned toward her. She was already in the hallway while I was still in the living room staring at her son like some groupie with a crush on a pop star. "Absolutely." I strode toward her.

* * *

We climbed a tall staircase with terra cotta Spanish paver tiles on the steps and a black ,wrought iron railing lining the sides. "Alejandro says you are from Wisconsin. Must be pretty different than our strange city. Are you enjoying your time in L.A.?"

"Yes."

"He said you're in summer session. But that he's helping to drive you to different healers in the city. Some project you're working on with your grandmother?"

"Oh yes. He's been great. I'm not sure I could have done this without him. This city's so overwhelming. It's huge, and unless you've got a photographic memory for numbers, who can remember and navigate all the freeways let alone the side streets?"

She smiled. "I remember when I first came to L.A. I felt like I landed in Oz."

"Exactly!" I said. "I keep wondering where the man behind the curtain is. But knowing me, I'd get lost on my way to the Emerald City and never find the curtain, let alone the man."

"I have a feeling you've found the man," she said.

My face turned hot and I sincerely hoped it was only pink and not bright red.

We walked down a long hallway with a series of closed, thick wooden doors. "Bedrooms, bathrooms, you're not missing anything," Alida said. "I grew up in Mexico. Didn't come here until I was around your age."

"What brought you to L.A.?" I asked.

She eyed me.

"I mean, if that's okay for me to ask? You don't have to tell me."

"*Está bien*, Sophie." Alida opened a door to a large modern office filled with a three-part desk unit and state of the art computers, printers and phones. The desk was filled with paperwork, a few headshots and stacks of scripts, as well as books. Movie and TV posters hung on the walls. There was a sweet view of the USCLA campus in the near distance. "This is Mr. Levine's office."

"It's nice." I realized I didn't know what Alex's parents did for a living. I'd been out of the dating scene for so long, that I didn't know if that was normal or not. Technically, Alex and I weren't dating. We'd only shared one kiss. He was just my Driver.

"Alejandro's dad is an Entertainment Manager. He guides the careers for screenwriters, a few novelists, showrunners and directors."

"Oh." Sounded kind of like an agent of sorts to me.

"Jacob works very hard. He's down to earth and honest. His clients love him. Producers and studios trust him." She beckoned. "Come with me."

We left the room and continued down the hallway. I noticed the framed photographs that hung on the walls. They all had a similar tone, a feel. Like they were taken by the same photographer. Someone who wasn't scared to dive into a subject's head. Root around, find the emotion and capture the real picture.

"You have a beautiful home, Mrs. Levine."

"Thank you. Call me Alida." She opened the door at the end of the hallway. "Nothing exciting. Just my studio."

I followed her inside a jewel of a room. French doors opened onto a small balcony that overlooked the back yard. Dozens of framed photos hung on the walls. A wide, dark, wooden Mission desk was located in the center of one wall under the photos.

I leaned in and examined a few. A photo of an orphanage in Mexico. A small, weathered woman wearing a nun's habit gazed directly into the camera, a patient look on her worn face. Around her, kids made faces, barely holding their energy inside for the second it took for the photographer to snap the picture. The signature at the bottom of the photo read: *Alida Hernandez Levine*. She was the photographer who wasn't scared to show someone's beauty or another's pain.

"These are all yours?" I asked.

"Yes."

"They're amazing. When did you start taking pictures?"

"When I was a child in Mexico City. My mother was Spanish and a teacher. My father was American and a salesman. I had one older sister and one younger. My parents separated when I was seven-years-old. We girls stayed with my mother and visited my father once a year in the States. The first trip I begged my dad for a camera so I could remember all our moments. Every piece of our stories."

"That must have been tough," I said.

She shrugged. "It was the only reality we knew. When I was fifteen, my mother remarried. Señor Perez was a nice enough man. A diplomat, of sorts. My mother offered my her daughters a choice: Travel the world, which meant changing schools once a year. Or go live with our father."

"What did you do?" I hadn't seen or even head from my dad in thirteen years. I couldn't even imagine making a crazy decision like that at such a young age.

"Have you ever been to Nebraska in the winter?" she asked.

"No."

"They have minus forty wind-chill and very large steaks."

"I'm used to minus forty. But I'd really like those steaks."

She cracked a smile. "My sisters stayed with my mama and explored the world. I chose my dad and traveled America. I learned not only about Nebraskan steaks, but Iowa corn, river rafting in Utah and picking blueberries in Michigan. When I was eighteen my dad got a job in L.A. There were beaches and mountains. Fall colors, skiing and deserts. And then I ran into the best part of Los Angeles."

Alida peered out the window at Alejandro's dad flipping burgers, brats and turning shish kebobs on the BBQ while he talked enthusiastically with his friends and clients. She smiled. "I met Jacob Levine at Universal City when we were young, stupid and impressionable. He was gorgeous, so smart and a charmer. Our religions were different, our backgrounds too, but we fell in love. We said yes to each other in Vegas. Our families were horrified but we decided to try and make it work. Twenty-five years later, I have no regrets in the marriage department."

"That's inspirational." I looked back up at the wall of photos. Dead center in front of the desk was a 10 X 12 glossy framed photo of a battered and crumpled SUV on the back of a flatbed tow truck. Fractured, tiny pieces of glass clung to the rim that would have held its intact windshield. The metal parts twisted into the guts of the car. There were faint smudges of dark red-brown splotches on the windshield fragments.

I couldn't help but take a step backward. Why did she have such a creepy photo on her wall?

"That photo's frightening, yes? But I keep it up there to remind myself every day that life isn't perfect. And yet we continue in spite of our fears. What's your story, Sophie? Do you like Alejandro? Because I know he likes you."

"Yes, ma'am. Yes, I do." When my stupid hand started shaking.

And Alida spotted it.

CHAPTER SEVENTEEN

Could there be a worse time for my hand to tremble? I covered it quickly with my other hand and held it next to my waist. How to distract Alejandro's mom? "I heard this used to be Gary Cooper's house. Did you buy it from his estate? What did you do to renovate it? I'd love to know more."

"So would I." She sighed. Took a seat in a chair adjacent to the large desk. Motioned for me to sit on the loveseat situated next to her. I did. "You haven't told Alejandro why you really hired him to drive you. Have you?" She reached out, took my good hand and placed it on my lap.

"No," I said.

She took my shaking hand and held it, gently, but firmly, between her hands. And gazed at me. "Why not?"

I met her gaze then peered down at my quivering hand that she squeezed between her two sturdy ones. And I just couldn't help it. I missed my mom and my Nana. I missed my home. A few tears leaked from the corners of my eyes. "I don't tell a lot of people. It scares me to tell people," I said. "That probably makes me a terrible person, but no, I haven't told him. Yet."

She sighed. "But he hasn't told you either."

What, I wondered. What hasn't he told me?

Alida took a long moment, then leaned in toward me. "Why are you really here, Sophie? Because as much as I believe you love your family? I don't believe you're here to write a book proposal with your Nana."

Busted. It was time for the truth. I just didn't expect to be sharing that with Alejandro's mom. Especially not the first time I met her.

I took a deep breath. "I'm petrified my grandmother's dying," I said. "She's had MS for thirty years. She's been in a wheelchair for five years. She's going downhill. I saw it. I knew it was happening. And I couldn't just sit still, do nothing and lose her without a fight."

Alida nodded.

"I traveled to L.A. to find a miracle. For my grandmother."

"Oh," she said.

"I'm not looking for sympathy or a donation to my favorite therapy or charity. I'm willing to be a guinea pig to find something, to find anything that can extend her life. Maybe that will be six months. Maybe I can find something that will buy her a year or two or five. Maybe I'll just stumble across a therapy that makes her more comfortable. Less pain. She's a really great person. She's kind and she's funny. And she wants people to follow their dreams. She just moved to Assisted Living but signed up for Berlitz to learn a foreign language. I think you'd like her."

"So basically you're in L.A. to save your grandmother? Is that the only reason?"

I shook my head. "I have early onset MS. I haven't told Alejandro for a lot of reasons. I didn't want him to feel sorry for me. I just wanted him to drive me. I hope he told you that I'm paying him. Right? I would never take advantage of him. I adore him."

"He adores you right back." She squeezed my hand. "I know a *curandero* in Rosarito, Mexico."

"A Latino healer?"

She nodded. "He's a trip, but he's powerful. He's also

booked solid."

"I don't think I have a lot of time."

"I can get you an appointment with him. Soon. I'm not going to tell Alejandro about our talk. But you both have stories. When or if you decide to share them with each other is between the two of you."

***

Alejandro lived in the converted pool house. His surfboards leaned against one wall. Pool nets hung on another wall next to a printout with contact information for a pool service company. He had a beat up leather couch, a desk with his laptop and printer. Some of his mom's photos hung on the walls. There were a few family photos, as well as candid shots of him and the other Drivers, as well as Jackson.

"Wow. Cool place. Rescue anyone with those nets?" I asked.

"I tried, once. My mom's dog, Miss Guadalajara, fell into the deep end and forgot the dog stroke. I tried to scoop her out, but the net scared her and she started drowning in the opposite direction. So I jumped in and saved her." He pointed to a photo on one of the walls. It was of a fully clothed, but drenched twelve-year-old Alejandro hugging an incredibly confused looking puppy.

"Which started your long string of saving bedraggled mutts. Like me, my first night in L.A."

"Bonita, you're a far cry from a bedraggled mutt." He took my hand and tugged me toward him.

I dropped his hand and backed away. "We're at your parents' home," I said.

He laughed. "We're also at my home. They're not going to break in and interrupt me. Besides they always knock first."

"Why'd you leave last night?"

He shrugged. "Someone had my Driver card and called me. The guy was a friend of a friend. I promised I'd take the calls. I had to go grab his keys as well as him before he got in the car. He was in West Hollywood. I had to make tracks."

"Do you have to do that every time?"

"No. We usually take turns. But Nick got a call right before mine. And I don't like to let people down. You just never know."

He glanced up to a framed photo on his wall. I followed his gaze and saw the same photo that was in his mom's office. The crumpled SUV that was on the back of the tow truck. "That photo was on your mom's wall. Why's it on your wall?"

He shook his head. "Today's a fun day. I don't want to get into it right now, okay? I'll tell you when the time is right. Come on, let's grab some BBQ before Cole finishes off what's left of the burgers."

He took my hand and we walked out of the pool house onto the lawn toward the picnic tables and the smiling, happy people.

I thought about it. I understood that dark matters were sometimes best kept hidden. A time and a place would arise that would necessitate sharing them. Like what just happened to me with his mom. I wasn't ready to tell Alejandro I had MS. So I didn't push him about the picture.

I wasn't the only one who had secrets.

* * *

The next day I was back at Walden hall where I turned in a term paper to the rumpled, but still sexy Dr. Schillinger. So far between quizzes, exams, papers and attendance I was pulling a 3.85 out of 4 in his class. Not bad considering all the other stuff I had going on.

"Hey, Sophie. I need to talk with you after class for a second," Dr. Schillinger said.

"Sure. No problem. I've got an appointment close by in a half hour or so. Maybe I can push it back?"

"We'll make it quick," he said.

***

I stood in front of his desk and tried not to fidget.

"You know how we did that genetic test with Spectrum labs?"

"Yes."

"That's the test where we learn part of our ancestry or what family genes we might carry for certain traits. Like who's likely to have blue eyes. Or brown eyes. Or oily skin. Or…"

This wasn't about my grades.

Schillinger looked down at a paper on his desk. That paper had my name on top. I guessed what he was examining.

"Or someone who might be pre-disposed to an autoimmune disease like Lupus, or MS, or Rheumatoid," I said.

"That's right." Dr. Schillinger gazed up at me and blinked. "You already know, don't you?"

"Yes, sir. I do. But thanks. You are awfully kind and incredibly sweet to try and break the news to me." I pushed away a tear, hoisted my backpack onto my shoulder and turned to walk out the door.

"Sophie."

"What?"

"You're young. It's not a death sentence. You can experiment. Try stem cell studies. Alternative therapies—"

"Thanks, Dr. Schillinger. Already on it." I turned and strode out the door.

***

I signed in at the receptionist's desk in the very bland USCLA Hospital stem cell central. "Hey Phil," I said. "Just here for a blood draw today. Think you can track down the tech that actually knows how to hit deep rolling veins? I'm missing the first half of the Packers-Viking game and I'm not all that happy about it."

"Let me see what I can do." Phil clicked on his computer keyboard and I walked toward the waiting area. "It's preseason football, Cheesehead. It doesn't really count."

I turned and stared at him. "Et tu, Phil with the Cheesehead reference? Of course I'm watching. Viking scum."

"Do not cast aspersions on my home people, Wisconsinite," he said.

I grinned. Never in a million years would I have guessed homogenous Phil with no-accent was from Minnesota. "Who do you think you're talking to, Fargo?"

But Phil was leaning into his computer screen, frowning, and didn't take my bait. "Sorry to say today is more than a blood draw. They've got you scheduled for an MRI."

"But, I just had an MRI."

"Apparently the powers that be have requested another one. Room 104. Nurse Michaels will check you in."

"If I miss the game I will be filing a complaint with the USCLA stem cell study program." I stomped down the hall.

"I don't blame you," Phil said.

***

Nurse Michaels asked me a slew of medical questions. If I had increased headaches, or dizziness, or nausea. Then took my blood—yes, three tries, again. "Why do I have to have another MRI so soon?" I asked.

He looked at my chart and no emotion what so ever slipped onto his deadpan face. How this was even possible was beyond me. "You need to talk to the doctors about that."

"But I'm in the room with you."

"I can't say, Sophie. I'm sorry."

"Can you hint?"

"No."

"Oh, come on," I said. "Blink once if it's good. Don't blink at all if it's bad. Or not good."

Nurse Michaels took my blood pressure and—Did. Not. Blink.

"Well this sucks, doesn't it?" I asked.

* * *

I was in the freaking MRI tube again. This time I opted for double earplugs and tried to remember what each moment of Pachelbel's Canon sounded like in my head. I even hummed it until the med tech behind the glass wall instructed me that humming would create movement that could interfere with my scan.

So I stopped humming for real, and just hummed in my head incredibly, amazingly, loudly. And thought about my mom and all her sacrifices. My Nana and how awesome she was. The joy when I watched Napoleon toddle around my apartment. How my breath vanished from my body when Alejandro kissed me. How it returned in a gasp when his tongue slipped inside my mouth and he kissed me stronger, harder and more intensely.

This is how I got through my most recent MRI, most recent assault and my most recent stress. I made it through this stupid, incredibly loud, headache producing medical procedure *by imagining love. In all shapes and forms.*

Two hours later I pulled my clothes back on in the small

exam room. Twisted my hair into a bun on the top of my head with a ponytail holder. Couldn't wait to get the hell out of Dodge.

I walked down the USCLA hall, the corridor, hit the elevator button and exited the building's doors. Made it to the park benches in front, sat my butt down and rested for a moment. I needed a little moral support. I needed to talk with a friend. I called Triple M back home.

She picked up, "Yo, what up, girlfriend?"

I heard football sounds in the background coming from her state of the art 42-inch flat screen TV mounted on her living room wall next to her glassed-in Barbie collection. "When did you become a rapster chick?" I asked.

"I'm not a rapster chick, homie, I am still your BFF. Wait... hold on... *flag on the play?* What do you mean freaking flag on the play? He was not offsides! *The ref is blind!* Viking bullshit!" She screamed.

I held the phone away from my ear but couldn't help smiling. "What's the score?"

"You're not watching the freaking game? What has L.A. done to you? Do I need to de-program you when you return home to Wisconsin?"

"No. I had something kind of weird happen today. I went to the clinic and—"

"*A ten yard penalty?* Kill me now! The score's 24—21, Vikings lead the Pack, two minute warning, end of the fourth quarter. And now, stupid asshat ref, we're out of field goal range. God dammit!"

This was not a good time to chat. "I love you Triple M. Let's talk later."

"Love you back, Sophie." And we both hung up.

I walked home and reminded myself that loneliness was part of moving away. I snagged a lemon from the tree close to my apartment. My phone rang and I picked up.

"What are you doing tonight, Cheesehead?" Blue asked.

"Well I missed the game. I guess working on the final

paper for Schillinger's class. My life is so exciting. Not."

"It's about to get a little more fun," she said. "Text me you address. We're picking you up at nine thirty p.m."

"I don't think so. I've got an appointment thing tomorrow and I'm going to Rosarito." I unlocked my door and reached my hand down to block any escape attempts by Napoleon. He attempted marching outside, but I plucked him up, shut the door, and plopped him back on the floor.

"Mexico?" Blue asked.

"Yeah. With my Driver."

"The good kisser?" She asked.

"Yes," I said.

"I'm assuming this means you made a good impression on his parents?"

I thought about the embarrassment I felt when Alex's mom spotted my trembling hand. "I definitely left *an impression* on his parents."

"Hah! Work on your Genetics paper this afternoon and screw the appointment unless it's super important. I swear, this outing is like kismet, or good karma for something you did in a past life. Or possibly even yesterday, because I don't believe karma is only past-life related."

"What are we going to do that starts at nine thirty at night, Blue? I'm not into clubbing or bar hopping. I'm totally not in the party mood. So thanks, I appreciate your offer, but whatever it is? It's just not my thing."

"Oh shut up. You're supposed to be the cheery one with the good attitude. You're not in a wheelchair. You're kissing a hot guy. And if you think I'd waste my time taking you to club in L.A? Well then, you're a moron. Because if you've seen one club in any city, you've pretty much seen them all."

"Okay," I said. "So what do you have planned?"

"My friends from the stem cell program are going bathing suit shopping."

"I don't swim. I don't need a suit."

"You're going to a romantic Mexican beach resort with your Driver. Do I even need to spell out the possible scenarios that might arise? You need a new bathing suit. Do you not remember the transformative power of beautification?"

"Don't the stores close at like nine?" I poured kibble into Napoleon's dish on my kitchen floor. He hovered next to it like he hadn't eaten in five days.

She laughed. "You've never been shopping with us before. It's kind of an adventure mixed with a party. Nine thirty sharp. In front of your apartment. Look for a pink limo."

"Pink?" I heard squeals of laughter in the background.

"Yes. Pink. It works for us." She hung up.

Napoleon pawed his food and gleefully tossed kibble onto my kitchen floor while he chowed down. And I wondered.

What had I gotten myself into?

CHAPTER EIGHTEEN

I stood outside on the sidewalk in front of my place at 9:25 p.m. I shivered. It wasn't Wisconsin cold, but it was a little chilly. I shrugged on the jean jacket I'd brought. I didn't want to be late. Everyone hated late. Cole popped out his door with Gidget tucked under his arm for their last run of the night.

He placed her gently on the ground and let her run around and sniff vile things. "What are you doing out here at this time of night?"

"Going shopping," I said.

"That's weird." Gidget ran off and stuck her nose in something that appeared disgusting next to the curb. "With the exception of Hollywood, I do believe most stores are closing about now."

"That's what I thought," I said. "But I've met a girl whose friends apparently have connections and I need a bathing suit for Mexico. You're still cool taking care of Napoleon for a few days?"

"Yeah."

"As much as I adore Gidget, don't let her in my place, okay? I worry. Napoleon's just so small and vulnerable and—"

Cole waved his hand at me. "You scored the Gary Cooper house tour for me. We're solid. Leave directions when to feed him, how much, and your contact info on the kitchen counter next to his food."

"Perfect. By the coffeepot," I said. "You can call me. Oh, shit. What if there's bad reception in Mexico? And I don't have a vet yet. But I did buy a cat carrier. Just in case—"

"Nothing's going to happen. Napoleon's young and perfect and adorable."

Because weird accidents and diseases never happened to young, perfect and adorable beings.

I shook my head. "But if something happens…"

"You worry too much. If one hair falls off his precious head, I'll take him to Gidget's vet. You just have to promise to include me at the next BBQ at the Cookie Monster's house."

"Okay?"

"And the séance. Promise."

"I promise. What séance?"

"Do you not understand that mediums attempt on a daily basis to contact the spirits of dead movie stars? Just think of the possibilities if I were actually inside a dead movie star's former abode, attempting to contact them? I could pitch this as a reality TV show. I have friends in the industry, you know," Cole said.

"Is this an L.A. thing? Because back in Wisconsin reality TV is either *The Bachelorette* or football."

When a bubblegum pink stretch limo pulled onto our street, windows down. Strangely enough, Pink—the singer—blared on its sound system.

Cole and I eyed it, incredulous.

"I think that's my ride," I said.

"I think you're going to have fun tonight," Cole grabbed Gidget, tucked her under his arm and hustled back inside his place.

The limo pulled to a stop next to the curb. A side door flew open. Blue poked her head out. "Welcome to the

Wheelie Girls' Bathing Suit Party, Cheesehead! Hop aboard."

Not something I would have done back in Wisconsin. But I wasn't in Wisconsin anymore.

"Hell yeah!" I punched my fist in the air and jogged toward her.

* * *

Blue and her three girlfriends were seat-belted into the comfy seats in the plush, tricked-out limo. Their wheelchairs were folded, stacked and secured with straps in the far back of the vehicle.

"This is my friend, Sophie," Blue said. "She's here from Wisconsin and is a rat in the MS stem cell study. Give her a Wheelie Girls' shout-out."

"Hey-Hey!" Blue's friends leaned toward me, smiled and lifted their glasses.

All I had was a bottle of water in my purse. I pulled it out and raised it to toast them—

"Bad luck! Don't drink!" A gorgeous brunette exclaimed.

The girls hastily lowered their glasses and leaned away from me.

"Had enough bad luck to last a life time," a pretty, mocha-skinned African American girl grimaced. "Nice to meet you Sophie. I'm Kiarah."

"It's super bad luck to toast with someone who only has water," the brunette said. "The new chick needs a party drink. Hey, Sophie. My name's Lulu." She poured some Dom Perignon champagne into a glass that was already partially filled with orange juice. She swirled it and passed it to me. "This is the sweetest mimosa you'll ever taste. Now we toast, ladies."

We clinked glasses and drank. "Cheers!"

"L'chaim!"

"Saluté!"

"To a most excellent adventure," Blue said.

I sipped. Yowsa. "Best mimosa ever," I said. "Thanks for including me."

"Thanks for joining us. I'm Amelia," a redheaded girl said and raised her glass to me. We toasted and took another drink.

"I'm calling truth or dare night. We haven't done that in a while." Blue pulled out her notepad and a pen from her purse. "Amelia, tell Sophie why you're in a chair. Or accept your dare."

Amelia made a face. "I don't think your friend wants to hear all the gory details the first night she meets us."

"So tell her your story in a non-gory fashion." Blue flipped to a page in her book and started scribbling. I spotted Amelia's name on top. Her notebook was like the Book of Scary Secrets. "Truth or dare, Amelia."

"Truth." Amelia took a sip of her drink. "I was in a car accident about three and a half years ago. My spinal cord was screwed up. I went from being a high school cheerleader to being the high school mascot."

"Pathetic, Amelia? *I don't think so.*" Lulu topped off Amelia's glass with more bubbly. "Chair or no chair you're so pretty, that every guy at Yale-Eastlake still wanted to bang you."

Amelia giggled. "Hah! Truth!"

"I'm calling truth before Blue bugs me," Kiarah said.

"You don't have to," I said.

"Have you ever argued with Blue?"

"Uh…"

"Mm hmm. She's relentless," Kiarah said. "I'm a Wheelie Girl because of a slip and fall. Can you freaking believe it? Stupid store didn't put up the yellow sign after they mopped the linoleum."

"You got a seven figure settlement," Lulu said.

"I'd rather be poor and able to walk," Kiarah

countered.

Lulu grabbed another champagne bottle from a built-in refrigerator, twisted off the netting and popped the cork. Blue and her friends held their glasses out and she poured more champagne. She tipped the bottle in my direction.

"Orange juice?" I asked.

Lulu arched one eyebrow. "Lightweight."

"Seizures," I said.

"Got it." She topped my glass off with fresh orange juice from a glass container.

"Truth or dare, Lulu," Blue said.

"Car accident. Old story. Drink up ladies. We are celebrating, tonight."

"I love celebrations," Amelia said.

"What are we celebrating?" Kiarah asked and sipped her mimosa.

"Well," Lulu sighed and gazed at the wheelchairs stacked in the back of the limo. "I've been in the stem cell program for over a year now. A week ago I bent down to put on a shoe. And no shit, first time in years, I could swear I wiggled a couple of my toes. Just a little. So, I did it like ten more times to check. But I could wiggle my freaking toes."

Kiarah nearly spit her drink out of her mouth. "Holy crap!"

"Oh my God!" Amelia squealed. "That's fabulous! What's next, I mean—"

"I don't even want to go there tonight. I just want to have fun," Lulu said.

"That's awesome news, Lulu," I said.

I caught the look on Blue's face. Happiness, envy. Back to happiness.

"I love you, Lu. I'm a little envious, but it couldn't happen to a more deserving chick," Blue said.

Lulu nodded. "Thanks! So, tonight's bathing suit party is on me, ladies. I do believe we are approaching the bathing suit capitol of L.A.'s Westside."

"Nordies!" Amelia said. "Double yay!"

*　*　*

The limo driver dropped us at a back entrance to Nordies at Westside Pavilion Shopping Center. A security guard knew we were coming and let us in a back door. A mid-thirties, coiffed, female shopping assistant led us to elevators and the bathing suit section in the sports wear department on the third floor.

Now Blue and me were sifting through suits on the racks. She was in the bikini section. I'd made a beeline for the one-piece rack. Amelia, Kiarah and Lulu already made their selections and the Nordies' sales assistant was helping them in the dressing room.

I hovered over the circular rack, flipping through suit after suit and carefully picked out five attractive pieces in an array of colors.

Blue wheeled up. "Show me you stash."

I held one suit in front of her. "This one's pink. Pretty color," I said.

"Boring," Blue said.

I stuck out the next. "The teal one has a scooped neckline and a built-in pushup bra. I could dazzle him with my cleavage."

"In that? Maybe if he was eighty-five years old and half blind."

I frowned and pushed another in front of her. "The white one's kind of retro. Like—maybe a Bond Girl wore something like this, fifty years ago. Sexy, yes?"

"Absolutely. Fifty years ago, Mamie Eisenhower."

I harrumphed. "The black one—the tag says it's slimming, and well, everyone looks good in black, right?"

"Houston, we have a problem. Why are you picking suits designed for middle-aged women when you're nineteen? Show off the goods, girlfriend."

"But I don't even swim!" I said.

"This isn't about swimming!"

Lulu, Kiarah and Amelia exited the dressing room. The sales lady trailed behind them carrying a hefty pile of swimwear.

"If it's not about swimming—then what's it about?" Lulu asked.

Kiarah wrinkled her up nose. "You're getting a one-piece?"

Blue smirked. "Truth or dare, Sophie. Truth—tell them what this is about, or accept your dare."

Oh crap. I did not want to tell these girls I was headed to Mexico with Alejandro. "I, I…"

"Fine. I'll tell them," Blue said. "Sophie's got a hot—"

"Dare!" I exclaimed.

"Ooh. A hot dare it is!" Amelia said.

"I'm a huge fan of hot dares." Kiarah smiled.

"Your dare, Sophie, is that we," Blue smiled at her friends, "get to pick out a suit for you. And you have to promise to wear it."

"Squee!" Amelia headed toward the clothing rack filled with bikinis.

"Wicked," Lulu wagged her finger at Blue and grinned. "That's what I like about you."

"Nothing too revealing!" I said.

"Take a risk, Cheesehead," Blue said. "We'll pick you out something semi-revealing, something super-revealing and maybe throw in a beach cover up if you give us a fashion show."

"Help me…"

But the Wheelie Girls just giggled and flipped through bikinis, because they were on a mission.

***

The outside of the high-rise hotel was sleek and modern, gleaming in the morning sun. It was situated in a pricey, well-kept section of L.A. called Century City, on a wide boulevard called the Avenue of the Stars.

"You're going to a Kelsey Vision Quest gathering?" Alejandro asked from the Jeep's driver seat.

"Yeah. I heard Dr. Kelsey speak at a seminar on the boardwalk before all the craziness with the Lowriders happened. He was really interesting."

Alex shook his head. "From what I've heard, the good doctor's a little crazy himself. A bunch of my mom's friends went to his Quests years ago. Everyone takes mushrooms, wanders around in the wilderness and speaks in tongues."

"I do believe speaking in tongues is a Pentecostal thing. Dr. Kelsey told me his program has been updated."

"Just because something's updated doesn't necessarily mean it's a good thing. Like—World War II Nazis versus the Neo-Nazis. The whole Quest thing creeps me out. It's not the safest, alternative healing modality." He pulled the Jeep into the sweep of the hotel entrance.

A man in a uniform rushed to the passenger door and opened it. "Valet?" he asked and opened the passenger door for me.

"Thanks. Just dropping off," Alex said. "How long is this get-together?"

"An hour," I said. "Hour and a half max?" I stepped out of the car and the valet closed the Jeep's door.

He shook his head. "Make it quicker. We need to beat the traffic and haul ass south of San Diego before gridlock. Gridlock doubles our commute. Passing Mexico's immigration can be quick or a long, slow nightmare with wait times. I'd like to cross the Tijuana border before rush hour."

"Okay. What are you going to do?" I asked.

"Westfield Mall's up the road. Grabbing more provisions."

"We're only staying one night, right? I only made a reservation for one night."

"I still don't understand why you don't want to stay at my parent's place. It's pretty. It's safe. I won't jump your bones." He waggled his eyebrows at me.

"Right. I'm staying at a hotel."

"Your call. Hey, Bonita. This Quest group feels a little cultish. If they ask you to sign an organ donation card, don't do it, okay?"

"You're bad," I said.

"Hah! You have no idea..." He grinned and peeled out of the driveway.

***

Dr. Kelsey's private seminar was held in an ultra modern two-bedroom, penthouse suite with sweeping eastern views of L.A.'s downtown miles in the distance, and the mountains rimming it even further away.

Meathead #1 stood by the suite's entrance door eyeing everyone as they came and went. He was probably on the lookout for someone pilfering hotel soap. Folks of all ages gathered around TV screens watching Youtube videos of Kelsey Vision Quests. A Greeter walked past handing out snacks and offering herbal tea. Another greeter lit a stick of sage leaves with a match and swished it around the room.

"You'd better wave that closer to the floor," I said. "You don't want to be setting off the fire alarms."

A thirty-something woman looked at the brochures and booklets on a small conference table covered in a white linen tablecloth. I picked up a few pamphlets and paged through them.

"Have you ever been on a Kelsey Vision Quest?" she asked.

"No. You?" I said.

"Absolutely. My first helped me get over my loser ex-boyfriend. I'm Beth."

"Sophie," I said. "So you've taken more than one?"

"Yes. My second Quest freed the energy of my bummer ex-husband. I'm thinking about going on a third."

"Oh," I said.

"Did you see the male greeter passing out the appetizers? I know he's like fifteen years younger than me but he's so hot."

Maybe Beth needed to change her choice in men.

"You should totally do the Quest," she said. "It's transformative."

"I'm thinking about it."

Dr. Kelsey squeezed my arm. I jumped, until I realized it was him, not a Meathead. And I relaxed. "I believe in honesty," he said. "How about you?"

"Absolutely." Considering how many half-truths and lies I'd told since I landed in L.A., that was actually a funny response.

"Great. Why don't you tell me more details about why you're here?" He took my arm and led me away through the crowded living room to a bedroom door.

I balked. "I'm not…"

"Neither am I," he said. "Just want to talk with you privately. Keep the door wide open should that make you more comfortable."

***

Dr. Kelsey sat at a small table next to the window while I paced. Finally *I* closed the bedroom door for more privacy. Then spilled everything to him about my MS, the alternative healers and the USCLA stem cell study.

"You got a lot on your plate. Take a Quest," he said. "Confront your fears. Meet your spiritual guardians. Ask them what they can do to help you battle MS."

"But it's not me I'm here for. It's not me who I'm

worried about. At least not right now."

He shook his head. "Then who is it?"

I bit my lip. "My grandmother. She's been in a wheelchair for over five years. She's had MS for thirty years. Her health's going downhill. I'm scared she might not have that much time left."

"That's why you're here in L.A? That's why you're researching alternative healers and doing the USCLA stem cell study?"

"Yes." I bit my lip. "I can't just let her wither away and die without a fight. It's not fair!"

"Well then, Sophie Marie Priebe." Dr. Kelsey held out his hand to me. "Let's get you on a Quest. You'll find your power. Become wiser than you ever dreamed possible. And quite possibly help your grandmother."

I looked at his hand, but hesitated. "The hallucinating drug part of the Quest thing scares me," I said. "Mushrooms? I think I'd like them on pizza. Not in my brain."

He laughed. "The drugs are different now. Even more natural than mushrooms. Plant medicine. South American Natives use it all the time."

"I'll think about it. I've got an appointment with—"

"Hello, Venusians!" a familiar male voice said. "I'm looking for Sophie Priebe. A pretty young lady with light brown hair, a twinkle in her eyes and flowers on her toes?"

I smiled. Apparently Alejandro had grown tired of waiting and busted in on the private, invite-only gathering.

Dr. Kelsey looked up for a second toward Alex's voice that boomed from the other room. His gaze swiveled back toward me. "Your friend?"

I nodded. "I've got to go. We've got an appointment with a *curandero*. Oh, and don't tell my... friend... anything I've shared with you."

"Patient doctor privilege," Dr. Kelsey said. "Whatever we discuss is between you and me. Completely private. Best of luck with the healer."

"Thanks." I turned to leave.

"In case you change your mind? We've got a Quest coming up next weekend. It's booked, but someone always backs out at the last minute. I can almost guarantee you a spot. Email or call me."

I wasn't sure I wanted to travel to a remote, nearly deserted mountain and take hallucinogenic drugs, let alone meet my "guides."

"Sure thing," I said.

Alex opened the door and strode into the room toward me. "Bonita?" He kissed me on my cheek, grabbed my hand and slid his fingers through mine.

"Hey," I said. "Right on time. Alejandro, I'd like you to meet Dr. Carlton Kelsey."

Dr. Kelsey stretched out his hand to Alex. "Pleased to meet you, son."

Alex's face was devoid of emotion as he shook Dr. Kelsey's hand. "Nice to make your acquaintance, Dr. Kelsey. Have we met before?"

"No." He smiled.

"Then, in all due respect, sir, I am not your son." Alejandro released my hand, wrapped his arm around my waist and hustled me out of the penthouse suite.

CHAPTER NINETEEN

Alejandro and I drove the 5 Freeway south toward Mexico. It was a behemoth beast of a road. It ran from Mexico to Canada and was the only Freeway in the U.S. to touch both borders. On average it had six lanes heading north and six venturing south. We passed signs for beach towns, industrial towns, airports, amusement parks and military base exits.

As we traveled farther south, I began to see signs that cautioned against running over people who were running across the road. We had the 'Watch for Deer' signs in Wisconsin, not the 'Watch for Illegal Immigrants'.

Mercury, the Roman God of Transportation, was with us. We had decent traffic 'till we hit the San Diego vicinity. That's when we slowed way down to a sputter and alternated between twenty and zero miles an hour.

Most of the vehicles surrounding us featured surfboards on top, bike racks attached to their backs and a wide variety of political bumper stickers. Cars jockeyed with each other to claim the lane that might be moving the quickest.

The reality was every lane was moving slowly. The commuters could have saved themselves future high blood pressure, doctors' visits and prescription meds if they'd just stayed put and skipped the 'I need to be one car ahead of you,' horn-honking dramas.

And speaking of drama, I dove right in. "Do you think you could have been a little more creeptastic when I introduced you to Dr. Kelsey?"

"Let's dissect 'creeptastic.' Dr. Kelsey is almost fifty years older than you," Alex said. "He's got you in a fancy suite filled with organic appetizers like hummus, tabouli, and organic energy drinks. His followers are hopped up on life, love, drugs and whatever else. They looked like they drank the Kool-Aid and can barely form coherent sentences, let alone retain memories of what they did five minutes previously."

"So? A lot of people have short-term memory loss. By the way—who are you? Why am I in this car and where are you taking me?" I grinned.

"Touché." He reached over with one hand tugged the bottom of my shirt and tickled my waist.

I squirmed. "Stop it!" I giggled and batted his hands away. My phone buzzed in my purse. I grabbed it, saw who was calling, hit accept and placed it to my ear. "Yay! Hi Nana! I'm so glad you called. What's up?"

"Nothing, really. I just miss you. Do you think you might get home soon for a visit?"

I frowned. "I'm coming home when the semester ends."

Alex shook his head. "No you're not," he said.

I shook my finger at him. "What's going on? Something you want to talk about?"

"Yes. I want to know where you are?"

I held the phone away from my ear. "Where are we?"

"La Jolla."

"We're in La Jolla."

"I was there once a long time ago," she said. "Beach town close to San Diego. They called it the Jewel by the Sea. Lots of cliffs and beaches. Very pretty. Who's driving you?"

"A nice young man. He's respectful and smart and funny. I think you'd like him. Maybe you and Mom should come out for a visit? You could see the ocean again and we could eat guacamole and visit La Jolla. Besides, I've met some healers and I think—"

"What's his name?" she asked. "The young man who's driving you?"

"Alejandro."

"He doesn't have a last name?"

"Of course he has a last name."

"So why don't you tell it to me?"

"His name is Alejandro Maxwell Levine."

Nana inhaled, sharp and raspy.

"You okay?" I asked.

"Never better. Is he Jewish?"

Alejandro shot me a questioning look. I shrugged. "Religion or heritage?"

"I don't discriminate. Put him on the phone with me. Right now."

My eyes widened. "My grandmother wants to talk with you."

"Huh. Okay. Why not? Guess it's only fair I get to meet your family," Alex said and beckoned to me with his index finger. "Can you put her on speaker?"

I clicked speaker and extended my phone close to his cheek. My face was next to his face. Our shoulders were touching. I remembered what he tasted like when he kissed me. I remembered what he felt like the first time he caught me when I nearly passed out in the Grill. "Nana. You're on speaker with Alejandro and me."

"Alejandro Maxwell Levine," she said. "Are you Jewish?"

"Half Jewish and half Latino," he said. "But my parents raised me with both cultures as well as faiths."

"You were baptized, confirmed and had a bar mitzvah?"

"Triple score," he said. "You should have seen the presents."

"Perfect!" She sighed and started coughing. "Hang on! Stupid allergies make me ferdrayt."

"She's learning Yiddish," I whispered.

"You're feeling dizzy? Confused?" Alejandro said. "Are you okay? Do you want to get off the phone?"

"You speak Yiddish too? Even better! No, I don't want to get off the phone. I am fine. Just a little ver klempt. I am Sophie's Bubba. My name is also Sophie Marie. You can call me Bubby Sophie. Even though my last name is Timmel, not Priebe. I don't want you to get us confused. Hah!"

Alex grinned at me and pushed the phone away from our faces for a second. "I've got this," he whispered. Pulled my hand that held the phone close to his face. "Yes, Bubby Sophie."

"Perfect, Alejandro," Nana said. "Are you in a romance with my granddaughter? You do know she is a shiksa, yes? It seems many young men of the Jewish faith will happily date shiksas, but not be serious about marrying them. Will this be a problem for you in the future?"

"Nana!" I hollered and collapsed back into my seat. I face palmed my hand into my forehead in sheer humiliation that only a family member could initiate.

Alejandro ran his finger over my cheek and traced my jaw. His fingers landed squarely under my chin that was collapsed in my hands on my chest. He gently lifted my head up. "Put the phone back toward me," he whispered.

I blushed but did as he asked.

"Bubby Sophie?" he asked.

"I thought for a second I lost you."

"You're not going to lose me, Bubby. In fact, I can't wait to meet you some day soon. In regards to your shiksa granddaughter? I'm crazy about her Wisconsin accent—"

"What accent?" I slapped Alejandro's thigh with my free hand. He caught my hand and interwove his fingers between mine and pulled me close to him. Which meant I was practically sitting in his lap.

A man in a truck in the next lane honked, leered and said, "Get a room!"

I glared at him. "Get a life!" I struggled to flip him my middle finger but it was currently engaged and wrapped tightly next to Alejandro's middle finger. He squeezed my hand and winked at me. "Ignore the assholes," he whispered into my ear and turned back toward the phone. "I adore your granddaughter's snarky sense of humor…"

I stuck my tongue out at him.

"… her beautiful dairy queen face, the fact that she's girlie but still thinks football is important and her sheer determination to get things done. So, no, I don't care that she's a shiksa. I also don't care that she's stubborn and that she's probably going to test me even further once I get off the phone with you. Can you live with that, Bubby Sophie?"

"Yes," Nana said. "You seem like a nice, young man, and I greatly appreciate you letting me practice my foreign language skills with you."

"You're welcome." Alejandro smiled at me.

"I must run or I'll be late for the sing-along in the lobby. We're performing a medley of Michael Jackson songs this week."

"It's my honor to have made your acquaintance," Alejandro said.

"And you, Alejandro Maxwell Levine."

I leaned into the phone. "I love you, Nana."

"I love you back, my favorite granddaughter."

"I'm your only granddaughter."

"I know," she said. "Which is number six on my top ten reasons why I love you the most."

She paused for a moment and I heard her breathing, hard and raspy into the phone. "Nana? You okay?"

"Never better. Just promise me one thing?"

"What?" I asked.

"Life is full of mysteries, odd twists and turns. You think you're traveling down one road only to discover you veered off and venturing down another. One that is completely unknown. And the new road has no fancy navigation system, no streetlights, or signs and you have no reception on your fancy phone. What do you do? Tell me, Sophie. What do you do?"

Alejandro squeezed my hand. He gazed into my eyes for a second. Smiled. Then turned his eyes back on the road. A lock of his black-brown hair escaped from behind his ear and fell onto his high, sharp cheekbone. He lifted my hand to his mouth and kissed it. Softly. Tenderly. I broke out in chills. Everywhere. "What should I do, Nana?"

"Be kind," she said. "Just be kind to each other."

"Okay," I said.

But she'd already hung up.

***

It took us a while to cross the U.S.-Mexico border. Luckily, I'd brought my passport with me. When I left Wisconsin to travel to L.A., I had no idea if I'd need to hop a plane, a train or take a ferry, or even a cargo ship, to a foreign country to meet a healer at a moment's notice. I was overly planning, but this is what I did best. Be stubborn. Be determined. And overly plan.

An hour after we crossed the border, Alejandro and I were in Rosarito, Mexico. It was a popular beach town filled with surfers, partiers, families and the occasional drug dealer. We were starving and grabbed a bite at a casual restaurant across from Rosarito Beach. People parked their surfboards next to their tables like most folks parked their bikes.

"I don't understand why you don't want to stay at my family's place." Alejandro said. "With the exception of the beach, it's gated, has security guards and, no, I'm not going to try and seduce you or sneak into your bedroom at night." He held up his hand in a Boy Scout salute. "Scout's honor."

"You were never a Scout, were you?" I asked.

He dropped his hand. "No, but it sounded good. Seriously, Sophie—you can trust me."

"I know I can trust you. That's not the point. The point is I rely on you to drive me. I'm not going to mooch off your family, or make your mom think you're hanging out with the wrong kind of girl."

"She likes you. She told me. She wouldn't have sent us down here to meet with Señor Morales, the *curandero*, unless she believed you were the right kind of girl."

"I've already got a reservation for a hotel room. I found a deal online. This is non-negotiable."

* * *

I stood at the front desk of the La Mar Hacienda and Suites, a festive, four-star beach hotel where I'd reserved a room. The lobby was packed with vacationers rolling their bags and clutching drinks. A uniformed male hotel clerk pounded away on his computer but shook his head. "I am so sorry, *Señorita*. There is no reservation under the name of Sophie Priebe. I would be happy to rent you a room, but La Mar is booked solid tonight."

I stuck my paper printed with my reservation confirmation number in front of him. "Here's my confirmation number. One person. One night. One queen bed. No oceanfront view." Alex was suddenly at my side with my suitcase.

"Problems?" he asked.

I rolled my eyes and nodded.

The clerk entered my confirmation number into the computer. "The confirmation code is for a reservation in combination with a cruise ship discount. Which cruise ship are you vacationing on?"

"I'm not vacationing on a cruise ship. I've never been on a cruise ship because I'm a sucky swimmer and water scares me. Why in God's creation would my confirmation number be connected to a cruise ship?"

"I do not know, *Señorita*. But if you give me the name of your cruise ship? We can probably figure this out, *muy pronto*."

I turned away from the clerk, looked at Alex and discretely sliced my finger across my throat.

He hacked and clamped his hand across his mouth for a moment. "*Señor, hablo español*," he said. "Can I help?"

"Yes," the clerk said. 'Do you know the name of the cruise ship your friend is vacationing on?"

* * *

Alex and I stood in front of a smaller, motel desk with a blinking, ancient, multi-colored neon sign on the wall behind the receptionist's counter. No one was in the lobby except for a short, round, older Latina woman behind the counter. Fine by me. "That will be sixty-two American dollars for a single room with a double bed."

I smiled. "Perfect! You take credit cards?"

"Of course. But we have to charge you ten dollars extra for credit card. Management policy. Seventy-two American dollars."

I thought about it. Looked around the lobby. It was kitschy, but clean. Dated, but sweet. And it was only ten more dollars. "Okay." I dug in my purse for my wallet.

"You share a bathroom. It is right down the hall."

I frowned. "There's no bathroom in my room?"

"It is practically across the hallway from your room."

A sunburnt, young couple that looked stoned stumbled through the lobby past us. "You have the key," the emaciated woman said to her male companion.

"No. You have the key." The skin and bones man rubbed his scruffy beard.

I half-expected insects or tiny marijuana plants to erupt from his facial hair. I backed away from them.

"What is it with you and keys!" the woman hissed. "I can't trust you with anything. What did you do with the stuff?"

"What stuff?"

She rolled her hazy eyes in her hollow eye sockets. "You know. The reason we came here. *The stuff?*"

"Oh," he scratched his greasy head. "The last time I saw the stuff was in the bathroom. Next to the spoon."

I gazed at the woman behind the counter, slack-jawed. "I'd be sharing a bathroom…" I lowered my voice. "…with them?"

"Yes," she said.

"Sophie. We're not seeing the *curandero* until tomorrow. You could stay at my family's place," Alejandro said. "There's plenty of room."

***

Alex and I exited his Jeep and stood in the parking lot of a little motel next to a small truck stop and diner. There was a Vacancy sign lit up in the front window. In the distance the sun started to make its way toward the horizon.

"Third time's the charm," I said. "This place is kind of cute. It's called Margarita Villa. Look—there's a van parked with a 'Child on Board' sign. What could possibly be wrong with this place?"

A man and woman burst out of the motel's entrance dragging suitcases as well as their two screaming kids. They raced toward the older Chevy van parked just yards away from us, scratching their heads, arms and ankles. The woman looked terrified. "Don't freaking do it! Lice. We are the walking dead. Save yourselves!"

"Thanks!" I hollered as Alex and I popped back in his Jeep and sped off.

CHAPTER TWENTY

Alejandro and I laid back on cushy recliners on a patio that faced the Pacific Ocean, about one hundred yards away. He was still in boardshorts and a T-shirt. I had changed into my new, slightly-revealing swimsuit with my V-neck, tangerine colored, beach cover-up. We sipped lemonades and watched the beginnings of another glorious sunset. I swiveled my neck and gazed back at the house attached to the patio.

His family's vacation home was a single story Spanish styled hacienda. The abode was simple, rustic, immaculate and on the freaking beach. It was all I could do not to grab my phone, snap a pic and send it to Triple M in Oconomowoc.

"So, on a scale of one to ten, how traumatized are you from your hotel experiences in Rosarito?" Alex asked.

"Six," I said and gazed at the sailboats making their way back into Rosarito's harbor toward their slips. "You knew, didn't you?"

"Knew what?" He slurped his lemonade and tried to hide a smile.

"You suspected that these hotels would be a bit of a nightmare." I kicked his bare shin with my foot.

He laughed. "Guilty." So I kicked his shin again. But this time he caught my ankle, held it between his hands, and pulled me and my beach chair toward him while I squirmed and kicked at him with my other foot.

"Bastard! Release my leg immediately!" I said. "What are you doing?"

"Moving you closer to me. Where you need to be. It's Mexico, Bonita. Mexico is beautiful and amazing and magical. But if you hit the wrong place at the wrong time, you could be a name in one of the news stories about twenty bodies without heads they found in a dump ten miles from here. That said? My family's had this place for years. We love it. And for the most part, it's safe. Except if you are taken prisoner." He tickled my foot.

"Stop it!" I squirmed. "Let me go!"

He wouldn't and even had the audacity to laugh. "Hah! You're mine! I'm in charge of this pretty foot with the flower on the big toe. I get to say when and where it will go. I will squeeze your toes better than any Chinese foot reflexologist ever could." He massaged my foot, pulling my toes.

"Ouch! Competitive much?" I shook my head. "You're the biggest dork I've ever met."

Alejandro laughed. "You're the biggest dork I've ever met. The biggest, cutest, funniest, Cheesehead dork."

I started laughing.

He dropped my foot. "Race you to the water. Whoever gets there first wins." He stood up and strode toward the ocean.

"What do I win?"

He turned and stared at me. "What do you mean, what do you win?"

"Well, if I have to go to all this effort, at least I should get something pretty spectacular if I win."

He grinned, stripped off his T-shirt and tossed it onto the sand. The sun glimmered like a mirage across his half-naked body: his built shoulders, tanned, muscular, wide chest with just the right amount of dark chest hair. His abdomen was ripped and the hair narrowed into a thin line, a tiny V below his belly button and disappeared beneath the waistband of his boardshorts.

Dear God, kill me now.

The sun on the waves reflected onto his smile and caught the sparkle in his hazel eyes. "If you win? You get to kiss me." He winked, then turned and jogged toward the surf.

"Go ahead!" I yelled. "I don't swim, remember?" I frowned and tapped my foot on the tiled floors.

"Who said anything about swimming?" He swiveled, faced me and jogged in place. "Don't you want to kiss me, Bonita?" He threw his arms out. "Like seriously, you're hurting my manly feelings."

"Fine." I stood up and strode out onto the beach toward him. The sand was soft and squished under my feet and between my toes, slowing me down.

"Nice acceleration. I'd estimate you're moving about two miles an hour. You're never going to win that kiss," he said. "And, I'm not bragging or anything, but it's a really good kiss. Because I like you something fierce. You're beautiful inside and out and you make me laugh, and that is so rare in my world. Seriously, you'd be missing out on something pretty darn great." He jogged toward the ocean.

I was too far away from him and completely out of the running on winning our current bet. Unless....

I put my two fingers to my mouth and whistled sharply. "Alejandro Maxell Levine!"

He whipped turned and regarded me, curious.

"If this was football, technically, you are offsides. I call a flag on the play. Ten yard penalty." I walked toward him, widening my strides. "Come on." I beckoned to him with my index finger. "You need to give me back those ten yards. What's fair is fair."

His eyes widened for a second and, shocker, he actually stopped in his tracks and then walked ten yards back toward me. I applauded and he looked surprised.

Game on, Alpha Boy.

I jogged toward him until we stood next to each other—still for a moment. He smiled down at me: full lips, white teeth, high cheekbones, a cleft in his chin and those freaking crazy-beautiful hazel eyes. He reached out, caught the waist of my beach cover-up and pulled me flush against him. My breath caught in my throat and my heart bounced around in my chest.

"Screw who gets to the ocean first. I'm kissing you now." He leaned down toward me. The second before his lips touched mine I ducked, tickled his waist and wiggled out of his grasp.

I raced toward the ocean, my legs pumping like a wide receiver headed toward the goal line. I stuck my feet in an inch of surf and jumped up and down on the sand. "I win!" I thrust one fist up in the air. "I win this one!" He strolled toward me. "I won." I repeated, breathless.

"I know. Thank God for football." He drew me toward him, wrapped one hand around my waist and the other hand behind my head. And he kissed me. The surf that lapped over my feet was cold. His breath against my lips and face was warm. He tasted sweet.

He was better than sweet. He was my Alejandro.

"You're my prisoner, Bonita," he whispered into my ear. "I'm not letting you go back to Wisconsin. You belong with me."

I don't know if it was him or the chill in the salt air, but I shivered and my skin tingled. Everywhere. I closed my eyes as he kissed my neck, his fingers tracing my skin down into the hollow of my throat while his other hand cupped my face. His fingers slid my sleeve down my arm and he kissed my bare shoulder. I felt a pulsing in my lower abdomen.

I fluttered my eyes open and spotted a small tattoo tucked in the curve under his chest muscles, right where they met his shoulder. It must have been the tat he had told me about earlier on Venice Beach. The one I'd never seen before. It consisted of three words and was inked in cursive.

Que nunca olvidaré.

What did that mean? I blinked and saw skinny, light-faded scars spider veining out from underneath his tat, wrapping below and over his collarbone. There was a larger, almost completely faded scar that jagged across his side ribs onto his shoulder. Another one that looked like a four-inch long surgical incision.

"Alex," I breathed. But his lips were buried in my shoulder. "Alejandro."

He looked up at me, breathless, a hungry look in his eyes. "What? Not a good kiss? Should we start over?"

"Best. Kiss. Ever." I traced his tat with my index finger. "What does '*Que nunca olvidaré*,' mean?"

He froze. In a heartbeat, he lost all interest in kissing me and instead reflexively clamped his hand firmly over his tat and scars, like he was attempting to squelch the bleeding of a gushing wound. He squatted, gazed out at the water and then dropped his head in his hands.

I had completely screwed up a perfect moment. Had I pried too deeply? If he'd wanted to share with me, he would have. How could I have been so stupid?

"I'm sorry," I said. "You don't have to tell me anything. I don't want to invade your privacy." I touched his arm.

He flinched.

And I cringed. "I'm so sorry," I said. "I'm so sorry, Alejandro. You are good and kind and sweet. And I adore you. Never in a million years would I want to hurt you." I paced back and forth in front of him as tears leaked from my eyes.

"It's fine," he said. "I only tell people I trust." He stood back up and held out his hand to me. "So, it's past time I told you."

* * *

The hacienda's living room had wood beamed ceilings and terra cotta pavers on the floor. A thick woven cotton rug rested in front of a Mexican tiled fireplace where a few logs were lit and burning. The room's west wall was primarily glass and shored up with beams that overlooked the patio we'd lounged on earlier. Sliding glass doors with full-length screens were built into their frames. The furniture was large and simple and comfy: Big chairs, big couches, big pillows. A large thin TV was mounted high on the wall. The surf crashed low on the beach.

I sat on a couch and leaned forward toward Alejandro. Once the sun had set, the beach fog rolled in and the temperature dropped almost twenty degrees in twenty minutes. We had changed into warmer clothes: jeans and long-sleeved cotton T-shirts. Funny that we'd picked basically the same outfit.

Alida had called ahead and the family help had stocked the kitchen with fresh fruits, veggies and ingredients for fajitas, juices and breakfast foods. A few small platters of food sat in front of us on a coffee table. Technically it was late for dinner. We both should have been hungry—but neither of us ate.

Alejandro sat on a chair close to me but wouldn't look me in the eyes. "'*Que nunca olvidaré*' is Spanish. It translates to, 'I will never forget.'"

"Okay," I said.

"When I was seventeen I was your basic high school kid," he said. "I had decent grades. Partied with my friends. Experimented a little bit with drugs, sex, alcohol and pushing my parents' limits."

"Sounds about right."

"One night changed everything."

I knew that night well. It was the night after I got my MS diagnosis.

"Jackson got a last minute invite to a party on the top of

the mountains on Mulholland Drive. He lived the closest, so I drove to his place in Malibu. We'd been friends since middle school and staying over wasn't unusual. I told my parents I'd be couch crashing at his place but didn't tell them about the party."

I nodded. Triple M and I had been sharing pajama parties forever.

"His friend, David, lived with his dad who had to leave town last minute. He usually stayed with his mom, but she had a new boyfriend and was occupied. David texted a few friends, who texted their friends, and the word spread like wildfire that it was *the* party to go to."

"We did that too," I said. "That's kind of a normal high school thing."

Alex nodded. "Jackson drove me, his sister, Lauren, and her friend Danielle up the mountain in his dad's SUV. The night was beautiful. Cool but not cold. The views that high up are amazing: the lights from the houses below looked like reflections of the stars above. I could vaguely make out the canyons hundreds of feet below the cliffs. There was awesome music and decent munchies. Beer, Patrón margaritas, shots and some medical grade weed. Everyone had a great time. Almost everyone had a little too much. Except for Jackson. He had way too much."

"It happens," I said.

"But this wasn't the first time it happened. He was on a strict curfew." Alex dragged his fingers through his hair, stood up and paced in front of the fireplace. "I knew I had to get him home or his father would ground his ass forever. I also knew there was no way in hell he could drive. Lauren and Danielle were somewhere between really buzzed and toasted. I'd only had two beers. I felt fine. I wasn't slurring, stumbling. I wasn't even mildly buzzed."

I flashed to the photo of the crumpled SUV in his mom's office, as well as a different shot of the same car on his wall in his pool house. I held my breath.

Alejandro squatted in front of the fireplace and rocked back and forth on his heels. "I haven't told anyone this story in three and a half years. So, forgive me if I meander a bit."

"Take your time." I stood up, walked the few steps and sat down next to him. Our knees touched. I brushed a lock of his hair that had fallen in front of his eyes across his cheek and tucked it behind his ear.

"I need to tell you. No more secrets," he said.

"Okay."

He sat down next to me. "I took the keys from Jackson and I drove. Malibu Canyon Road gets dicey in areas with all the switchbacks and drop offs. The girls were singing along to Pink. Jackson was passed out in the back seat next to Danielle. There were signs warning that the road was narrowing to one lane. I'd seen it on the way up, it was scary, but I could handle it. I stopped at the stop sign. Flashed my brights. Didn't spot any headlights from the other side. Didn't hear another engine. I inched the SUV forward. There were chewed up holes in the road and the shoulder was barely a foot wide with scrub brush clinging to the edges. It was all so freaking narrow."

I shuddered. "That would have scared the hell out of me."

He shrugged. "Once I navigated through that one lane, I was so happy that I hollered. The girls cheered and raised their fists high in the air toward me. I turned and we fist bumped. That must have been when the deer ran out in front of the car."

I inhaled sharply.

"Danielle saw it first and screamed. I turned, spotted the animal in the headlights, slammed on the brakes and yanked the wheel, hard. I felt a thud. Heard the deer shriek. The next thing I knew we were flying off the road through the air. It felt like an eternity. It felt like a heartbeat." He sat down, hugged his knees into his chest and his entire body started shaking.

One of my hands flew to my heart. The other to his shoulder. This time he didn't flinch. Tears seeped out his eyes and down his cheeks as he dropped his forehead into his hands.

"It's okay. It's okay, you can tell me." I leaned in and wrapped my arms around his shoulders, cradling him. "Tell me the rest."

"The girls screamed. I slammed my arm over Lauren's chest, pushing her back against the passenger seat. She never wore a seatbelt. She hated them. I don't know why."

"Oh, my God." Tears coursed down my cheeks.

Alejandro kept rocking. I held onto him. Tight. Firm.

"We landed nose down on a rocky cliff. We hit hard and the SUV rolled. My air bag deployed. I thought it was over. But we skidded off the incline and dove again. My head and shoulder smashed against the driver's window. My left arm twisted and punched through the glass and metal. I heard the windshield shatter and felt a weird crunch as my arm and my collarbone splintered. I tasted blood in my mouth. Jackson was silent. I prayed he was still passed out—not anything worse. Danielle screamed, 'My leg, my leg!' And I blacked out."

"It's okay." I pulled him closer to me, if that were even possible.

"I came to in hazy pain. Like, I knew it was bad, but there was this weird element to it that didn't feel real. Danielle kept complaining about her leg. But she wasn't screaming anymore. Just stumbling over her words, like she was out of breath, really tired. I twisted, glanced over my left shoulder and saw Jackson out of the corner of my eye. He was unconscious and propped up by his seatbelt. The pain in my shoulder and arm was fierce. I swiveled back and looked to the right at Lauren in the passenger seat. But she wasn't there. She was just gone. I passed out again. The next time I surfaced was in the ICU."

All this time he drove me and I didn't know. This strong man, this sweet man, this man I was falling for had been through hell.

"The only thing the docs and my parents told me before my shoulder surgery was that everyone lived. Everyone in that car was still alive when I went into surgery."

"Oh my God, Alejandro." I rested my face on his good shoulder and cried.

He clutched me around my waist and I hugged him back. "I came out of the surgery with screws and plates in my arm. I was messed up from the pain and the anesthesia and the painkillers. When I could finally wrap my brain around what happened, I asked my folks for more details. Jackson escaped with some mild sprains and strains, a few cuts and some bruises. He had walked out of the hospital the next morning with a really bad hangover. I was so relieved."

"What happened to Lauren?" I asked.

"She flew through the windshield after our first impact. She broke her back and her spinal cord was totally messed. She's had surgery after surgery but she's still in a wheelchair. Lauren forgave me. Jackson thanked me. It took about a year, but eventually their parents forgave me, too. I think they figured if Jackson had been driving, all of us in that car would be dead."

"They're probably right, Alex." I wiped a tear from his cheek, then one from mine. "What about Danielle? Her leg was broken, right?"

"Yeah. Her leg was broken. Her spleen was ruptured. Her liver and kidneys were torn. She had emergency surgery." He broke down and started to breathe from the bottom of his lungs—guttural. "She died on the operating table. She didn't make it. She was nineteen years old."

"Oh my God, Alejandro. I'm sorry. I'm so very sorry."

"I've been living with this darkness in my heart, in my head, every single waking moment of every day since the accident. I not only broke one person—I killed another."

CHAPTER TWENTY-ONE

Alejandro's usual smiling face was grim. He appeared tortured, haunted. His entire body shook.

"I was arrested when I was still in the hospital and charged with DUI and involuntary manslaughter. There's zero tolerance for under aged drinking. I spent a year in jail. After that was probation and my license was suspended for another year. I paid a fine and performed community service. The best part of my messed up journey was meeting Nick, Tyler and Nathan. They'd been through something different, but in their own way, similar."

How he met his friends, the other Drivers—it finally made sense why they did what they did.

"We talked about a way—even if it was grassroots and small—a way we could make a difference. We unofficially banded together to start the Drivers. It's my way to make amends. So now you know my story. Feel free to run for the hills."

He had been through so much. He owned it. He made amends. I shook my head. "I'm not running anywhere. Everybody screws up. Everybody has secrets."

"I never planned on meeting you, Sophie. I hooked up with girls, but frankly, I don't date. But you were different and you weren't from here. There was a crazy part of me that hoped, that in spite of the Internet and YouTube and

Facebook and Twitter, that you could just get to know me, not already see or know me for the stupid asshole that I was. There was a part of me—I guess it was my heart—that hoped you wouldn't look at me with disdain or disgust and think—Alejandro Maxwell Levine—what a monster."

"I would never think you were a monster." I climbed onto his lap and straddled him. One of my legs on each side of his. My inner thighs hugging his outer thighs. I cupped his face in my hands. "Look at me," I said.

But he wouldn't.

I grabbed his shoulders and shook them. "Look at me, Alejandro!"

He finally looked up at me: regret, fear, humiliation, sadness played across his beautiful face.

"After everything you have done to help people, to change lives for the better, you still believe you're a bad person?"

"I break people."

"You can't break me, Alejandro."

He shuddered and clung to me like I was his refuge. We lay back on the rug in front of the fire, facing each other. He traced my face with his fingers. I wrapped my leg over his.

"Sophie?" He asked.

"What, baby?" I asked. "You can tell me."

"You give me shelter." He reached for me, wrapped his arms around me, buried his face in my neck and his chest heaved.

I held him until he fell asleep. Then it was my turn to cry. I knew the real reason he couldn't break me. But I didn't know if I had the guts, if I had the courage to tell him:

I was already broken.

* * *

We parked and walked up a street in the middle of the ramshackle, non-touristy section of Rosarito. Alejandro held my hand.

"About last night," I said. "Thank you for telling me. I know it must have been difficult."

"I don't tell it all that often. And for some reason I think that each time I share it, that it'll get easier. But it doesn't."

I squeezed his hand. "I need to share some things with you."

"Not now, okay. Let's leave last night for what it was. It stirred up stuff. Can we talk about it in a couple of days? You cool with that?"

"Yeah."

Not really and yet at the same time? Relieved.

There were no taco stands or T-shirt shops in this part of Rosarito. Just tiny, musty shops selling tobacco, food and groceries. Laundry hung on skinny, fraying lines outside shabby apartments, as if waiting for the occasional sea breeze to venture away from the beach to dry it.

A one-story, cinder-block building stood out from the others surrounding it because of its fierce fence: it was ten feet tall, chain-link and encircled the property's perimeter with barbed-wire coils on the top that curled in. A blood red metal door in the front of the building featured several small laminated photos of saints glued to its front. A hand-written sign read, *"Por favor llama a este número para hacer una cita."*

I regarded Alex and raised one eyebrow.

"Please call this number to make an appointment."

"Do we need to—"

"Already taken care of," he said.

I peered through the fence at a long, narrow back yard that was primarily concrete, broken up by skinny patches of yellowed grass. There was an ancient plastic jungle gym, a drooping basketball hoop and a dilapidated dollhouse in the corner of the property.

"We're here," Alejandro said.

"A world famous *curandero* practices out of this place?" I asked. "It looks a little—"

"Magical." Alex looked at his watch. "It's noon. They run a tight ship around here. Three, two, one…"

As if on cue, there was a loud creak as a metal security door swung open behind the fence. About twenty kids ranging in age from four to fifteen raced out into the yard hollering excitedly. A few girls made a break for the dollhouse. A group of boys and girls grabbed a soccer ball and started kicking it. The four and five-year-olds headed for the plastic jungle gym.

An older, lean woman with a kind face followed them outside. She wore a wimple on her head, a knee-length gray skirt, sensible shoes and a T-shirt with an image of John Lennon and an inscription that read, "Imagine." "Children!" she said. "Back inside in one hour. Practice your English."

"*Sí Hermana Lennon!*" a boy shouted.

All the kids were dressed in clean, simple clothes, most likely hand-me downs. The children appeared well cared for, nourished and happy. The exception being one girl who was around five-years-old. She stumbled dramatically out the door, plopped down on the back step and burst into tears, wailing at the top of what sounded like healthy lungs.

Sister Lennon sat down and wrapped her arm around the girl's waist, hugging her gently. "*Está bien, Maria. Está bien.*" Maria's cries diminished. The nun whispered into her tiny ear and she hiccupped.

"This place is an orphanage," I said. "A pretty orphanage. One that looks clean with caring people. The world-famous *curandero* works out of an orphanage?"

"Yes." Alex nodded and took my hand. Wove his fingers through mine. Brought my hand to his lips and kissed it. "Funny, yes?" he asked. "Lost souls seem to find each other. Oftentimes they want to help them."

Funny, yes, I thought. Alejandro and I seemed to be lost souls and we were finding each other. "Tell me more." I squeezed his hand.

"At age fourteen, the *curandero*, Padre Morales, was a drug dealer. He got arrested. Went to prison. Found his version of God. And soon thereafter realized he had a gift."

"Which is?" I asked.

"He can see energy blockages. He prays to the saints. His prayers are powerful. Local legend has it they are heard. He gives herbs and performs the laying on of hands. He helps people heal," Alex said.

"Did he help you?"

"He helped my mother after my accident. So that would be, yes." Alex knocked on the red door and a small, wizened man answered it.

His eyes lit up when he saw Alex. "Alejandro! So good to see you. You've gotten so tall! You need to come visit us more often. How is your wonderful mother?"

"She's great Padre, thank you!"

"And this must be Sophie." He took my hand. "I am so pleased to meet you. We have some work to do, yes? Come with me." He led me inside the building.

Alex stood in front. "Padre?" he asked. "Can I take the usual suspects surfing?"

"Good idea, Alejandro." The Padre dug in his pants pockets, grabbed a key ring and tossed it to him.

Alex caught it in one hand.

"Have fun. And thank you," Padre said.

Alex handed him the keys to his Jeep. "Meet up later?"

The Padre nodded.

Alex went to the side fence and hollered something in Spanish. A bunch of the older kids squealed in joy, disappeared back inside the house and came running out the entrance carrying three, old surfboards. They strapped the boards on top of an ancient, beat-up VW van and piled in. He coaxed the engine to start on the third attempt, cranked the passenger window down and waved at me from the driver's seat as they sputtered away. "You're in good hands, Bonita."

"He gives the older kids surf lessons whenever he comes down here. They adore him." Padre led me inside the small building.

I did too.

* * *

I lay on my back on a skinny massage table on top of a comfy, cotton sheet. We were in a small room with a fan located next to an open window with bars on it. The table stood in front of a petite altar decorated with richly colored silks, satins and painted cotton fabrics draped across it. A prayer box, a few rosaries, tiny framed pictures of saints, Eastern Indian gurus, Jesus, the Virgin Mary and a bust of the Buddha were prominently displayed on the rustic shrine. Freshly cut flowers in a simple, blue glass vase rested on one corner. Votive candles were lit, their flames flickering with the fan.

The Padre chanted in Spanish and dabbed scented oil on my forehead, then held his hands lightly on my head. He was barely touching me but his hands were hot. He repeated his prayers and the laying on of his hands on my neck, my upper back and my lower back. After about an hour, he went to the altar, said one more prayer, crossed himself, genuflected and picked a white and a red rose from the vase.

"You can sit up when you like," he said. "How do you feel?"

I sat up a little light-headed but filled with energy. Like I'd taken five yoga classes in a row. "I feel amazing. Warm. Filled with energy."

He handed me the red rose. "This is for your heart. For love and kindness. Caring and truth."

"Thank you, Padre."

He handed me the white rose. "This is for honor. For respect. To remember life changes but souls never die. I'll say prayers for you, Sophie Marie Priebe. But God has already seen fit to answer your most essential requisite."

***

The Padre parked the Jeep next to the sand by a small beach. Alex was in the water, helping a kid kneel on a surfboard. All around him the children were in various states of surfing. Some were on their stomachs on the boards, bobbing in the water. Others waded out into the ocean or dogpaddled next to their friends. There were three kids to every board. One young teenage girl squealed as she crouched on her board, caught a wave, paddled and pulled herself to standing.

And then there was Alejandro.

A look of sheer delight glowed on his face. And in that moment the rest of my heart cracked open and I knew. I absolutely knew I found healing. It didn't take the form of acupuncture needles, or aura cleansing, or even Chinese foot massage. My healing was six-foot two-inches tall, had dark hair, hazel eyes and was the embodiment of kindness. My healing was Alejandro.

He smiled and waved at me. "Bonita! Isn't this magical?"

"It's the best, Alejandro."

My phone buzzed in my purse. I picked it up and saw I'd gotten a text from Mom. "Don't panic. Nana's in the hospital. I think it's under control. But call me."

***

We sat in the Jeep in a long line of cars at the Mexican-American border when I finally scored spotty cell reception and was able to get through to my mom. Nana's coughs had turned into bronchitis, which landed her in the hospital. The doctors ran a cardiac workup. She had atrial fibrillation: erratic or extra signals were going to her heart, making it beat faster or even tremble. This wasn't the good kind of trembling, like falling in love.

"Her fibrillation could go into blood clots or heart failure," Mom said. "So, the doctors stopped her heart and re-started it."

One of my hands flew to my chest. "I'll get on a plane," I said as we inched forward in line toward the checkpoint.

"No. The worst is over. They gave her antibiotics for her bronchitis, an inhaler and they're keeping her at the hospital for one night. They're going to discharge her tomorrow. The worst case scenario—the day after."

"Are you sure?"

"Yes. She didn't even want me to tell you. She wants you to finish summer school and whatever the secret project you're working on, that she's all furry fempt about," Mom said.

"You mean 'ver klempt'," I said.

"I thought you were taking Genetics in summer school. Are you learning a foreign language too? You really do take after your grandmother, you know. More so than you do me. I love you, sweets. I miss you. We will weather this small storm, and we will see each other soon."

I made Mom promise to call or text me with updates. Hung up and sent Dr. Kelsey an email, and a text asking him if there was still an opening for the Vision Quest that night. He replied immediately, saying he'd make one for me. To say that Alejandro wasn't all that thrilled about this would be an understatement.

But I was going. I might have found my own healing, but I hadn't tracked it down yet for my grandmother.

CHAPTER TWENTY-TWO

I sat on my living room floor across from Alejandro. I'd borrowed a large hiker's backpack from him. It lay on the ground between us as Napoleon played with its straps and cords: biting one, then getting distracted and pouncing on another. There was a pile of items on the rug next to the backpack.

"I don't understand why taking a Vision Quest is going to help your Nana with atrial fibrillation?" He asked.

"Because, Alejandro. It isn't just her heart problem. It's because she's had MS for thirty years. MS eats away at a person over time. It can take away your ability to function and move and walk. And once you're in a wheelchair—the longer you're in it the more susceptible you become to infections. The more complications develop with all your other organs. So, every single healer you drove me to? Was one more person that might be able to help Nana. Maybe I could find something to give her relief or buy her time. Maybe I'd find a miracle."

"Oh," he said. "I'm really sorry."

"Me too."

"Is that what you wanted to talk about earlier?"

"Yeah. That's one of my secrets." *Just not the biggest one. And I didn't have it in me to tell him, yet.*

"There was never a book, was there?" He asked.

"No, there was never a book," I said. "I'm sorry. That was kind-of a lie. Because I really wanted, I really needed you to drive me. Help me."

"It's cool, Bonita." He sighed. "I wish your grandmother wasn't going through this."

"Me too. Life isn't for the faint of heart," I said and picked up a printed piece of paper and read from it. "Recommended items to bring on your Kelsey Vision Quest. #1. Drinking water."

Alejandro sighed. "Check," he said. "Aren't you glad I made you buy bottled water?"

"*You* bought the bottled water. I would have been happy with a container of tap." I drew a line through the item. "Matches."

"Check." He held them up and shook them at me. "You know it's fire season and it's like a tinderbox up in the mountains. I don't understand what you need the matches for."

"It's on the list." I drew another line on the list. "A functioning, fully charged flashlight." I grabbed a flashlight from the pile and flipped it on. A decent-sized beam shone from it. "It works."

"I'll put new batteries in it," he said.

I shone it on his face. He blinked and squinted. "I asked you to hand it to me, not blind me."

"You are my prisoner," I said in my best eastern European accent. "Kiss me immediately, prisoner, or I will interrogate you. I will tickle your…" I glanced down at the list and spotted, "Mouthwash? Why is mouthwash on the list? Are we Vision Questing for oral hygiene? What do I need—"

He kissed me. His hands cradled the sides of my face, pulling me toward him as he kneeled on the floor, leaning over the pile of survival items. His tongue traced my upper lip. I sighed and closed my eyes. He bit gently on my lower lip and then slid his tongue inside my mouth. He was exploring. Inviting. Tempting. My breath caught.

But then he stopped kissing me. I blinked my eyes open. He'd retreated a few inches. "You're a tease," I said.

He looked me square in my eyes. "Skip the Quest. Stay here with me. I'd be more than happy to tease you all night."

I reminded myself to breathe and shook my head. "I have to go."

"But you don't. I don't want you to go to this Vision Quest tonight, Sophie. It doesn't feel safe. It doesn't feel right."

"Alejandro. I would prefer to stay here with you. I'd like to lie on a carpet of grass next to you while we eat magical guacamole and chips, as planes take off over our heads. But I can't do that right now."

"Why not?"

"Because my grandmother's in the hospital with something that might make her heart explode. So you don't get a vote on this one. I'm doing the Quest." My own heart was pounding, but I forced myself to gaze back at the pile of survival gear. "Sturdy athletic shoes," I said.

"Check." Alex sighed and reached to put them in the backpack. I intercepted them as we tugged the sneakers in opposite directions. "No. I'll wear them."

He let go of the shoes, but grabbed my hand. "I'm driving you and staying with you through your entire Questy experience."

"No." I shook my head. "You can't be there. You can drive me to their lodge. It's on the way. After that, I have to do this with other people on the Quest. No outsiders allowed. Besides, Dr. Kelsey personally offered to drive me."

"Dr. McKreepy? You think that I'm going to let you get in a car with bad Santa's doppelganger who's imbibed too many feel-good drugs and most likely lost a significant amount of his brain cells? No freaking way."

"Hello? I'm nineteen. Not twelve. If I don't do this one thing that could help my Nana? I'm not only a shitty granddaughter, I'm a shitty person."

He sighed and scratched Napoleon's belly. "Did you charge your cell phone? The reception can be hit or miss in the mountains."

I yanked my cell out of my purse and plugged it into the wall socket.

He nodded. "Did you pack warm socks?"

"Yes, Nana."

"I'm driving you to their lodge. Where is it?"

"Halfway up the mountain."

"We have a ton of mountains in L.A. An address would be helpful, Sophie."

"Oh, you know me. I'll find it somehow." I picked up the list and waved it at him. "Check out where it says, 'Location.'"

He snatched the paper from me, looked at the "Location," and inhaled sharply.

"What?" I swear his face paled. "You, okay?"

"Yeah. I know exactly where this place is."

"Great. Where?"

"Right down the road from where I drove three people over a cliff and killed a girl."

Oh crap, no. "You don't have to drive me," I said.

"Actually? I do."

***

After all the packing and the discussions and the arguments we started kissing again and somehow found our way into my bedroom. I tugged his shirt off and we made out on my bed. We ran our hands over each other's bodies. His mouth explored the curve of my neck.

I ran my hands over the muscles in his shoulder.

He traced my breastbone—from the top below my

throat, to the bottom beneath my breasts—with the flat of his hand. My breath hitched in my chest.

I ran my hands over his chest and stomach, and somehow ended up at the waistline of his jeans.

He slid a hand underneath my ass and cupped it, pulling me toward him as he rolled us over so I was on top of him. He gazed into my face, his eyes glazed, his mouth moist and open, his breath ragged. "Sophie."

We kissed and caressed each other when Napoleon skidded across us, back and forth, like we were speed bumps on his way to life.

"Aah!" I hollered as Napoleon attacked my hair. Alejandro scooped him up gently and deposited him on the floor. "Go play with your other cat toys, dude. I want to bury my lips in the skin on your stomach, Bonita." He slid his hand up my shirt exposing the skin on my waist.

Kill me now.

When I caught a glimpse of the clock on the wall. It was time. "I hate to say this." I swatted his hand away and pushed my shirt back down. "I've got to be wide awake in an hour so I can tackle climbing a mountain and talking to nature Gods. Which, by the way, scares the shit out of me."

"So, cancel. Stay here with me." He wrapped his arms around me and tugged me close to him.

It felt exquisite to be cradled in Alejandro's arms. There was no place else I'd rather be. It was time to confess my secrets. Expose my real self to him. Be honest.

There's an old saying that there are no accidents in life. As much as I thought Alejandro and I had begun because of an accident that night at the Grill, here we were a couple of months later, lying in each others' arms. Here we were falling for each other. Okay, truth be told, I was totally falling for him. "Alejandro, I need to tell you something."

"Tell me anything," he said.

I sighed. "I'm not just here at USCLA for summer school."

"I know, Bonita. You're here to research alternative healers. You're here to find healing for your Nana."

"Yes. I twisted away him and rolled over on my bed, so I wouldn't have to look him in the eyes when I told him the truth. "But, there's something else."

What if once he heard I had MS, it sickened him as much as it sickened me and he left? What would I do without him?

My stupid hand started quivering, and I grabbed it with my other hand and pulled it close to my side, so, hopefully, he wouldn't see. "My Nana's not the only one with health issues. Turns out—"

When his cell phone blasted "Gimme Shelter."

"No," Alejandro said. "No. I am not doing this tonight. Whoever it is can call another Driver, or call a cab or sleep it off next to a sack of potatoes…" He peered at his phone. "Dammit!" He jumped out of my bed and punched the screen on his phone. "Nick? What the?" Alex strode out of my bedroom, yanking his shirt back on.

I extricated Napoleon from my hair, again, and pushed myself to sitting. I looked at the clock—it was time. I had to rock and roll or I'd be late.

"What do you mean, *you can't?*" Alejandro paced through my living room. "We already talked about this. Yes, I know he's been for-the-most-part clean for a while. Yes, he used to be my best friend. How come, tonight of all nights, you can't?"

"It's fine," I whispered. "I can get a ride." I pulled out my phone from the plug on the wall, fired it up and dialed.

"Hang on." Alejandro waved his finger at me.

"Hey, Beth," I said into my phone. "It's Sophie Priebe. I met you at the Kelsey Vision Quest gathering at the hotel yesterday." I nodded and listened. "Yes, I'm taking my first Quest tonight. I'm sorry, this is totally last minute. But Dr. Kelsey told me that you live close to me and that I could call you should my ride fall through. That seems to be happening." I listened. "Cool! Do you know where the

Grill is? Awesome! I'll meet you outside in like fifteen minutes. Thanks. You rock."

"He used to be troubled. Now he's just an asshole," Alejandro said into the phone. "Yeah, got it. Yes, we'll talk. The timing sucks, you know." He looked at me.

"Stop worrying before I punch you," I said. "Trust me, I'm tempted."

"This is the last time, Nick." Alejandro said into the phone. "I'll text you if it all goes to hell. And, thanks for the heads up." He hung up and shoved the phone into his jeans pocket.

"You can't drive me, can you?" I asked.

"No. Not tonight," he said. "Duties. Loyalties. Damn it, Sophie. I'm just trying to be myself with you. Break free of my past. And yet, here it is. Obligation city."

"Got it." My heart sank. "Your first priorities are your friends and driving. That's fine. That's normal. I guess I rank third or fourth or fifth on your scale of important things. That's cool. That's reality. I'd rather deal in reality than fantasy."

"After tonight, I plan on redefining my reality. And Bonita? Trust me, you and I have never been fantasy."

* * *

Alejandro drove me to the Grill. He parked in the No-Parking zone, threw the car in neutral and the engine idled. He leaned over, put his hands on top of my shoulders and kissed me hungrily.

I pushed him away. Gently. "I've got to go."

"I'm sorry," he said. "I'm getting this thing done with Jackson, then I'll drive up to the lodge."

"Sounds good." I stepped out the passenger door and adjusted my backpack so it was positioned more evenly across my shoulder blades. I looked at him. He stared at me while regret, fear and even hunger played across his beautiful face.

"Sophie?" a woman yelled, interrupting my thoughts, our gaze.

I turned and saw Beth waving at me from the open window of her sturdy, older, Toyota hatchback that was double-parked, about a quarter block away.

"Beth!"

"Hurry up. We've got to get to the lodge on time." She popped back in her car.

I gazed at Alejandro. "I've got to go."

"I do too," he said.

But neither of us moved.

"Sophie!" Beth yelled from her driver's window as she edged out into traffic and headed toward me.

"Coming!" I rounded the front of Alex's Jeep, and got stuck behind a couple of drunken tourists who staggered in front of me. One tripped and lurched toward me. I ducked and dodged out of his way.

Alex hit his horn, hard.

"Chill!" I hollered and made it to his window that was rolled all the way down.

"I should be there for you." His brows were knit and he slammed the dashboard with his fist.

"You're helping your friend. Tonight is no big deal. I'll see you after."

"Just one more thing," he said.

I watched as Beth's car crawled toward me through traffic. "What?"

"I love you, Sophie," Alejandro said. "I think I've loved you since the holy guacamole under the airplanes that were taking off. I knew I loved you in Mexico. But I need to make it official. So, right now, I'd like to call this official. Okay?"

"Okay." I wiped the back of my hand across my stupid crying eyes. "It's official."

"Kiss me."

I leaned through the open driver's window and I kissed him on his beautiful lips.

Beth blared her horn.

We separated and I stumbled backward.

"I'll see you in a little bit. Be careful." He pulled away from the curb out into Westwood traffic. Gazed at me for a second from his driver's window. "Promise me you won't do anything you're not completely comfortable doing."

"Promise," I said and watched him leave.

* * *

Beth drove us out of local traffic onto a few highways and turned off an exit. She drove up into the heart of the Santa Monica Mountains.

The roads were curvy, narrow and dark. In the distance I could see the lights from the houses in the Valley below. The other side featured a layer of fog and below it the twinkles of city lights in West L.A. and Santa Monica. It was like we were on top of L.A.'s world, looking down.

Beth chatted on about how this was her third Quest. She'd plopped down six hundred bucks because she had a crush on one of Dr. Kelsey's guides who'd be accompanying the Questers tonight. "If I'm lucky, he'll chaperone me tonight," she said.

I think what she actually meant to say was, *"If I'm lucky, he'll bone me tonight."* But I didn't verbalize that because I didn't want to be too much of a smartass considering she was being so nice, driving me and all.

We pulled into the lodge's parking lot filled with a variety of cars and SUVS. A three-story, non-descript, concrete-block structure housed the headquarters for Kelsey Vision Quest. I ascertained this because "KELSEY VISION QUEST" was painted in block letters on its exterior walls. Meathead #1 stood by the front door. Meathead #2 was in the driver's seat of Dr. Kelsey's SUV and drove off, a cloud of dust in his wake.

We were late. Folks were already piling into vans, SUVs and trucks. Beth threw her car in park, yanked her keys out of the ignition and yelled, "Hurry up!" She grabbed her backpack from the backseat and I grabbed mine.

The next thing I knew, a greeter guy in the back of an open truck offered me a hand and hoisted me up. "You are?" he asked.

"Sophie Marie Priebe. Thanks for the help."

"Sophie Priebe? Dr. Kelsey's been looking for you." He grabbed a pager and keyed in a message. Then handed me a form. "You need to read and sign the paperwork. Print your name next to your signature and the date."

I grabbed the pen, signed on the line and dated. Always with the paperwork.

* * *

A group of about twenty of us sat in a circle on the dirt ground in the high desert in the Santa Monica Mountains. It was chilly, remote, no buildings in sight, the trucks parked far in the background on a patch of dried grass next to the narrow road. A couple of lanterns were positioned around our gathering and barely lit the place.

Dr. Kelsey stood in the middle of the circle and held court. "Everyone will have a human guide who stays with them during their Kelsey Vision Quest," he said.

A middle-aged man seated across from me pulled out his matches and lit a small stick of bundled leaves. He blew on the leaves, fanned the flames and waved the smoke into our circle.

Dr. Kelsey practically tackled the guy and grabbed the lit stick. "What are you doing?" He jammed the lit end into the ground, twisting it until the embers disappeared.

"It's sage. Typical Native American way to cleanse the energy. I've been on Quests before you know," the man said.

"I know very well what sage is. And we don't use it on my Quest," Dr. Kelsey said. "This is my program. You follow my rules and everything will be fine. Even better than fine." He stepped back into the center of the circle. "You'll see things you've never seen before. Experience profound openings. Maybe meet your power animals, or even your spiritual guardians. Your human guide will keep you safe in the rare case that you have anxiety or concerns." He pointed to two twenty-something guys and two women wearing Kelsey Vision Quest logos on their long-sleeved T-shirts. "Feel free to ask them questions."

The guides waved to us. One woman held a large thermos and poured liquid into outstretched paper cups that the others held in front of her. They passed them to people in the circle. My cup arrived and I accepted it. Its contents were brown, smelled a little funky and I wrinkled up my nose. I wished Alejandro was close by at the lodge, instead of picking up Jackson who-knows-where.

"Good luck, everyone," Dr. Kelsey said. "I can't wait for you to experience the mind-blowing bliss and freedom this program gives people. To life! Bottoms up."

"To life!" We collectively said and raised our cups.

I belted the concoction back. It tasted a little bitter. But not half as bad as many herbal teas. This Quest experience was going to be cake. Maybe I'd even learn something to help my Nana. What was I worried about?

CHAPTER TWENTY-THREE

I kneeled on the dirt and vomited into scrub brush that kept weaving back and forth in front of me like it was drunk. "I don't understand?" I retched again. "I don't get it?" My stomach wouldn't stop heaving. "I'm sick. Am I supposed to be sick? Is everyone sick?" I pushed my grimy hair back from my sweaty forehead, rolled onto my ass and propped myself up with one hand on the ground behind me.

"You aren't sick, Sophie. You're actually becoming healthy." Dr. Kelsey sat across from me on the earth, his legs akimbo, about twelve feet away. Several lanterns flanking him cast ominous shadows onto the rocks and cliffs around us. "The plant medicine is helping you expunge all the poisons in your life that are keeping you imprisoned. That are stopping you from knowing your truth." All three versions of him leaned back against a huge boulder as he fidgeted with something rectangular and silver colored in his lap.

I felt feverish and dabbed my forehead with the sleeve of my shirt. Moments later I was freezing and shivered. My skin started crawling and felt like it was peeling off. I feared I'd be left with bloody muscles and tendons and visible bones. I peered down at my hand—it was still intact. "I feel like shit."

"It'll pass," Dr. Kelsey said. "Nothing bad can happen

to you. I'm your guide for tonight. All the other Quest participants share a guide with four other people. You lucked out. You've got me all to yourself." He didn't make eye contact—just kept peering down at his shiny toy.

I gazed around. There was a full moon overhead. We were on top of a mountain cliff that jutted out high over a canyon. Below was scruffy, dried out looking vegetation, most likely due to the summer heat and lack of rain. Hooded areas mottled the canyon walls. Darkness filled their interiors and possibly led to caves. Steep precipices dropped abruptly to rocky tunnels.

Wild animals wailed in the distance. At first their cries were faint but quickly increased in volume until their screams rippled through the air around me. I clamped my hands over my ears. But now I could not only hear them, but see and practically touch them.

An enormous owl with a wingspan of ten or more feet swooped toward my face, talons extended, shrieking.

I flinched, ducked and squeezed my eyes shut. When I opened them the owl perched on a sturdy branch in a tall pine tree and peered down at me with yellow saucer shaped eyes. "Hoo!" the owl screeched.

"Hoo back." I huddled into a ball, squeezing my knees toward my chest.

Dr. Kelsey's magnetic voice echoed around me. "Tell the owl you are not scared of it. It has no power over you."

"What if it flies into my hair and gets caught? What if it attacks me? What if it lands on me and sticks its long spiky talons into my shoulders? And they jab into my heart and then I die?" I shuddered. "What the freak should I do then?" I pushed myself to standing and stumbled away from the scrub brush toward the cliff, toward a precipice.

"What the owl does is up to you, Sophie. You tell the owl what to do. Just like you can tell MS what to do."

"Hah! You're a riot."

"That's why you're on the Quest. You need to learn this

information so you can help yourself as well as your grandmother. Integrate it. Believe it. Live it."

Everything was becoming even ore hazy around me. But I could swear Dr. Kelsey was holding that silver thing to his face.

"Ask yourself the important questions, Sophie. The questions that can change lives," Dr. Kelsey's voice boomed and echoed from some place close to me. Or maybe it was far away from me. Really, it was too difficult, or possibly too easy, to figure out. But then I experienced a brief moment of clarity, where I saw something too familiar.

"Important question. Why do you have a camera pointed at me?" I asked.

"Because we need to share your journey with others. We need to help people with cancer or MS. People in wheelchairs," he said. "You're ripping your mind open to discover your essence. Save people. Just like you want to save your grandmother."

"My essence believes that you have a flipping camera pointed at me," I said. "Turn it off."

"You need to tell the owl to leave and turn it off," Dr. Kelsey said. "Not me."

I swiveled. "I am not scared of you, owl," I said.

The gigantic bird's feathers morphed from dark green to gray to turquoise and then to black. All in a matter of seconds. Funny thing was, the owl's eyes stayed the same. Yellow. Round. Creepy. No matter what color the owl was, its enormous round yellow eyes stayed the same color and glared at me. Then blinked.

I looked around. I saw stony cliffs while snippets of songs played in my head. I heard a few lines from the Rolling Stones' "Sympathy for the Devil". Lynyrd Skynyrd's "Free Bird" made me wonder if I could fly.

I felt my soul split from my body and fly high into the sky toward a cliff that jutted out over the canyon below. My grandmother stood on that cliff and shook her finger at me. "Go back, Sophie. Stop it, now!"

But blood wasn't the only thing that coursed through my veins. Power and hunger mingled with my blood, circulated through my brain and poured through my body. Suddenly I no longer felt sick.

I felt amazing.

Invincible.

Omnipotent.

I started to giggle.

I wanted to fly.

I smelled smoke.

I held my hands out like airplane wings and skipped across the cliff, swerving to and fro. That rock in front of me—that I almost banged into—was the most beautiful rock I'd ever seen in my life. That plant above my head talked to me. An enormous spider that was even taller than me stood up on its back legs, regarded me through fiery flickers that illuminated it and said, "Sophie! Follow me. Something bad's happening. This place, this beautiful place is burning." The spider waddled away from me.

"Hey!" I watched the flickers grow into flames that licked the scrub brush on the cliff. "Like—spiders creep me out. Seriously. Why should I follow you?"

"Because if you stay here, you'll burn," the spider said. "Come on!"

"But," I said. "If you're a spider—why do you have a camera?"

The spider paused and morphed back into a glistening, sweaty, corpulent version of Dr. Kelsey. "Sophie. There's a fire! We have to go! Come with me," he held out his hand—which morphed back into hairy spider legs curling toward me.

I shuddered. "You go. I'll be fine. I'm good in emergencies. Always have been."

Flames popped up around Dr. Kelsey. He dropped his

camera, turned hairy tail and lumbered away until he was out of sight.

I watched as the camera fell in slow motion into a scratchy-looking bush, close to the cliff's edge. The fires grew. I heard the dead plants scream as the flames lit them and they sizzled, their bodies lighting like corpses lined up on a conveyor belt in a crematorium. One after the next.

I didn't know why, but I needed to get that camera. Thick clouds of smoke congealed in the canyons and billowed in the air around me. Colonies of bats squealed as they flew out from caves in the cliffs around me, winging their way through the smoke. One large flock exploded out of the rocks just feet above my head, screeching and flapping their wings around me as they escaped into the night sky.

I screamed, ducked low to the ground and coughed. I clawed my way on the earth toward the camera that lay discarded, like a flashy toy the day after Christmas. It stuck out of scrub brush that clung to the edge of the cliff. It was illuminated by other plants as the flames licked their bases, expanded upward and popped as they ignited like tiny bombs.

But I didn't care about bombs, or other acts of warfare. I was here to save a life. I was a good soldier and I would carry on. I crawled toward the scrub brush, snaked my hand close to its flames and snatched the camera. My hand started to burn. I dropped the camera, looked up and saw flames circling me. Engulfing me.

If I ran, I'd be burned. If I stayed, I'd die.

I looked around for my power animals: no owl, no spider. No bliss coursing through my veins. Only flames making their way toward me. I searched for a way out of this mess. There were flames everywhere: smoke congealing and people screamed in the distance. I shook my head and realized: I was screwed. There was only one way out, and it was if I dropped off the edge of the stony cliff.

There was a ledge below it. Unless I wanted to die right now, this was my only option. I stood up and walked to the cliff's edge. Balanced on the precipice as the flames snaked their way closer to me.

Now was the time. I could just let go. Surrender to the moment. The heat. The inevitability. Really? What did I have to lose? I leaned forward. Just let go Sophie, I told myself. Really, death is inevitable.

But I didn't want to die, her or now. I wanted to live. I wanted to love.

I heard the revs of a loud car engine, its horn honking like crazy. A guy yelled, "Sophie Marie Priebe! Step away from that damn cliff. I'm coming for you."

I turned and saw him. He wasn't a spider. He wasn't an action figure with a D emblazoned on his long-sleeved T-shirt.

He was simply my Alejandro.

"You're here," I said as he scooped me up in hi arms and hauled ass back to his Jeep, throwing me in the passenger seat and belting me in.

"You bet your ass I'm here." He hopped in the driver's seat and revved the enigre. "Hang on. I'm going to get us out of this mess."

* * *

I was back at USCLA emergency room, lying on a gurney sucking oxygen out of a mask while Alejandro held my hand and texted Nick on his cell. "Damn," he said.

I pulled the mask off my face. "What?"

"Do you remember passing out on the way down the mountain?"

"No," I said and immediately wondered if it was from the hallucinogenic plant medicine or a seizure.

Alejandro nodded. "Well you did. I think you had a seizure."

Great.

"I thought you were dying. It freaked the hell out of me and I didn't know if I should stop or keep driving, but the flames were on our ass, so I just kept driving and held your hand. I got cell coverage about a quarter of a mile down and called 911. They were already on it. I got through to Nick and Tyler. They're freaking crazy, but they were already in Malibu and went up into the hills. Nick found Beth—"

"Oh my God, I said. "Is she okay?"

He shook his head. "She'll live. Things could be worse. She'll need some skin grafts on her arms. Tyler managed to help some locals evacuate with their two dogs, four cats and two horses. Dr. Carlton Kelsey was treated for smoke inhalation and has left the building. No comment on his part. Most of the people on the Quest are accounted for."

"Most?"

"A few people on their roster are missing. Police have opened an investigation into Kelsey Vision Quest."

The nurses kept monitoring my blood pressure and my oxygen intake.

"Alejandro," I said and reached for his hand. "You rescued me. You saved my life. I've got to tell you something. I tried to tell you before."

He wove his fingers through mine. "Anything."

"I've been diagnosed with—"

A harried, young, female doctor burst into our semi-private curtained area. She flipped through my chart. "You're nineteen-years-old, you're in a USCLA stem cell study for early onset MS *and* you just survived a forest fire," she said. "Someone needs to call Lifetime Network and option your rights for a TV movie." She examined me and my burns.

I looked at Alejandro. The truth was out, and not in the way that I hoped it would happen.

Would he shun me? Would he judge me? Was I tainted in his

eyes?

Alex squeezed my hand then released it, leaned down and kissed me on the top of my smoke scented hair.

"You lucked out, young lady," the doctor said. "Your burns are first degree and for the most part minor. But your blood pressure's high. That happens when you suffer from smoke inhalation. The hallucinogenic you took can really mess people up. You could have ended up as a guest in our Psych Ward. I'm assuming you voluntarily took this stuff."

"Yes. But I was told the plant medicine was harmless."

"You were told wrong. You're dehydrated from vomiting. I see here in the chart you had seizures. The plant medicine could have kicked your MS symptoms into overdrive. The fire you escaped has already consumed a couple hundred acres. You should probably stay overnight for observation. I'll have you transferred to—"

"No," I said. "Please. I hate hospitals. I really want to go home."

She sighed. "Do you have a roommate? A friend to stay with you?" She eyed me and then Alex, with a questioning look.

"Yes. She has me." Alejandro took my hand and squeezed it, again. "I'm staying with her. Do you have any instructions? A number I should call if she gets worse? Has more seizures?"

"911 in case of emergency." She dug in her pocket and pulled out a business card and handed it to him. "I'm only here for another couple of hours. You can page me or the nurse's station if you have questions. I'm prescribing a creme for your burns. Pick it up on your way out." She turned and I swear, shook her finger at me. "You're going to feel like crap for a couple of days. Rest, hydrate and eat something bland like chicken soup and crackers No excessive physical exertion if your know what I mean." She scribbled in my chart.

"Thank you Doctor," I said.

"You're welcome." She left the cubicle.

I looked at Alejandro. "I think I figured out why the Vision Quest's provision list included mouthwash."

And despite everything, we both cracked smiles. Here we were again—full circle.

CHAPTER TWENTY-FOUR

Alejandro ran a bath for me in my ancient clawfoot tub. I brushed my teeth for the third time and spit into the bathroom sink. That simple effort made me feel even weaker. Like I'd just taken a five-mile hike instead a three-gargle spit. I ignored the elephant in the room—he finally knew my biggest secret—I had MS.

"My mom always said lavender and Aloe Vera are healing for burns and stuff." Alejandro poured a concoction from a box directly under the faucet. "The description on this bath soak package says the ingredients are organic and natural."

"Sounds like the plant medicine," I said.

"Oh crap. I'll empty it." He plunged his hand down into the water toward the stopper.

"No," I said. "Keep it." I leaned forward over the sink and stared into the mirror. My face was red and covered in soot. I was really lucky that I hadn't been badly burned. I had a few blisters and minor burns on my hand and other areas. I was, however missing half an eyebrow: the fire had singed it off. "You must think I'm hideous."

Alejandro stood behind me, wrapped his arms around my waist, leaned his sooty face next to mine and peered into the mirror. "Nah. I think you look kind of exotic. Like that chick in *The Girl with The Dragon Tattoo* who had really skinny eyebrows."

"She had *two* skinny eyebrows," I said. "Where would I be if you hadn't shown up?"

"Probably with a normal man without all the baggage who would've been there for you from the get go. A guy who doesn't break people."

"Excuse me. *Without you* I'd be on a slab in the county morgue." I said. "Going on this stupid Quest wasn't about me. Well—it kind of was. But for the most part, it was for Nana." My legs trembled. My hands started shaking. I couldn't hide my shame or my symptoms any longer and a few tears leaked out.

He hugged me tighter and nuzzled his chin against my face. "It's okay to cry, Bonita. Do you want to skip the bath and just hit the bed?"

I wiped my eyes with the back of my hand. "God, no." I said. "I'm a stinky creature from Middle-earth." I looked at the tub. The water looked warm, the bubbles inviting. And yet… "Truth?"

"Truth," he said.

"If I have a seizure in liquid deeper than a glass of orange juice tonight—I'd drown."

He nodded. "This explains your freaky aversion to surfing."

"You're discovering all my secrets."

He stepped away and ran his fingers through the water. "The temperature's perfect. Your carriage awaits." He gestured to the tub. "I'll even give you privacy. I'll sit right outside the door and I won't even peek. But if I hear anything unusual, I'll rescue you. You're not drowning tonight."

I didn't know whether to feel grateful or embarrassed. "I have MS, Alejandro. No matter how many herbal baths I take, it's incredibly doubtful that I'll be a person who lives a long, rich, healthy life."

"Bonita—just take a bath. One small thing to help you

relax and feel better. Okay? We'll deal with the rest of it later."

"Really?"

"Really," he said. "And no worries about me seducing you tonight. I'm a total gentleman. I wouldn't lay one finger on you, in that kind of way, even if you handed me an engraved invitation."

Hmm. That almost sounded like an Alpha Boy challenge.

"Your puke-stained shirt," he said. "What do you think? Should we take it off?"

"Yes." I stretched my arms up over my head.

He tugged on my shirt and slowly peeled it over my head, leaving me naked from the waist up except for my sweat-drenched bra.

He held the shirt balled up in his hand. "Keep it or toss it?"

"Toss it."

"Agree." He pitched it into the wastebasket in the corner of the bathroom. His eyes landed on my chest and swept slowly down my body. He cleared his throat. "Your jeans," he said. "They're dirty. Again, puke-stained. Smell like smoke and probably have bat shit on them. What do you think?"

"I think you're going to help me get out of them."

He kneeled and unbuttoned my jeans. Slowly. I heard his breath catch. He placed one large hand on each side of my waistband and eased my Levis down my hips.

My stomach did flip-flops and seemed to drop low into my pelvis. I started feeling hot and my heart pounded in my chest.

How could I be dehydrated, burnt, exhausted and massively turned on all at the same time? When my jeans chafed against something painful on my thigh. "Ow!" I flinched.

He gazed up at me, concerned. "A bruise or a burn?"

"A burn, I think."

"Where?"

My hand traveled down directly in front of his face, grazed his lower lip, (by mistake I swear,) and I tapped a spot on my thigh just inches from his mouth. His breath quickened and warmed my leg.

"Hang on." He stood up, opened the mirrored bathroom cabinet door, peered inside and grabbed a pair of scissors. "I'm cutting this pant leg off right above where it hurts. Okay?"

"Okay," I said.

He knelt back on the floor and punctured a hole in my threadbare jeans with the tip of the scissors and started cutting off my pant leg.

I tried not to fidget, but I was sprouting goose bumps and suddenly had the shivers. He cut around my entire thigh until the filthy pant leg collapsed around my ankle. "Better," I said.

"Good. You were right," he said. "It's a burn and a bruise. Nasty. Where's that cream the ER doctor gave you?"

"In my purse," I said. "On the kitchen counter."

He sighed, got up and left the bathroom. "I hope Dr. Carlton Kelsey uses his time wisely to cross a whole lot of state lines far away from California."

I wriggled out of what remained of my jeans.

"Because if I see him, I will kick his flabby ass from here to—"

He froze in the bathroom's entrance and gazed at me, speechless.

I stood before him in only my bra and panties. Pointed to the clothing on the floor. "Could you throw that in the trash as well?"

"Um." His eyes glazed over. "Yes." He picked the pile off the floor and pitched it into the wastebasket.

"Thanks. You said you'd sit outside the bathroom door to make sure I didn't drown. You still okay with that?"

"Oh." He frowned and shook his head. "Yes. Absolutely." He stepped the few feet outside the door. I heard him sit down and lean back against the hallway wall. And sigh.

I smiled. He was still my Alpha Boy. I unhooked my bra and shimmied out of my underwear. Dropped both on the floor. Stepped gingerly into the tub.

The water was warm, but not hot. I sat down, sighed, dunked under the surface for a few seconds and wet my hair. I resurfaced dripping wet and reclined against the back of the porcelain tub. I grabbed the bar of soap and carefully cleaned the blood, soot and smoke from my skin. "This feels great," I said. "Thank you."

"You're welcome."

I reached for the shampoo on the side of the tub and winced when squeezing the bottle caused the burn on my hand to flare. Thought about it. There weren't a ton of bubbles left. And then I wondered after all we'd been through, if I really needed them.

"I need your help, Alejandro," I said. "If you're up for it."

"What?" he sounded interested.

"Would you wash my hair? The burn on my hand hurts."

"Okay," he said, still outside the bathroom door.

"That means you can come back inside."

He walked in with his eyes squinted shut.

"Open your eyes, before you fall, dork."

"But I promised," he said.

"And I promise you're not going to see anything you haven't seen before."

He smiled and blinked his eyes open. It was like watching a kid on Christmas morning seeing presents for the first time. (Yippee! Santa made it after all!)

He kneeled next to the tub, reached over me, grabbed the bottle of shampoo from the far corner, flipped open the top and poured a dab into his palm. His gaze danced over my body submerged under the water and landed on my face. His lips were full. I wanted to kiss him. He massaged the shampoo into my scalp. I closed my eyes.

Heavenly. He was freaking heavenly. "Why you haven't become a hair stylist is a question that will always haunt me," I said.

"I could be like that Warren Beatty character in the old movie, *Shampoo.*"

"I've never seen that movie, but trust me if Warren's character did half of what you're doing now—sign me up."

I slid under the water for a second and wondered what to do. I had MS. But I'd fallen in love for the first time with Alejandro: a gorgeous, smart man who loved me back. *I was safe. I was cared for. I was in love. Seriously? My decision wasn't all that difficult.*

I slid back up out of the water, my hair slicked against my neck, chest and back. I blinked my eyes open and realized the bubbles were gone. Alejandro was deliberately avoiding eye contact, staring at something on the ceiling. "Look at me," I said.

"Nah. We'd be getting into dicey territory. I think it's safer to look at that spot on the wall."

"No." I grabbed his hand. "I want you to look at me. *All of me.* The good, the bad… I'm bruised. I'm burnt. I have this stupid disease that could be inactive for years and one day might decide to eat me up and leave me in a wheelchair. Most nineteen-year-old girls are close to being perfect people. *But I'm not.* I'll never be a perfect person. I need you to know that."

"Bonita," he said. "I'm the guy who will love you, no matter what."

I pushed myself half out of the bath water and clasped his face between my hands.

"Kiss me," I said.

"I can't. I promised to be a gentleman."

"Kiss me, or I'll pull you in this tub on top of me. And don't think just because I had a really shitty night that I can't do that. I'm a midwestern chick and I've completely fallen in love with you, you big, gorgeous dork. And midwestern chicks know what they want, when they want it, and they get it done. So kiss me," I insisted, more than a little breathless.

He smiled, pulled me toward him and kissed me. Our hands flew across each other's bodies: cupping, caressing, gliding. I giggled and splashed his shirt.

"I knew you were going to do that," he said.

"I want to feel you. I want to touch you," I said.

He ripped off his shirt and reached his hand out to me. I took his hand and stepped out of that tub wet from head to toe: scarred, bruised, burnt and naked.

He inhaled sharply and eyed me. "You're fucking beautiful."

"Prove it to me," I wrapped my arms around his neck and pulled him toward me.

He lifted me up. I wrapped my legs around the top of his hips. He carried me out of the bathroom through my hallway and into my bedroom.

He lowered me on my back onto my bed.

"Protection?" I asked.

He grabbed his wallet and pulled out a condom. He shrugged off his jeans in seconds and rolled on the condom.

"I want you, Alejandro," I said, my breath heavy.

He straddled me. He was naked. And he was beautiful. Truth be told, I hadn't seen a lot of erections. But I do think his might have been perfect. That this moment might be perfect. "I want you to be my first love," I said.

"You sure? That's not the plant medicine talking?"

"You better believe I'm sure."

He lowered himself against me firmly. I looked up into his beautiful face. His hazel eyes flecked with gold were hungry, filled with desire. He entered me as gently as possible and I gasped. After the first few moments, I knew this was by far the best decision of my entire life. "I love you, Bonita," he said as we found our rhythm, lost our breath, and melded into each other's bodies.

* * *

Our first time making love was sweet and tender and, well, interesting. Afterward we were famished. It had been a long night filled with all kinds of excitement. He ordered takeout. The sun rose as we sat on my living room floor sharing pizza, fresh chicken soup with noodles and bagels with cream cheese.

We were exhausted, went back to my bed and napped for a couple of hours. We woke up in each other's arms when Napoleon skittered across the blanket and pounced on our feet.

Our second time making love lasted longer and seemed a little more intense. Definitely more goosebumps.

But the third time we made love? I realized that even a semi-orgasmic Chinese foot massage wouldn't ever come close to satisfying my needs the way Alejandro did.

* * *

Pacific Coast Highway was an amazing expanse of winding road that ran along California's coast. In some areas it was blocks from the ocean. In other stretches it was actually adjacent to the coast. The highway was one of the few access roads in and out of Malibu and was the address for celebrities, moguls and a few rehab centers.

Alex and I drove on PCH up the Malibu bluffs, the sun off to our left over the waves breaking on the beautiful SoCal beaches. I wasn't sure if I should venture out so soon after my nearly disastrous, healing experiment. I didn't want be a burden, nor did I care to be an eyesore or bear the brunt of gossip. But when Alex said Jackson's folks had whipped together a fund-raiser for the Malibu Fire Department, I was game, and pulled my attitude, as well as a pretty outfit together. I did my hair and applied some makeup. Tried my best to pencil in my half-missing eyebrow.

"I'm glad you're doing this with me, Bonita." He grabbed my hand and kissed it. "You'll see. People will be supportive. If they're not, give me a nod and I'll run interference. If you get tired, we'll leave."

"You sure?"

"Positive," he said. "Did I tell you the past couple of months driving and hanging out with you have been the best months of my life?"

"About twenty times." I covered a smile. "Tell me Alejandro—what did I do to win you over? Like—when was the moment? Was it the first night I met you when I was drenched in beer and bleeding all over your favorite T-shirt? Was it when the girls hid me under the picnic table in Venice Beach and I smelled like Coppertone mixed with dog poop? Or possibly when after I puked my guts out during the Vision Quest? I've provided you with so many magical moments."

"I was intrigued by the beer and blood but thought the gang banger and poop thing was different from the average girl. You definitely had me with the fire and puking incident. But I think the clincher was when your Nana talked Yiddish as an excuse to discover my intentions regarding you. I already knew you were pretty, smart and funny, but the fact that you came from a great family did me in."

He slowed the Jeep and waited in the center turning lane for a few moments until oncoming traffic broke. He pulled a U-ie, accelerated for seconds, then braked and pulled over to the side of the road. We were in line behind twenty cars snaking their way to the front of a white, curved, concrete-walled entrance with tall plants overhead, so no one could see in.

"Jackson's house?" I asked.

He nodded. "Pricey benefit. Big turnout. Casual party, but splashy." He grabbed my hand. "Do you want to skip it?"

Absolutely I wanted to skip this. I'd rather be alone with him in front of a fireplace. I'd rather he kiss me as he stripped off my clothes.

"All the money's going to the firefighters?"

Alex nodded.

"Let's do it."

"Okay." He put the car in park, exited the driver's door and tossed his keys to a Valet Guy. "Keep it close, yes?" He slipped the Valet a twenty, walked around to the passenger side of his Jeep. But another Valet had already opened my door and I'd stepped out.

"You cheating on me with another Driver?"

"Yes," I whispered. "The tiny, middle-aged man in the shiny, black jacket who reaches my shoulder if he stands on his tiptoes is a huge turn on. Sorry."

Alejandro laughed and wrapped his arm around my waist. We moved past security guards through the open gates onto the biggest estate I'd seen in my entire life, a movie, TV show, or even *People Magazine*.

* * *

Unlike Alejandro's family, Jackson's parents did have their BBQ catered. Half of their manicured, very green front yard was filled with food tents manned by servers. Casually attired, well-groomed guests stood knee deep in line in front of the stands waiting for tacos, burgers, Thai, vegetarian, hot dogs, as well as BBQ chicken and ribs.

We passed a booth filled with bowls, platters and bushels of fruit. There were oranges, tangerines, strawberries, blueberries and blackberries. Alex grabbed several peeled tangerine wedges that were speared with festive toothpicks, as well as one orange. "This is all from Jackson's family's orchard," he said. "You've never tasted a tangerine like this, ever." He fed me a small slice, popped another in his mouth and started peeling the orange.

I munched. "Yowsa!"

A guesthouse was located next to a basketball court that had been transformed into a small, upscale playground. There was a section where kids and adults slid down blown up slides and jumped on trampolines. A tightrope stretched between two platforms towered high above a safety net below it. Tyler walked across the rope holding a balancing rod; a safety harness was securely strapped around his waist and legs.

"Yo, Cirque you are so laid," Alex hollered up at him. "Showing off your fancy moves?"

Tyler grinned and glanced down at us. He hit the middle of the tightrope's expanse and wobbled precariously, the balancing rod teetering from side to side as he tried not to fall. "Hey, Sophie. You look pretty hot, no pun intended, for someone who just escaped a major fire."

"Thanks!" I glanced at Alex, who frowned. "I'm missing half an eyebrow."

"Eyebrows come and go, sweets. I have 'fancy moves' that could make you forget all about that missing brow."

Alex pulled out the orange and pitched it at Tyler. It bounced off his stomach and he grunted. "Stop flirting with my girl."

"Orange you going to ask me nicely?" Tyler wobbled back and forth on the line. It looked like he was going to lose his balance and fall. But he made it to end of the rope without assistance. "Yes!" He reached the tiny platform high over the ground.

"Thank God. I hated the thought of seeing such a pretty

boy crash again," Alex said.

I applauded along with a couple of cute, coiffed chicks who made googly eyes at Tyler.

"You're always jealous that I'm prettier than you." Tyler climbed down the ladder.

Alex snorted and then tried to stuff back his laughter back by clamping one hand over his mouth. I wondered why Tyler was still single. When five girls threw themselves at him, I stopped speculating.

Alex and I walked away from The Tyler Show toward the main house. "That used to be you, didn't it?" I frowned.

"I'm not like him anymore." He pulled me toward him and kissed me on my lips.

"Get a room!" Tyler yelled.

"Get a life!" Alex hollered, and they both laughed.

I spotted Gabriella, the makeup artist who helped hide me from Oscar and his gang bangers that day on Venice Beach. She was at a table about ten yards way, face painting an elaborate design on a teenage girl. She waved at me. "Sophie! Come on over. Let me draw something magical on your face."

"How about an eyebrow?" I waved back.

"Yes!"

"Let's go!" I tugged on Alex's arm.

"Yo, Alex!" Nick waved to us from the tall, sleek front doors of the ultra-modern house at the deep end of the property. "Jackson wants to show us something."

"Come on, hon. Just for a couple of minutes," Alex said.

The mansion was on a tall bluff overlooking the Pacific. We entered the foyer. "Hey," Nick said and squeezed my hand. "Thank God you made it out all right. Damn fire's still chewing up acres, destroying people's homes and dreams."

"Sucks," I said. "Nice of Jackson's folks to host the benefit."

We wandered around the house looking for Jackson. The rear living room's ceiling vaulted three stories tall. With the exception of doors and nearly invisible framework, the walls were glass. The back doors led to a rectangular shaped pool with a smattering of sleek lawn chairs on the concrete slab surrounding it. Twenty white picnic tables were set up on the grassy yard that spread out around it. There were more food kiosks and servers. Party guests roamed around. They chatted with each other at the tables and around the pool.

A low, modern fence surrounded the edge of the property. It protected folks from falling off the lawn and skittering down the bluff high up over the beach below it. There were steps built into the cliff that descended, tier by tier, to the sands below.

"What do you think?" Alex asked.

"Someone needs to call God and tell Her Jackson's parents stole heaven," I said.

Nathan, Jackson and Tyler, and one of the adoring girls from his fan club, walked toward us. "Yo!" Jackson hoisted his glass in the air. "My dad just got the newest Ferrari. The first one of the new model in the entire country. Want to check it out?"

"Seriously?" Nick asked.

"Why not," Nathan said.

Alejandro looked at me.

"Go. I'm going to get my eyebrow and possibly other body parts painted."

"Color me interested," he whispered. "I'm right behind you," he said to his friends. " They sauntered off and he turned toward me. "I'll stake out a place for us at a picnic table next to the big pool. Not the other pool. This one. Get here before the sun goes down the fireworks starting over the ocean."

"Fireworks for a benefit *for a fire* in the hills?" I asked.

"Just go with it. Jackson's folks are probably raising over

a 100 K tonight for the Malibu Fire Department. Everything they've spent money on is a tax write off. Yeah, it's a bit of a joke, but…" He lifted his hands up in the air. "So's the Ferrari. Do you really think I give a rat's ass about checking out the newest Ferrari in the entire U.S. of A?"

"You tell me," I said.

He cradled my face in his hands and stared down into my eyes. "I don't care about that stuff, Sophie. I haven't cared about that since the accident." He leaned in and kissed me on my lips.

I reluctantly pushed him away. "Go!" I said.

"I'll see you at sundown next to the backyard pool. I'll get us plates. By the way, we're leaving the party early. We've got better things to do."

CHAPTER TWENTY-FIVE

I chatted with Gabriella. She gave me a temporary eyebrow with a henna tattoo. Then painted a sun, a moon and glittering falling stars on the same side of my face. She confided that she and Javier were starting to date. It probably wouldn't have happened if they hadn't run into each other that day they helped rescue me on Venice Beach.

I thought of the funny ways our lives twist, turn and collide. We think something's truly terrible—and it might be—but then sometimes magic happens. You meet someone. You find healing. You fall in love. I thanked Gabriella and tipped her.

It wasn't dusk yet and I couldn't help myself. I thought of Cole's obsession with Gary Cooper as I explored Jackson's parents' estate.

I meandered past a small orchard with avocado trees, orange, lemon, lime, fig, and... more orange trees. Different varieties, I assumed, as their fruit had a slightly different scent. I passed an herb garden that smelled of basil, rosemary, thyme and sage. Lavender plants and roses were planted among the herbs.

I closed my eyes and inhaled. It smelled intoxicating—like if God had created Her own potpourri and gave it free of charge to whoever prayed for healing. "Hold this close to your heart. Squeeze it between your hands when you doubt. Breathe in its essence. This could make you well."

I spotted another swimming pool adjacent to the herb garden and orchards. There was what looked like a barn styled, two-car garage behind it. This pool was smaller than the one behind the main house. A slate gray, unbroken concrete pathway led to its placement on the property, which was a little odd—almost as though it was meant to be hidden, to be secret. A private, secluded body of water for a special person who deserved to be surrounded by the beauty of the trees and embraced by the scent of the flowers.

I was curious and walked toward it. I was the only person wandering this section of the estate. Guess this wasn't part of the party. Secure guardrails surrounded the pool. Not the kind of fence to keep people out, but rails to help persons get in and out of the water. Most likely a person with a disability. There was lift platform for a wheelchair in the shallow end.

This had to be Lauren's pool. Jackson's sister had suffered a life-changing spinal cord injury when they drove off Malibu Canyon Road. The accident put her into a wheelchair and left her a paraplegic.

It was getting darker. Time to get back. But then I spotted the rear end of a limo sticking out of the two-car garage. Its custom paint job was colored Pepto-Bismol pink.

A screech overhead startled me and I jumped. The black sky above lit up as a white flame ascended into it and a single firework exploded. Spider-like long, hairy legs materialized from its hub and arced down away from it. I cringed for a second as funky memories of the fire and the hallucination poured into my brain. I quickly realized this was the barge of fireworks Alejandro had talked about. And it was past time that I needed to meet up with him.

I turned and made tracks.

"I'm surprised you didn't figure it out, yet," a guy said,

as he stepped from the garage's shadows directly in front of me.

I backed away. Until I saw that the guy was Jackson, his hands in his pockets, slumped a little casually, like he always was. And I stopped.

"Hey!" I said. "Your folks have an amazing house. Fierce benefit. I could swear I've seen that pink limo before."

"Yeah. You have. You rode in it the night of my sister's bathing suit party."

"Your sister?" Something felt a little off with Jackson. Maybe he'd been drinking. Maybe he was on meds. Maybe his meds were off. "I've never met Lauren. Although, Alejandro told me all about her and the accident. What a nightmare you all went through. I told Alejandro I'd meet him before the fireworks started Can we talk later?"

When Jackson didn't answer, I turned, wondered if he had a hearing problem and strode back to the main house. He followed me—his toes practically clipping my heels.

"You've met my sister," Jackson said. "Lulu told me all about you. Blue's friend, Sophie. The girl from Wisconsin who was in the MS stem cell study. Who else could it be?"

Whoa. I froze, but then swiveled back toward him. Alex told me Jackson's sister's name was Lauren. And it hit me. "Your sister's *Lulu?*"

"Yeah. Happy that you're stealing the guy she's been in love with forever away from her?"

"What do you mean?"

He guzzled his drink and tossed the glass onto the grass behind him. "Lulu's been in love with Alex since grade school. She's in a chair, going through therapies, surgeries and experimental procedures. Finally she's seeing progress. Her toes are starting to move. The MRIs are coming back positive, for a change."

"She told me," I said. "I mean, I didn't know it was Lauren, but, the girl I met—Lulu—told us the night of the bathing suit party."

"She's a good girl," he slurred. "But you on the other hand. You waltz in here this summer, randomly meet Alex at the Grill. Then you," he made quotation mark symbols in the air, "'hire him,' to be your Driver. And the next thing we know is that after four years of being shut down? Alex is seriously falling for someone. Some sweet little 'Aw-shucks I'm-just-a down-on-her-luck girl' that none of us know. He's got his pick of any chick in L.A. And he's falling for a girl from bumfuck, Wisconsin. Really?"

My temper flared from his insinuations but I kicked it back down. "Jackson. There's a serious misunderstanding happening here. I'm going to find Alejandro. We'll leave. And then maybe, we can figure this all out tomorrow. Okay?" I backed away from him, turned and walked toward the house.

But Jackson lurched behind me, grabbed my arm, twisted it hard behind my back and spun me around. He shoved me back against a thick hedge. I screamed, but he clamped his hand over my mouth. "You just waltz in here, mess up all our lives and think that's okay. That it's fine? It's *not* fine. It's *not* okay."

And I realized—Jackson was messed up—and not just a little. Hopefully not completely 'round the bend. But enough that I needed—"Help!" I screamed at the same time as the fireworks ripped through the sky and exploded overhead.

I saw Nathan in the distance on his cell, jogging toward the mansion's front gates. God, if I could just get his attention. "Hel—"

Jackson clamped his hand over my mouth. "I don't want to hurt you, Sophie. I just want you to go away. *Forever.* Could you just go away forever? And our lives can return to normal." Red, white and blue fireworks pierced the layer of smoke from the fire that hovered heavy in the night sky.

When Nathan ripped Jackson off me and we both

stumbled. "Jackson! What are you doing?" Nathan asked. "Take your hands off her, now! Alex will kill you."

I shivered and hugged my arms over my chest. Jackson sprawled on the lawn just a few yards from me. Was it true about Lulu and Alejandro? Had I screwed things up for her? For them? I had this sinking realization that quite possibly, someday, I'd be the girl in the wheelchair.

If I stayed with Alex, I'd be a constant reminder of his excruciating past. Everything he was trying so hard to leave behind would be shoved in his face. Every time he'd look at me, every conversation, every time he touched me he'd be transported back to that awful time when he grew to believe he was a monster.

Jackson lumbered off. "Sophie just tripped. I was trying to help her. Guess you called that one wrong, Mr. Driver."

Nathan scowled, shook his head and asked me, "Are you okay?"

I nodded. I felt like a poisonous cocktail was pouring down through my body just like that smoke from the fire. It was worse than the bad trip from the plant medicine. It was killing one hope and one dream at a time then moving on to the next.

"You need to get your act together, Jackson," Nathan said.

Jackson waved 'goodbye' over his shoulder and kept weaving.

My cell buzzed and I plucked it out of my purse. It was a text from Mom.

"Sophie," Nathan said. "I'm on my way back to the Westside for a Driver thing. I'm calling Alex. He'll come get you. Everything will be fine."

I tapped the box on my phone and read the text—

Nana had a stroke. She's not well. Come home tonight. I love you Sophie. Mom.

My knees felt weak and I plopped my ass down on the ground. "No. Everything's not going to be fine," I said. "I'm going with you, Nathan. You can drop me wherever on the Westside. But I need to leave. Now."

"But—what about Alex?"

"What about him?" I pushed myself to standing. Walked past Nathan, past the security guards, the valet attendants, the late-arriving partiers out the mansion's front gates. I turned right and strode down the side of the road next to Pacific Coast Highway. I stuck my thumb out in the universal sign that I was looking to hitch a ride.

This couldn't be happening. It simply couldn't. My shoulders felt numb. Ice water coursed from my heart down into the rest of my body. Maybe this was just a really bad dream.

A car horn beeped repeatedly and an Escalade veered in front of me and parked, the engine running. Nathan jumped out of the driver's door and strode toward me. "What are you doing? You can't hitchhike down PCH at night? You'll get plowed over in a heartbeat or a whack job will pick you up and kill you."

"I have to get back to my place." I said.

"I already texted Alex. Twice. He's on his way."

"I can't wait for Alex. I can't wait for anybody." I kept on walking past his Escalade.

"Fine," Nathan said. "I'll catch major shit for this. But fine, I'll drive you."

* * *

Nathan drove me back from the party in Malibu to West L.A. At first he tried to ask questions. "Did Jackson hurt you?"

"No."

"Did you and Alex have a fight?"

"No."

"Anything you want to share? Get off your chest?"

"No and no."

Because, how do you tell a guy you barely know about a person you've known forever? Out of all the words in our language, how do you pick the ones to describe the woman who recorded your very first steps with a clunky video camera? The angel with a huge heart who attended your ballet recitals in kindergarten, every horrific grade school play, each volleyball tournament in high school? How do you tell an acquaintance that my Nana had a stroke, is in a coma two thousand miles away and might not make it?

Me? I couldn't find the words. So I didn't even try. I just told Nathan my address and I stared in silence out the window the rest of the trip back to the Westside.

He dropped me in front of my apartment. "Do you need anything else?"

I shook my head. "Thank you," I said. "Go yank that person's keys away."

Nathan smiled at me from behind the wheel. "You're a sweetheart, Sophie. I hope you and Alex can figure it out." He peeled away from the curb.

* * *

I fed Napoleon. Marched into my bedroom, hauled my suitcases out of my closet, placed them on my bed and unzipped their tops. I yanked clothes from my closet as well as the chest of drawers, and pitched everything into my suitcases. Grabbed the framed photos of my Nana, Mom and the selfie shot of Triple M and I, rolled them in clothing and stuck them in my traveling bag along with my laptop and everything in my desk.

Next stop the bathroom. It took me five minutes to fill a few zip-lock bags with liquidy things and shove that in one suitcase, as well. Hauled a few things to the trash.

I looked around the apartment. It was empty of my presence except for some food in the fridge and cabinets, as well as shampoo and bubble bath I was leaving behind in the bathroom. I called a cab. Wrote a note for Cole, included a spare key. I told him to take the food, that I had a family emergency and that I'd be in touch. I stuffed the note in an envelope and shoved it under his doormat, the edge peeking out.

I called the airlines, booked something last minute—red-eye, *with* a connection through Chicago to Milwaukee—and argued with the operator for the family emergency rate. After several heated rounds, she and I agreed on an exorbitantly priced faire accompanied by a case number that I could re-open and attempt to re-negotiate the price, *after* I got home to Milwaukee. I hung up and cursed her. I shoved Napoleon inside the cat carrier as he complained loudly.

I dragged my large suitcases out to the curb. Walked back to my front stoop and grabbed Napoleon's cage, my purse and my carry on.

Cole's door popped open. "Hey—what's going on?" He was dressed in crisp Polo cotton men's pajamas and cradled Gidget in his arms.

"I'm going home. It's an emergency. I can't talk about it. I left you a note and a key." I pointed at the envelope sticking out from under his front mat. "Take all the food and beauty products in my place."

"Oh, thanks," he said. "Are you coming back?"

"Shit if I know."

"Are you okay?"

"I don't think so."

"I'm sorry…" his eyes widened as he and I both spotted Alejandro's Jeep burning rubber down our small street and screeching to a stop at the curb.

"Uh-oh. You need help, just yell. For someone. I guess." Cole jumped back inside his place. Slammed the door. Shut his windows. Then peeked out the side of the curtains.

Alejandro hopped out the driver's side and strode

toward me. He was dark and brooding and didn't look happy. "I got a text that Jackson was a dick to you at the party. That he might even have tried to hurt you. I showed up ready to kick his ass, but he was gone and you were too. Then I got a text that you're walking down PCH—hitchhiking. The third text was that you didn't want to wait for me. That Nathan was driving you home."

I nodded. "That sounds about right."

"What the hell is going on?" He pointed to my suitcases.

"I've been thinking, Alejandro. I've been thinking that you are finally getting over the worst thing that ever happened to you. A nightmare moment that crushed you. Tonight, I realized, I would always be part of that. I will forever be the girl who makes you remember that you once believed you were a monster."

"That's not true." He paced in front of me. "You brought me back to life. You made me laugh again. Smile. You made me think that tomorrow would be a fun adventure instead of a tunnel of darkness." He grabbed my shoulders. "Why Sophie? Why do you think you could undo me?"

"Because, Alejandro. I have MS. And MS is a stupid, mean disease. Someday, I might be in a wheelchair. And that'll put you right back in that tunnel."

"That's not true! I'm bigger than that."

I saw the cab turn onto my block. "You *are* bigger than that. Which means you belong to the world. You belong to every single soul that needs your help, because you've never forgiven yourself. Your mind and your heart and your entire life is still with that girl who died the night you drove over the cliff." I shook my head, pulled away from him and lifted my hand up in the air so the cabbie would see me.

He pulled over to the curb, behind the Jeep.

"I want you to forget about me, Alejandro." I said. "We had an amazing story that lasted for one magical summer. But you'll never belong to me."

"But I do. I do belong to you Sophie. And our story doesn't have to end."

"Our story's complicated," I said. "Complicated stories usually end badly."

The cabbie was out of the car and regarded me, curious. "LAX?" He asked.

I nodded. He popped the trunk, started grabbing my bags and hoisted them in.

"You can't go," Alejandro said. "What we have isn't that complicated. It's real and it's simple. What we have is love."

I willed myself not to cry. Not to lose it. Forced myself not to tell him about Nana. Because if I did? He'd come back to Wisconsin with me. I gazed at him, under the streetlight, the moon shining high behind him. He was my dark beautiful angel without the wings. He was my Alejandro.

And I had to let him go.

CHAPTER TWENTY-SIX

I stood on my tiptoes and kissed him on the cheek. "Whoever writes the fairy tales never tells you that eventually the magic ends. Cinderella grows older, develops bunions and can't wear her slipper," I said. "Snow White eats apple pies instead of just apples and loses her girlish figure. The Prince cheats on her. Sleeping Beauty develops insomnia and gets addicted to Ambien."

"You and I are not a freaking fairy tale."

I stepped into the cab with my purse and Napoleon in the car carrier. "Drive," I hissed to him. "Now!" I shut the door.

The cabbie shook his head as he peered back at me. "Lady, I can't."

"Of course you can," I said.

"Look behind you."

I swiveled my head and saw Alejandro standing directly behind the cab, one foot on the bumper. "If you're leaving, I'm coming with you."

I wished with all my heart that he could.

"Meter's ticking, lady."

And I realized one way to get rid of him.

"Hang on," I said, and grabbed my purse. Opened the cab door. Stepped out and walked the few feet toward Alejandro, my heart banging against my ribs like those fireworks exploding in the night sky. "I forgot something." I fumbled through my bag and pulled out my checkbook and a pen. "We had a deal. I was supposed to pay you for your services. I'm so sorry. I temporarily forgot." I filled in the date out the check as my hand trembled. "Alejandro Maxwell Levine. For—Driving services. How much do I owe you?" I gathered all my false courage and gazed up at him.

His face turned crimson. "You're freaking kidding me."

"No. You rendered a service. I always pay my bills. So, how much should I make this out for?"

"I don't want your money."

"Okay then." I signed my name with a flourish. "I'll let you fill in the amount." I ripped the check out of the book. "You can text me the total later. Try and keep it under fifteen hundred, okay? I think I've got enough to cover that." I handed it to him.

He took it, gazed at it for a second as his eyes turned to ice and his face hardened. "This is how much you owe me." He ripped the check up into pieces and dropped them. They fell to the ground as he turned and strode toward his Jeep.

"We're just a dream, Alejandro," I hollered after him. "And eventually you've got to wake up from a dream." I got back inside the cab and shut the door.

Alejandro screeched off. The cabbie pulled away from the curb. I waited until we had rounded the corner before I started sobbing.

***

My mom had texted that she'd pick me up on the curb under the Great Lakes Airlines sign in Milwaukee's Mitchell Airport arrivals section. I hadn't slept a wink on the flight and was freaking exhausted from worry and sadness. The sun had already risen by the time we landed. I carted Napoleon and my carry on bag off the plane and walked toward baggage claim. I passed Security. That's when I saw her.

Mary Martha Mapleson held two large cups of Starbucks, waiting for me. We spotted each other and we both froze. Tears streamed down her face. And I knew the worst had happened.

* * *

We didn't have a funeral for Nana. We had a party.

We held it in the activities room at her most recent home at The Seasons Assisted Living Center. We served cupcakes, an assortment of deli meats, as well as a cheese and cracker plate. We had two punch bowls: The contents of one was gently spiked with a touch of vodka, the other was just punch.

We decorated a table with an assortment of framed photos of Nana throughout her life: as a chubby blonde toddler with meticulous ringlets and a huge smile. As a young woman wearing red lipstick dressed in a fashionable suit, her arm draped comfortably across the arm of a well-suited man, who was my grandfather. A photo of Nana, joyous, holding my mom when she was a newborn. A candid shot of her and five-year-old me at my ballet recital. The last picture was a group shot of Nana with her new girlfriends from the Assisted Living community. They all wore makeup, were decked out, held their cocktails toward the camera and smiled.

Our party—or should I more accurately say—Nana's going away gig—had a big turnout and the spiked punch was popular. Mom had to leave in the middle to make a run to the liquor store for more vodka. The Seasons' choral group delivered an *X Factor* worthy rendition of Michael Jackson's "Man in the Mirror." I don't think there was a dry eye in the house.

Everyone wanted to share a memory with Mom and me. They'd pull us aside and confide a moment they treasured about Nana. We even had a Sophie Marie Timmel Book of Memories left out on one of the dining tables and encouraged folks to write something. Most of them did.

The event went by in a flash. At the end, Mom and I were exhausted. As we cleaned up the room with the help of Triple M, I paid attention to Mom to see if she was okay, or losing it. I think she was somewhere in-between, which seemed pretty normal.

Triple M took out the large Hefty bags filled with trash. The dishes were washed, dried and returned to their cabinets. Mom and I carefully took down Nana's pictures, wrapped them in towels and placed them in a box. "She was so beautiful," I said and started crying.

My mom hugged me. "Yeah she was, sweetie. A force to be reckoned with. Which is why I named you after her. You've got her spirit. Her drive. Or as she recently liked to say, her 'chutzpah.'"

***

Two weeks passed since that awful night I left L.A. I heard from Blue, but didn't have the heart to call her back and tell her my sob story. Cole called. Apparently someone had already moved into my former apartment and replaced the see-through curtains. He was having a difficult time spying on them and was peeved I'd moved out for good.

I heard nothing from Alejandro. I gathered my courage and called him a couple of times. I even left a few messages. He never called back.

But I did hear from a representative for the USCLA stem cell study. They weren't all that pleased that I'd missed several appointments. I contacted them and told them what happened. They were polite, but insisted I get my butt back there for a clinical check in. I agreed and booked my plane reservation.

Mom and I visited Nana's plot to check the installation of her headstone. She was buried in a cemetery on the top of a relatively steep hill overlooking Lac LaBelle. She always loved the lake. It seemed fitting she would get to gaze upon it for eternity.

Mom and I held hands and watched the workers cement her simple headstone into the ground.

"I'll miss her," I said.

"Understatement," Mom said.

"I wish I didn't have to go back to L.A. It was good in so many ways, but it was also really tough."

"Nana wanted you to take that trip. She financed it, against my better wishes, might I add. One night after you left, she told me, 'You need to let Sophie go. She's not a kid anymore. She needs to stretch her boundaries and find her strength.'"

The workers looked down at Nana's grave. One crossed himself. The other nodded at us respectfully.

"Thank you," Mom told them, and they left.

"I tried everything to save her, Mom. Stem cells. Acupuncture. Vision Quest. Healing prayers. Chiropractic. A medical intuitive. Aura healing. Yoga intensives—"

"I know you tried everything. She knew it too. You took this incredible journey for her—and yet at the same time, she wanted it to be about you."

"But maybe I didn't do enough. Maybe if I had—"

"Stop! If Nana were sitting in her wheelchair right here, right now, she'd say, *'Sophie. My favorite granddaughter—'*"

And I smiled for the first time since I got the dreadful text at Jackson's party. Since the night I said heartless words to Alejandro. "I'd say, 'I'm your *only* granddaughter, Nana.'"

My mom cracked a smile and reached her hand out to me. We held hands and walked down the hill around tombstones and markers. Fall was hitting Oconomowoc early, a sudden gust of wind swirled around us raining down jewel-colored leaves.

"I bet Nana would say, *'Sophie, I feel ferdrayt. Out of all these exotic experiences, out of all your adventures—what made the biggest difference in your life? What was the most healing?'"*

The opening music to "Gimme Shelter" by the Rolling Stones started playing in my brain as I thought about all the therapies. Some I liked. Some were silly, others scary, a few even dangerous. But with each memory, I thought of Alejandro. He gave me shelter. *And my heart clenched as I realized I would never feel sheltered like that again.*

* * *

My flight back to L.A. was uneventful. I stood on the curb holding the handle of my wheeled luggage as my cab peeled off. I recognized the sweet scent of oranges down the block as I gazed at my old sublet. The new tenant had replaced the ugly lace curtains with fresh new ones.

I closed my eyes and a wave of memories washed over me: the stinging from the slivers of glass in my face. My shock when Alejandro caught me as I fell that first night at the Grill. The laughter that bubbled up within me when he was covered in acupuncture needles. The heat that consumed my body when he kissed me for the first time, right on that doorstep. The bathroom after the fire where he helped me clean up, told me my eyebrow would grow back and carried me to bed where we'd made love for my first time.

It all seemed so far away—like it was a different lifetime ago.

I walked down the narrow, concrete path and knocked on Cole's door. He opened it wearing Ralph Lauren pajamas. Gidget burst from the open doorway like the monster-out-of-the-body in *Alien*, leaping up and down and scratching my shins as she alternated between barking and howling.

"Ow! Hey! You're super cute and I missed you too." I tried to rub her ears and her sloppy little face, but winced as she nipped my ankles. "Stop biting me you little ragamuffin."

"I might be casually attired, but I am not a ragamuffin," Cole leaned in and smooched me on my cheek. "Missed you. I'm really, really sorry about your grandmother." He grabbed my carry-on-bag and pulled it inside his living room.

"Me too." I took a breath and willed myself to not go to the emotional place. I was practicing saving my tears for private moments.

"My house is your house." He gestured to his living room and I entered. "Gidget! Get your derriere in here. Now." She waddled inside and Cole shut the door. "How's Napoleon?

"Being doted on by my friend, Mary. She's feeding him cheese and tuna in front of her TV during Packer games. She thinks if she trains or tricks him into doing something YouTube worthy, she can film him and make millions."

"Cat videos sell you know. Give Mary my number," Cole said. "Glad you're back. Second bedroom's made up. You talk to the Cookie Monster?"

I must have looked sad because Cole pinched my arm. "Hey!" I said.

"Hey back! You're young and cute. Don't worry about him. Besides, I've got just the ticket to distract you. I tracked down Clark Gable's old house. It's for sale in the hills above Sunset. There's an open house this weekend..."

Besides putting a fork in my eye or running into Pintdick again, I couldn't think of anything else that I'd prefer less.

"I know. You're totally tempted," Cole said. "Thank me later."

"I'll thank you now. Unfortunately, I have no time for dead celebrities on this trip. I'm just in town to tie up my loose ends."

***

Early the next morning I handed in my final Genetics 300 term paper to Professor Schillinger. He'd given me an extension when I contacted him about Nana. Next up was a trip to USCLA for the stem cell study. I sat in a small hospital room, fully clothed with my sleeve rolled up above my elbow. Nurse Michaels drew three vials of my blood on his third attempt. "Have you ever considered another profession?" I asked.

He sighed. "I'm still paying off my student loans." He walked out the door passing Dr. Goddard, who entered and took a seat on the swiveling stool.

He sat across from me and flipped open my chart. "Well Sophie, there's good news and bad news," he said and frowned. "Which do you want to start with?"

I couldn't save my Nana. She lay deep in the ground on top of a pretty hill. A carved marble angel rested on top of her plot, guarding her journey to Heaven. I was half-tempted to get her a Star of David to attract some dear departed souls who might speak Yiddish with her. I'd screwed up Lulu's relationship with Alejandro.

And I messed with the same beautiful man who would always have trust issues. The guy I missed with every breath I took and every beat of the few pieces that remained of my battered and broken heart. What could be worse? Perhaps I could invade a small third world country and become a dictator.

When it dawned on me. Why did they make me endure the extra MRI? There must have been suspicious results on the previous one. The stem cells were probably going bad. Quite possibly forming tumors in my brain or pushing against my spinal cord. I took a deep breath. "I'd like to start with the bad, please."

CHAPTER TWENTY-SEVEN

My legs were weak as I trudged down the USCLA hospital corridors for the last time. I didn't know whether it was from my MS, or nerves.

Turns out the stem cells weren't hurting me. The jury was still out. We wouldn't know for a while. There would be new medical breakthroughs and discoveries happening every year for people like me: people that had weird diseases and conditions and frightening situations. Not that these treatments would be approved overnight.

The bad news was I was released, aka, kicked-out-of the stem cell study for non-sanctioned drug use. My post-fire blood draw had found its way back to the powers-that-be who ran the research. My blood showed traces of hallucinogenic plant medicine. And I had signed paperwork out the yin-yang, promising not to do anything that would interfere with the study's rules and regulations.

Therefore when it came to me, USCLA's tests were null and void. Which cost them time and money and screwed them over. I apologized to Dr. Goddard and tried to explain my reasons, my motivation about my grandmother, but he was a busy man. He informed me that I could obtain follow-up MRIs performed at the facility of my future doctor's choice. But my participation here was officially over. He graciously wished me the best of luck, shook my hand and left the room.

I felt like an ass. I came to L.A. with hope and determination. I was leaving for the second time, hopeless—and I had no one to blame but myself. I wiped a few tears away, trudged past command central and the two receptionists manning its desk.

"See you in a couple of days," Phil said.

"Nope, Viking scum, I'm out of here."

"Oh." He raised an eyebrow, but didn't ask the obvious.

I stopped in my tracks. "Send me an email now and again, would you?" I asked. "Let me know how you are."

"I don't have your email."

"Pilfer it from my chart."

"That's in violation of—"

"HIPPA." I sighed, went to the desk, scrawled my email on a piece of scratch paper and handed it to him. "If I don't hear from you in two weeks? I'll track down your email and sign you up for every Green Bay Packer fan club website in North America."

"I knew you were trouble the minute you walked in the door." He smiled and pocketed it. "Good luck, Sophie."

I'd almost made it to the elevator when a magazine skimmed my scalp and landed with a smack on the floor in front of me. "Hey!" Blue yelled. "Not only do you not call me. But then you move, come back into town and don't call me some more?" She wheeled up to me and ran over my foot. Twice. Then parked on it.

"Ow," I winced.

"Ow, back." She reached down, picked up the copy of Cosmo on the floor and smacked my thigh. "How many times have I called, emailed and texted?" She hit my thigh again. "Am I not worthy of at least one return message?"

"Stop! Yes! I think you're breaking my toe and for God's sakes I bruise easily."

"Good. Something to remember me."

"Look. I didn't call because…" My heart dove into my

stomach and I felt sick. "My grandmother died."

"Oh no!" Blue exclaimed and started to cry as she backed off my foot. "I'm so sorry. Do you want to talk about it? I'm meeting Lulu, but she'd be cool if I postponed..."

Lulu turned the corner and wheeled toward us in her chair.

Aw shit. But I needed to have this conversation. Do the right thing, even if it was the tough thing. Lulu regarded Blue and me quizzically. "What's going on?"

"Sophie needs to talk. Can we postpone—"

"I'd like to talk to Lulu privately, if that's okay?" I asked.

"Anything you need to say to me," Lulu nodded, "you can say in front of Blue."

* * *

I sat on a park bench off a pathway that ran between USCLA campus buildings. Lulu and Blue were huddled in close to me. There was a smattering of subtle fall colors on the leaves. Delicate hued yellows, oranges and reds. As if the California trees couldn't commit to the whole change of season thing.

Fall semester was in full gear and a wide array of students carried backpacks and checked their cells as they walked, looking up at the names on the brick buildings, searching for their classes. A new, exciting journey was beginning for them. My journey was over. The exception being the apologies I needed to offer.

"Lulu—I had no idea you were in love with Alejandro when I met him. If I knew, if I had an inkling? I would have removed myself from that picture so quickly it would have made your head spin. Never in a thousand years would I have wanted to hurt you, Jackson, or Alejandro."

"Got it," she said. "But—"

"No buts. The night of your folks' party, this whole thing

just came out of nowhere and smacked me in the face. I was shocked when Jackson told me I'd hurt you. I'm so sorry. I'll never interfere in anything between you and Alejandro ever again. If it makes you feel any better, we haven't even spoken since the night of the party."

I'd stay away from Alejandro. But, I'd miss him for a lifetime.

"Sophie. You and I need to get something straight," Lulu said. "My brother might run his mouth off, but he doesn't speak for me."

"Okay," I said.

Blue rolled her eyes. "Just tell her, Lulu."

"Jackson has always wanted Alex and I to be a couple. And don't get me wrong. I've always liked the guy. We grew up together. Shared a couple of make out sessions in high school. After the accident everyone just assumed because we spent so much time together, we'd fall in love. But I never felt it for him. I never felt anything profound for anybody until a while after my accident. And no, I'm not going to tell you his name."

"So this means, this means..." I stumbled with my words. "This means you're not in love with Alejandro?"

"Good God, no," Lulu said. "Maybe Jackson is. He's been an asshat ever since we hit puberty. If you love Alex— by all means, go for it. And I apologize to you for not making this clear the night of the benefit. But everything that night was bat shit crazy."

"It really was," I said as my mind whirled with the possibilities. *Could we still have a chance? Would he take me back?* "Thank you," I said and fumbled through my purse and pulled out a business card. Lizzie Sparks's private email was inscribed on it. "Thank you so much." I stood up and despite their protests, kissed them both on their cheeks. "You and Blue are the best. And I will keep in touch. I promise."

"Or next time, I *will* break your toe," Blue said.

THE STORY OF YOU AND ME

* * *

I was back in Lizzie Sparks' cozy office room with one barred window that was cracked open. She was in demand, so popular as a medical intuitive and so wise. I was so clueless. It felt like a lifetime ago that I'd first met with her. I scrunched forward on an older, upholstered chair and she sat across from me, holding my hand.

"I'm so glad you came back Sophie. How has your journey been?"

I didn't know what to say. The world, my life, everything was all so different from three and a half months ago, when I first consulted with her.

"I came here for healing," I said. "I thought I found it. But it wasn't a modality or a guru. It wasn't a technique or a surgical procedure. It was guy."

She nodded. "Tell me his name. A little about him."

"Alejandro Maxwell Levine. He's kind. Funny. Loving. Sexy as sin…"

"Handsome." Lizzie smiled.

"Oh my God, you have no idea!" I returned her smile. "He drove me all over Los Angeles looking for healing. He helped me so much. Then he told me his secrets. And they weren't simple. He said he felt like a monster. That he broke people. But, honestly? He never meant to hurt anyone. He made a bad decision. He's been paying for it ever since. He's more than owned it."

"Did you tell him your secrets?"

I extricated my hand from Lizzie's, stood up and paced the small room.

"I tried. Our timing sucked."

"Your timing was perfect," Lizzie said.

"How can that be? I screwed up everything between us. He rescued me, you know." I glared down at her. "From a bad choice I made. And then someone accidentally revealed my biggest secret. So I told him— everything."

"But you didn't," Lizzie said. "You didn't tell him everything."

I shook my head. "I did. I'd already told him about my Nana. I told him about my MS. I told him the healers weren't for a book. They were to save Nana's life."

"But you didn't tell him the truth about why you left him. Why you pushed him away."

"That's obvious. I did it for him! With me out of the picture, I can practically predict his story. Some day when he's living in his beautiful house, with his perfect wife and their two smart, healthy children that aren't staring down the gun, scared about contracting some dreadful genetic-related disease—he'll thank me."

"He won't. Because that's not his story," she said.

"Why not? If I could save one life out of this whole journey, at least I've saved his."

"But you didn't. You took it away when you didn't allow him to make up his own mind. Because in this young man's 'story'—with his perfect house, wife and children—his life will still be incomplete. There will always be a missing puzzle piece. Why did the girl who said she loved him walked away so callously. He'll never know. And that will eat at him like an ulcer."

I started crying. "Have I screwed us up forever?"

"Maybe," Lizzie said. "Maybe not. You need to track him down. Have a conversation with him. You need to make it right. No matter what the outcome."

* * *

I thanked Lizzie. I was back in Venice and a plan was percolating in my brain. I wasn't going to risk running into Pintdick today, so her assistant ordered a taxi for me.

My first visit was to Javier's tattoo place, Inkbaby, on the boardwalk. I instructed the cabbie to wait for me, meter running, on the closest cross street. I walked half a block and entered the shop. Javier chatted with a potential customer, showing him a variety of template designs for tats. I bided my time pretending to check out designs for a few minutes until the man left. Javier swiveled his attention to me. "Sophie!"

"Javier. Famous Venice Beach artist!"

He walked from behind the counter and regarded me with concern. "You're all right. Thank God." he said. "We didn't hear anything about you and we were worried. You look thin. But you're well, yes?"

"Kind of. My grandmother died." I thumped my fist on top of my chest right over my heart. "My heart's a little broken."

"*Siento mucho la perdida.*" He leaned in and bear-hugged me with his muscular, painted up arms. "I'm so sorry for your loss." He released me. "It's going to take a while, you know."

"I know. Javier, look. I need to talk to Alejandro. He won't return my calls. Have you seen him?"

He dropped my hands and sighed. "He was here a couple of weeks ago. But I haven't heard from him since. Have you talked to one of the other Drivers? Like Nick?"

"Not yet. Great idea. Can I have his number?"

Javier pulled a card from his pocket and handed it to me. It read, "DRIVER," and had Nick's name and contact info.

"You're the best! I've got to run. If you see Alejandro or if he calls, would you tell him I was here? That I really need to talk with him?"

"You got it."

* * *

The cabbie drove me to Alejandro's house on Copa del Oro. The fare kept ticking skyward. When we arrived I paid him. Even if Alejandro wasn't here, it would only take me a half hour or so to walk back to Cole's place. Also, it wouldn't hurt to have a little money left over for things like food. He peeled off as I hit the call button next to the closed gates and waited.

A few windows were open in the front of the house and I heard the gate's buzzer ring lowly from inside. But no one answered. I fidgeted and then pushed the call button again. Waited another couple of minutes. Contemplated climbing the fence, then thought what a great impression that would make on Alejandro's folks when I was arrested for breaking and entering. So I pushed the button again. Okay, truth be told, I banged on that damn buzzer five times in a row. I had to find Alejandro.

Thirty seconds later a short man marched from the side of the house toward the front gates and me.

"Oh yay!" I said. "You're the same gentleman who wore the sombrero at the Levine's picnic. I'm looking for Alejandro? Is he here?"

"No, miss." He shrugged and eyed me through the slats.

"Do you expect him back today? Soon?"

"I do not know, miss."

"Oh," I said. "His parents? Are they here? Could I talk to them?"

"I'm sorry, miss, no. They are out of town."

"Oh," my heart sunk. "Can I leave you my contact info? My phone number, email? You could give it to his parents when they come back or if they call."

"Yes, miss," he said." I scribbled my info onto a piece of scratch paper I dug out of my purse and handed it to him. I watched as he walked away. "Thank you, sir," I hollered. "Thank you very much."

I sighed and slumped back against their gate but an alarm went off and I jumped. Dang! I walked down Copa de Oro, past the mansions attended by the gardeners and maids and pool service trucks. I plucked the Driver's card and my phone from my purse. I punched in a number and waited while it rang. He picked up. "Nick, it's Sophie. You've got to help me."

* * *

I sat in the passenger seat of Nick's immaculate truck and watched the heat simmer in waves off the pavement lining the entrance to Union Station. Folks of all races, ages, walks of life entered and exited the doorways to this gorgeous Spanish styled train station. Two security guards kept an eye on them.

"Alejandro said he needed to get away. Go some place where he could just be himself, chill out and find shelter. He was torn up, Sophie. I haven't seen him like that in years," Nick said.

I was a terrible person. I had done a horrible thing to someone I loved.

"Shit," I said. "Has he called? Is he all right?"

Nick shrugged. "Haven't heard from him. Hey, I wish I could drive you farther, but things are tight around here with the new semester, the frat parties and the newly liberated, heads-up-their-collective-asses freshmen. We're training a few new Drivers, but as you know, we're missing one of our best."

"I miss him too," I said.

Nick slammed the steering wheel with his fist.

I jumped. "You okay?" I asked.

"Yeah. For someone who just gave away his best buddy's secret to the girl who broke his heart? I'm great."

"I love him, Nick."

He looked out his driver's window. "I know, Sophie. Just don't mess him up more than you already have."

I placed my hand on top of his fist and squeezed it for a second. "Thank you."

CHAPTER TWENTY-EIGHT

I took the train to San Diego and then caught a tour bus to Rosarito. Strangely enough it dropped me off at La Mar Hotel, where I grabbed a taxi. I tried to explain to the cabbie what Alejandro's parents house looked like: gorgeous beachfront hacienda. Located in a gated community with security guards. But, unfortunately, there were over a hundred houses that matched that description.

He drove me to community after community, guardhouse after guardhouse. He'd pull up, say hello to the guards and inquire using Alejandro's last name. "*La casa de Levine?*" The guards just shook their heads. I was frustrated, but it wasn't really their fault. They were paid to protect—not offer up private information.

So here I was again, thousands of miles away from home. Feeling those glass shards from the broken beer bottle digging back into my face, migrating down through my chest and piercing my heart.

The sun was making its way toward the Pacific Ocean and I still hadn't found Alejandro. I felt exhausted, weak and my hand started trembling. What was I thinking? At least I could have tried to track him down a little while longer before I ventured to a foreign country on my own. Why had I journeyed so far away, all by myself? And it hit me.

I raced down paths most people wouldn't tiptoe onto because it was out of their comfort zone, perhaps even dangerous. I traveled thousands of miles, crossed mountains, deserts and fires because I had hope. And if you had hope, maybe you could conquer a disease. Perhaps you could save a life.

So I journeyed for love: the first time for my Nana. The second time for Alejandro. No matter how we ended up—together or apart—I knew that I'd always love him. He'd always hold an exceptional piece of my soul, my heart, my mind. He was my first love. He sheltered me.

And it dawned on me...I asked the cab driver if he knew where Padre Morales's orphanage was. His eyes widened in the rearview mirror's reflection. He nodded and turned onto a road that led back into town. Fifteen minutes later we were in the midst of Rosarito's non-touristy, gritty neighborhoods, with the hole-in-the-wall apartments and mom and pop stores.

The cabbie slowed to a stop next to the plain concrete block building surrounded by barbwire fence. *"Padre Morales."*

"Yes." I opened the passenger door, stepped out and glanced at the blood red door. The cabbie popped open the trunk, hauled out my suitcase and plopped it in front on the pavement. I knocked on the door, really hoped someone was home, dug through my purse for twenties and paid the cabbie. He pocketed the cash, eyed me and said, *"Buena suerte, señorita."*

"Gracias." I would take all the luck offered to me.

He drove off as I knocked on the door. But there was no answer. I dragged my bag around to the fence. There were no kids playing in the playground. That's when I heard a song coming from the inside of the orphanage. It was John Lennon's voice singing "Imagine." I couldn't help but smile. When the red door flew open and the Padre stuck his head out and stared at me.

"Dios mío!" He said. "I was wondering when you were

going to arrive. Come inside. *Pronto!*

* * *

The Padre made me a sandwich and insisted I drink two glasses of juice. I changed into my swimsuit and my beach cover up back at the orphanage. Now I stood on a calm patch of a local Rosarito beach and watched Alejandro in the ocean waves. The sun was a few feet above the horizon, but he was still helping a half dozen kids learn to surf.

Alex was half naked, wearing board shorts, bronzed and laughing. His black hair was wet and even longer than last time I saw him. He looked carefree. He looked happy. Did I even dare interrupt him?

Padre Morales poked my arm and I flinched. "Do you love him?"

"I do."

"Then for him, and I plead with you—for all of us? Talk with him." He turned and walked away.

My first love, Alejandro Maxwell Levine, dove under the ocean waters, resurfaced and pretended to be a shark attacking a twelve-year-old boy's surfboard. The boy screamed with delight, stood up on the board and rode it to shore.

Alejandro stuck both his arms up in the air and yelled, "Raphael! You did it!"

Raphael dragged his board out of the water and collapsed onto the wet sand next to me, his wet, bare, skinny chest heaving.

"Alejandro," I said. But his attention was already focused on his next student.

Raphael squinted at me. "You're the pretty lady in the picture," he said and pushed himself up on one elbow.

I shook my head. "What?"

"You're the pretty lady in the picture on Alejandro's phone. I think he likes you. Alejandro! Alejandro!

Alejandro!" Raphael hollered.

"Shhh! Be quiet, kiddo. Just be a nice, silent, young man. Okay?" I dug in my purse. "I'll give you a quarter."

"Alejandro! I have a new friend. You must meet her."

"No," I hissed. "I need to... I must... I can handle this..."

Alejandro was waist deep in the surf but swiveled toward Raphael's voice. And froze when he spotted me. "Bonita. What are you doing here?"

I gathered my courage, stood up and walked into the water. The waves lapped over my ankles and surf sprayed onto my legs. "I'm here because someone wise once told me, 'Life is short.' He said, 'We are not perfect people. We don't know how much time we will have together.'"

"Hmm. That guy sounds like a pompous dick."

I looked at the ocean waters that scared the shit out of me. Then gazed at Alejandro. "No, he's not, actually. He's perceptive. He's smart." I waded into the ocean up to my hips and the waves drenched my cover-up.

"You're petrified of water. What are you doing?" He asked.

"Remember when we first came down here and we were on the phone with my Nana?"

"Yeah?"

"Remember when she said 'Just be kind to each other.'"

"Yeah?"

"Those were her last words to me before she died."

"Oh, Bonita. Your Nana died?"

"Yeah. That's one of the reasons I left you the night of the party."

"I'm so sorry. I didn't know," he said.

"I didn't want you to know. But, I didn't follow my Nana's last words. I wasn't kind to you. And I regret it. I regret every mean thing I said. And I want to take it all back. But I can't." I tugged my cover-up over my shoulders and tossed it behind me onto the ocean. I strode toward him clad in that really-revealing bikini the Wheelie Girls truth or dared me to get during our Bathing Suit party.

I felt exposed. Raw. Vulnerable.

"I can never take away hurting you or the mean things I said the night of the party. But I promise to try with every inch of my frightened heart to trust you, Alejandro. You're the first man I've ever fallen in love with. You will be the man I'll never forget. And I don't care if you belong to the world. I still want you to belong to me." I waded toward him until the waves crested up to my chest.

"I'll always belong to you."

"No matter what happens with us, Alejandro? You and I have a hell of a story."

He dove into the water and swam toward me.

I tried not to be scared as the waves splashed against my neck, my face.

He hit sand, strode toward and reached me. One muscular arm encircled my waist as he pulled me toward him. I wrapped my arms around his neck, my legs around his hips. He kissed me hard and full on my lips. "I love you Sophie Marie Priebe. I'll always love you." He walked us into shallower waters, where the waves splashed around our waists.

"I love you back."

And we kissed in the surf; surrounded by giggling children, a priest, surfers, a few tourists and sailboats making their way back to a marina. And it was magical.

He stopped for a second, pulled his head back and smiled at me. "I think our story deserves a name. What do you think we should call it?"

"Let's keep it simple," I said.

"I like simple. How about The Story of You and Me?" And he kissed me again.

The End

AUTHOR NOTE

Dear Reader:

Thank you for reading *The Story of You and Me*. I hope you enjoyed Sophie and Alejandro's story as much as I enjoyed writing it.

I'd be so grateful if you would take a moment of your valuable time to write a brief review on the site where you purchased this book and even Goodreads, if you have the stamina.

Every single honest book review helps an author. *A lot.*

Thank you again,

Pamela DuMond

GoodreadsLink:
http://www.goodreads.com/author/show/4430293.Pamela_DuMond

On a Personal Note

About a year before I started writing *The Story of You and Me*, a woman reached out to me on Facebook. She asked me a few questions about where I grew up. We determined that her brother, R, was my first love. She was his sister, and even though many years had passed I remembered her fondly. We became FB friends.

This encounter from my past made my mind spin about *first loves*.

First loves are all about magic and romance, hope and tears. Your heart clutches and your skin tingles simply by thinking about this person. You're grateful and beyond happy that you found this amazing being whom you believe you can't live without.

I reminisced about R.

We met at the end of my senior year in high school. I was eighteen, cute, an A student and painfully shy. He was seventeen, handsome, squeezed by on his grades, but was in a garage band (which automatically made him cool.) We couldn't be more different, but we fell crazy in love.

He made me laugh. It was okay to be my slightly dorky self around him. He introduced to me to his loving family. He was the first guy who sent me roses. When I moved away to college he visited almost every weekend. I stayed away from all the cute frat guys because I was in love with a hometown boy.

We went to dances and concerts and (first time for me) made love—usually on my skinny mattress, on a bunk bed in my dorm room. And yeah, we did that a lot.

We talked marriage. I wanted to wait. He didn't. He proposed on my 19th birthday. He couldn't afford a ring, so he handed me a box of Oreos and a little silver cross. He asked me a big question and offered a bigger promise. I said yes, but with the caveat that I needed to wait a few years to get through school.

We were so young—it's not a huge surprise that we broke up five months later. But it was brutal. My heart felt like it was being ripped out of my chest. I remember sitting on my family's kitchen counter sobbing, while my dad paced, trying to explain to me about life and love and that it's not fair and not right, but that there would be more. There would be more people to love. There would be more stories to share.

And yet I found myself, years after R and I broke up, poking around on his sister's FB page looking for a link to him.

But there was no link.

That's when I noticed her son was also named R. And suddenly a piece of my heart knew. His sister confirmed it:

R had died during a drunk driving accident. He was thirty-seven years old.

I wept for first loves. I spilled tears for a boy I thought I was all wept out over. I cried for innocence lost as well as the sheer sadness that burrows into your bones when you realize that you'll never have a chance for re-connection. When you feel the profound sadness that someone you love, or loved, is never coming home again.

Life is precious, but it isn't always perfect or easy or pretty.

Follow your dreams.

Tell the people you hold close to your heart that you love them.

And live life bravely.

Thanks for being part of my journey.

Pamela DuMond

ACKNOWLEDGMENTS

A huge thanks to my readers who have been loyal as I jump around genres. There are so many types of books I love and so many I want to write.

I couldn't have written this novel without the help of Dr. Andrew Goldstein. Thank you, Andrew, for your amazing on-going help with stem cell research and medical procedures. (All mistakes and liberties taken in this book regarding medical procedures are mine and not his.)

Thanks Regina Wamba at http://www.maeidesign.com for an awesome book cover. Thanks to Michael James Canales for all your web support and graphics. http://www.mjcimageworks.com. Thanks Ramona DeFelice Long for your insightful content editing. Thanks Chase Heiland for copy-editing. Thanks author Rita Kempley for your notes on my first draft. (Holy cow, you're brave!) Author Bob Bernstein you are a Prince among men! Thanks for all your help with Scrivenor and Createspace. Thanks Deborah Daly Roelandts for your help with police procedures as well as all things Oconomowoc, Wisconsin related. (All police/legal mistakes are mine and not hers.) Melissa Black Ford – You, señorita, are my secret author weapon. Thanks Naomi Richman (Acupuncturist).

Thanks to my early readers: Kristin Warren and Shelly Fredman.

A shout-out to my Entertainment Manager Jeffrey Thal at Ensemble Entertainment: I'm grateful you believe in me as well as my stories. You rock, dude!

A special thanks to Cheyenne and Monica Mason for all your help inside, as well as outside of the box and for being so incredibly cool.

Thanks to my writer buds and inspirations: Jamie Dunier, Shelly Fredman, Rita Kempley, Jenny Milchman,

Grant Jerkins, Laura Schultz, Ed Schneider, Joe Wilson, Carlette Norwood, JM Kelley, Mike Snyder, Jacqueline Carey, Dave Thome, Doug Solter, Melanie Abed, Allie Sinclair, Julie Weathers, POV, (and apologies to whoever I'm forgetting.)

Thanks to my amazing friends who are savvy, kind and helped and encouraged me when I couldn't quite find my way through the story, or at times, life: Joan Brady, Marsha Boyer, Melissa Stead, Kimberly Goddard Kuskin, Sadie Gilliam, Dr. Carrie Hartney, Elise Ford, Lynne Massey, Dorothy Hattan Mcqueen and Samantha Mehra (yogi extraordinaire.) A huge shout out to all my DG North and Wheaton Academy HS buddies.

Thanks to the amazing bloggers who give so much of their time and encouraged me: Sassy Girls' Book Club, Forever Young Adult, Chick-Lit Central. A shout out to all you folks on Goodreads! I'm still getting to know you. Thanks for your patience.

To my family: I love you *mucho*.

Go read a good book and tell someone you love about it.

Xo,

Pamela DuMond

ABOUT THE AUTHOR

Pamela DuMond is the writer who discovered Erin Brockovich's life story, thought it would make a great movie and pitched it to 'Hollywood'.

She's addicted to *The Voice*, and *Reign*. The movies *Love Actually* and *The Bourne* trilogy (with Matt Damon -- not that other actor guy,) make her cry every time she watches them. (Like -- a thousand.)

She likes her coffee dark, her cabernet hearty, her chocolate dark and she lives for a good giggle.

When she's not writing Pamela's also a chiropractor and cat wrangler. She loves reading, the beach, working out, movies, TV, animals, her family and friends. She lives in Venice, California with her fur-babies.

Visit her website at www.pameladumond.com for news, reviews and info on upcoming books and whatever else is up there.

Printed in Great Britain
by Amazon